S0-BFC-397

PORTAL COMBAT

Bryan Cohen

This publication is protected under the US Copyright Act of 1976 and all other applicable international, federal, state and local laws, and all rights are reserved, including resale rights: you are not allowed to give or sell this book to anyone else. If you received this publication from anyone other than Bryan Cohen or Amazon, you've received a pirated copy. Please contact us via BryanCohen.com and notify us of the situation.

All contents Copyright © 2014 by Bryan Cohen. All rights reserved. No part of this document or the related files may be reproduced or transmitted in any form, by any means (electronic, photocopying, recording, or otherwise) without the prior written permission of the publisher.

Limit of Liability and Disclaimer of Warranty: The publisher has used its best efforts in preparing this book, and the information provided herein is provided "as is." Bryan Cohen makes no representation or warranties with respect to the accuracy or completeness of the contents of this book and specifically disclaims any implied warranties of merchantability or fitness for any particular purpose and shall in no event be liable for any loss of profit or any other commercial damage, including but not limited to special, incidental, consequential, or other damages. All characters appearing in this work are fictitious. Any resemblance to real persons, living or dead, is purely coincidental.

Trademarks: This book identifies product names and services known to be trademarks, registered trademarks, or service marks of their respective holders. They are used throughout this book in an editorial fashion only. In addition, terms suspected of being trademarks, registered trademarks, or service marks have been appropriately capitalized, although Bryan Cohen cannot attest to the accuracy of this information. Use of a term in this book should not be regarded as affecting the validity of any trademark, registered trademark, or service mark. Bryan Cohen is not associated with any product or vendor mentioned in this book.

Book cover designed by James Olsen of Robot Brain Design.
Photo by Oomphotography. Edited by Ashley Gainer.

Copyright © 2014 Bryan Cohen

All rights reserved.

ISBN-13: 978-1505556438
ISBN-10: 1505556430

To Julie, Tim, and Ashley for being just a phone call away.

Contents

Author's Note

While life as an author be a lonely one, the writers who find the most success are the ones who have a team. I knew that when I planned to write three novels in the second half of 2014, I was going to need some help. At first, this help focused on shoring up plot points and casting away grammatical errors. By the time I reached *Portal Combat*, I really felt the strain of writing significantly more fiction than I'd ever attempted.

I sat down to outline *Portal Combat* in late October. Despite my best efforts, I didn't seem to have enough in my creative reserves to come up with a story I could be proud of. It didn't take long to realize that I'd need help to make this book a crowd pleaser that continued the story effectively.

I reached out to my team. In the same way that Ted calls on Erica, Natalie, Dhiraj and Jennifer to fight the forces of evil, I called on my friends to help me out of this creative pickle. A few brainstorming phone calls later, and I had the skeleton of the plot I needed to truly tell this story.

It can be hard to admit when you need help, but there are few downsides to forming your own team. An acronym I recall from my high school days is Together Everyone Achieves More (TEAM). That phrase was certainly proved true when I wrote this book. Many thanks to everybody who has helped me to grow and refine my creative process.

I hope you enjoy Ted's next adventure. It's a real team effort!

Sincerely,
Bryan Cohen
Author of *Portal Combat*

Acknowledgements

Thank you to everybody who made this book possible.

My beta readers Julianne Clancy, Tim Matson, Barbara Pohland and Torsten Spooner made a difficult project much easier with their notes.

James Olsen did a great cover, and Oomphotography did an amazing job with the key art.

Thanks to Alisa Rosenthal for helping out and to Michael Silberblatt and Cordelia Dewdney for bringing the characters to life.

Ashley Gainer went so far above and beyond this time. Craziness.

My wife put up with a lot of late hours on this one, and I'm so lucky she keeps me around.

PART ONE

CHAPTER

1

Sela Fortbright cracked her knuckles as she guarded the gateway between two worlds. She was stout, like most of the members of her family, but the light souls had said she was something special. That's the reason they gave for taking her away before she could know who she really was. As a result, she was part of an esteemed order of defenders who made sure all the realms were safe, but she wondered how her life would've been if a different path had been presented.

The same thoughts clouded her mind as she saw three hooded figures approach the gate. It was an odd sight, as few strangers came within a league of her station. Most of the travelers who needed to pass from this world to the Realm of Souls or another destination were familiar faces. The dim lights of the gateway arch reflected against the black hood of the man in the front of the trio. He seemed about as tall and wide as she was, so he wouldn't present much of a problem if things went south. His two counterparts were each the width of several men, and a faint gurgling sound emanated from one of them. Sela gave her knuckles one final crack before crouching into a defensive position.

"State your business."

The man in front lifted his hood just enough to reveal a smile. "Don't get your tights in a bunch, noble gatekeeper. We're simply passing through to

Earth." He extended a glowing document to Sela. "I believe you'll see that everything's in order."

Sela relaxed her shoulders and took the document. She leaned against an ancient stone behind her, which once formed a great castle that towered above everything else. Now, like most of the world, it had been abandoned and seemed more likely to crumble than offer any sort of protection. Built into the stone was an arch that was as wide as her powerful metal staff. The stones that formed the gateway itself glowed with mystical energy, much like the document Sela leafed through. Through the arch, there was a hole that seemed to lead to nothingness. Without Sela's assistance, that's about where the people attempting to pass through would end up.

Sela handed the document back to the man in front. The journey to her station would take a toll on most, but the leader of this pack seemed unfazed. When his fingers brushed hers during the handoff, Sela's first instinct was to tear his wrist off.

"Documents can lie, but eyes can't. Remove your hoods."

The man's crooked smile beneath the hood gave Sela a hint of recognition. The hint changed to a flood of memories when he removed his hood.

The man was a boy the last time she'd seen him. Pink cheeks had since given way to a thin, black beard. His hair was the same color, though it now hung down around his shoulders. The man's eyes were the same dark green hue as they'd been when the two of them grew up together.

"Hello, sister."

Her face strained to smile; it'd been so long since she'd done so. The warmth inside threatened to cut through the ice that had surrounded her heart. Sela shook her head.

"Brother." She was half-startled by the laugh that escaped her mouth. "You were running around the house naked the last time I saw you."

Cal Fortbright chuckled. "Little has changed, Sela."

The laughter was far different from the coos Sela remembered him for. Would the revived love for her brother and family change everything she'd become?

If Cal sensed her thoughts, he didn't let on. "I'd love to catch up, but my associates and I really should be leaving."

Typically, Sela didn't mind keeping small talk concise. After all, her training taught her that sentences should be short and battles long. Her current chat with her brother might have been the lengthiest exchange she'd had since she was assigned this gate.

As her brother took a step forward, Sela moved to block him. The warmth had given way to a warning in the back of her mind.

What you see can't be trusted.

The training had informed many of her actions up to this point, and the lessons she'd learned tended to emerge exactly when she needed them.

Sela put up a hand. "Brother, forgive me, but we're not through here."

Cal crossed his arms. "You're not sure it's really me, are you?"

Even as a child, Cal had been perceptive. He was the kind of precocious kid who would tell adults how things really were. When he guessed why people were acting a certain way, he was typically right. But his perception alone wasn't enough to convince the gatekeeper.

"It is a time of war." She studied her brother. "Precautions must be taken."

Cal nodded. "Ask me anything you want."

Sela rambled off question after question that only Cal could answer: the location of their house in their home village, their mother's ancestors and even a nickname she'd had as a little girl. Cal answered all of them without hesitation. Still, there was something unsettling about seeing her brother here after all these years. It reeked of an appeal to the heart by the dark souls.

"I'm sorry, Cal." She stood up as straight as she possibly could. "I believe you're my brother, but I'm going to have to deny you passage."

Her brother's eyes glistened. His sly smile told her he'd been expecting this outcome all along.

"You know, Sela, I even still have that scar on my arm from when we were little. Would you like to see?"

Cal removed the cloak and tossed it to the ground. The sweat covering his arms and chest made his rippling muscles stick out in the dim lights of the gateway. As Sela glanced at the scar on his right arm, her worst fears were confirmed. She fought the anxiety that built in her stomach as she spied the dark soul tattoo that had been painted all around the childhood injury.

"See, Sela?" Cal removed a sword from its scabbard. "I really am your brother."

Sela pulled the metal staff from her back pouch. "My brother is dead."

She let Cal strike first. The sword clanged against the staff, sending a vibration through Sela's hands and generating sparks with the impact. The other members of Cal's party removed their cloaks as well. They were green, lizard-like creatures that Sela recognized as Draconfolk. Carved into the scaly appendages of one creature were the same images as the ones on her brother's arm. The other creature was tattoo-free. The blood glistening on one of its claws made it apparent that the gate had not been the trio's first stop that night.

Cal grunted and spun his weapon toward Sela again. She moved to counter with ease, causing another blast of sparks to illuminate the four of them.

Cal pressed down with his sword, attempting to bring Sela to her knees. "The light souls chose their gatekeeper well."

Sela pushed against him with all her might, causing Cal to stumble backward. "Jealous?"

As one of the two Draconfolk got within range, Sela pushed off her staff and kicked the beast right in the chest. The creature clutched at the spot and let out a wheeze. Sela planted both feet on the ground and swung the staff into the head of the other beast. The creature groaned and tumbled to the ground.

Cal let a flurry of blows fly, each one sending Sela a little further back. Her arms grew sore, but she ignored the pain. When she made contact with the wall, she took a big swing with her staff and sent both weapons to the ground.

Cal winked. "Guess we'll settle this like brothers and sisters should. With fists."

Sela's brother crouched down, and she mimicked the position. This time, she opted to take the offensive. She swung her fists with such speed that even the dark soul couldn't block more than a couple. One blow hit Cal's face so hard that she felt a tooth pop loose. Another cracked him on the temple and caused him to lose his balance. Sela wiped her bloody knuckles on her side and stepped toward her brother.

"How many people did you have to kill to get to me?"

Cal rubbed at his eye, which began turning black and blue. "Eleven. Twelve if you count your dear, sweet brother. You'll make 13."

Just then, Sela felt a sharp pain through her back. She looked down to see the point of her brother's blade exiting her stomach. She didn't need to turn around to realize that the Draconfolk without the tattoo had thrown the sword like a spear and scored a direct hit.

Sela could barely hear the chanting noises above the pounding of her own heart. The pain from her back and chest made it impossible to feel the burning sensation on her arm. She looked to see the dark soul tattoo brandishing her flesh before glancing back into the smiling eyes of her former brother.

"There's a living soul on Earth. He'll kill you. Easily." Sela coughed out blood as she went to her knees.

Cal touched her shoulder and moved around to her back. "As long as he doesn't kill you, the war is won."

Sela felt her brother pull the sword out of her body as she took her final breath.

Sela's eyes opened and she felt the burden of the past dozen years disappear off her shoulders. All these years of protecting the realms and secluding herself were over. She looked down at her abdomen to see the wound closing up.

"Welcome to the other side." Cal offered her a hand.

She took it with a smile and brought in a deep breath. The quiet night sky falling over the desolate land surrounding her was no longer oppressive. The infinity around her wasn't lonely — it was a chance for freedom.

"What's the plan?"

"You always were impatient." Cal gestured to the arch. "I'll tell you on the way."

Sela nodded. She picked up her staff and slammed it into the ground. As she did so, a small, blue sphere formed in the center of the arch. It grew taller and wider and cast its bright light on the four of them. Before long, it had formed a glowing portal.

Cal stood in awe for a moment. "It's mesmerizing."

Sela smirked. "You'll get used to it. Shall we?"

She took Cal's hand once more and the two of them walked through the portal to Earth.

CHAPTER
2

Ted gripped the armrest tightly as the government-chartered plane shuddered once more. The plush seats and furnished décor reflected what he'd been told was the latest in aeronautical technology. He'd give it all up for a propeller plane and a smooth ride. Ted looked over at Agents Vott and Harding. Vott was going over some documents and seemed like he barely even noticed the turbulence. Harding was asleep. He was always asleep.

Ted reached for a cup of water, but another shake caused it to spill over. He blotted the liquid off his pants with a napkin. "Are we safe in this thing?"

Vott glanced up from his work. "You're safer than we are. If we go down, you can just fly out of here."

Ted knew Vott was right, but the fear sensors in his brain still hadn't quite gotten used to his superpowers. He attempted to grin for Vott, but it wasn't very convincing.

"Don't worry, Ted." He looked back down at his paperwork. "We'll land as soft as a pillow in a couple of minutes."

Ted looked at Vott again, this time concentrating on what he was thinking. After wading through thoughts of Vott's wife and the man's last bank statement, Ted found that Vott truly believed his words. In Ted's two and a half months away from Treasure, he'd used his new mental powers constantly, though he'd only applied them to gather information. He'd promised Erica he wouldn't use the powers to change someone's mind, and if he couldn't see the girl he loved, he had to maintain her trust. He wished keeping his word let him hold her in his arms again.

As Vott had predicted, the plane landing was uneventful despite the torrential downpour. The three of them, as well as a few other Department of Homeland Security agents on the special project, exited the plane. Brandishing umbrellas and microphones, reporters of all kinds stood outside in the havoc that was Hurricane Winston. Beside them were Ted's supporters, hoping for autographs and a chance to shake the hero's hand. Ted was relieved the crowds were less than half as large as usual. He hoped that most people had evacuated the area as instructed by the state's governor.

Harding opened an umbrella above Ted's head. "You've got about five minutes here. Don't forget, you still have to sign a football for my niece."

Ted didn't understand why it had to be a football, but he nodded regardless. They walked down the steps to cheers and questions all at once. The wind blew stinging rain into his face. After dealing with fires and mudslides earlier that season, Ted figured he was getting close to his elemental merit badge. He did his best to smile and nod for the cameras as he signed everything from t-shirts to the self-published and semi-authorized biography Dhiraj had commissioned over the summer. Between the squeals of fans came the stumpers.

"Ted, will you be going back to high school in the fall?"

"What's it like saving the lives of hundreds of people every week?"

"Will you go to college next year or be a full-time hero?"

The last question was one he'd been pondering all summer. And all the time he'd spent thinking about it didn't get him any closer to an answer. He let out a polite "no comment" before Harding brought Ted into a vehicle that seemed to combine an SUV and an armored car. This was the kind of vehicle they built for hurricanes.

Ted wiped his face on a DHS embroidered towel and looked up at his handlers. "So, how are we gonna do this?"

Vott smiled. "I like it when you're all business."

"Two weeks left." Ted turned his head to the side, allowing the accumulated liquid in his ear to dribble out. "I might as well do as much good as I can."

Vott explained they'd go just outside the city's most populated area. Once they'd set up camp, Ted would go off and do his thing. They'd be in radio contact the entire time through the earpiece Ted was putting in place. Just as Ted thought the vehicle was about to speed away, a man who seemed vaguely familiar popped into the seat beside Ted.

It was becoming instinct for Ted to learn as much as he could about a person by doing a quick scan of his thoughts. Before he could help himself, he often knew the name, occupation and general disposition of an individual. As the man began to speak, Ted already knew everything he needed to.

"Ted Finley, it's an honor."

Senator Christopher "Kit" Kable looked stronger than most politicians he'd encountered, and during the last few months, that number continued to grow. Congressmen in particular had a thing for roping him into selfies. Kable filled out his black suit from top to bottom and had a beaming smile that illuminated the vehicle.

"Senator Kable." Butterflies fluttered in Ted's stomach. "I'm surprised to see you off the campaign trail."

Kable smirked. "It's a trail with many paths. Your associates here said I could have a few minutes of your time."

Ted raised his eyebrows at Vott and Harding. The latter gave him a shrug in return.

"Sure." Ted fumbled with his earpiece. "If you're trying to get my vote, keep in mind that I won't be 18 by Election Day."

The senator let out a belly laugh. While his physique was that of a body builder, his laugh reminded Ted of a cartoon Santa Claus.

"Of course. Of course. Despite that technicality, you hold a lot of sway in this country. After the earthquake in California and the wildfires in Colorado. Heck, what you did off the coast of Louisiana was—"

"Senator."

"Please, call me Kit."

Ted had been given too many names to remember this summer. He wished people hadn't given him the permission to be more personal.

"Kit. What do you want?"

"All business, I see." The senator straightened his tie. "Ted, I'd like you to endorse me for President of the United States."

Ted had figured that was coming. With election season impending, he'd been asked to join dozens of campaigns, from the school board to the office of local representative, but none of them came close to a request for a Presidential endorsement. Ted didn't know much about either candidate's platform; all he knew was that his parents voted for President Blake in the last election.

The car pulled to a stop. Agent Harding hopped out and Vott made a gesture that showed how little time they had to talk.

Ted nodded. "I'm flattered, Senator... Kit. Get up with my manager, Dhiraj Patel. He handles these kinds of decisions. I just do the dirty work."

Kable laughed again. "And you do it so well, Ted." He extended his hand. "Good luck out there."

Ted thanked him and followed Agent Vott to a makeshift shelter. The howling winds were so strong they almost pushed Ted over.

"He sure went to a lot of trouble." Ted yanked the shelter door closed behind him. "And I can't even vote."

Vott furrowed his brow. "If you told people to vote for Kable in November, he'd win the election."

Ted didn't need to read Vott's thoughts to know that was true. He also wasn't sure that was the kind of responsibility one person should have.

A gruff-looking man in his late 50s greeted Ted and the agents as they walked into an emergency operations center for the city. The man barked orders to over a dozen people sitting in front of laptop screens. It was like a disaster movie, and he was the reluctant star. With Ted's help, this would be the team that would save as many lives as possible during the Category 3 storm.

"We're happy to have you here, Finley." The man had a gruff tone of voice to boot. "What you've done in just the last few months has been inspiring."

Pride ballooned in Ted's chest. "Thanks, sir. How can I help?"

The first pressing need was a levee that was about to break on the east side of town. Vott and Harding radioed in the directions on his headset as he took to the skies. Flying through the rain and wind took some getting used to, but it was much easier than zipping through smoke and fire in a full fireman's getup as he'd done in Colorado. By the time he reached the levee, Ted could see the problem. There was so much water attempting to stream through the sandbags, it would be a matter of seconds before things got hairy.

Ted landed behind the levee. Two firefighters called out to him, but he could only hear half their words. Ted instructed the men to stand back as he floated above the scene. He pushed his hands outward and watched as the water began to recede. As he did so, he used his powers to move a few dozen sandbags from the back of a truck to the levee. When he let the water go, he watched as the waves lapped harmlessly at the reinforced wall. The firefighters' cheers filled Ted with confidence. He grinned at the men behind the levee when the he heard Vott's voice.

"There's a problem, Ted. We need you on the other side of town."

"Ten-four."

Ted followed the instructions from his handlers and rocketed across the city much too fast to take in any sights. When he reached the front of a seven-story hospital, his feeling of strength and pride diminished. He could hear the crunching of metal and see the building start to lurch to one side. Somehow, the water had caused the building's foundation to crumble. He thought of Natalie recovering from her stab wound last year, and his mother coping with her second-degree burns from the Go Home Alien attack. Nobody he loved was inside that building, but they still deserved his best effort.

"How many people are inside?"

Vott paused. "At least 20 who haven't gotten out yet."

Ted sighed. "Alright."

He took a deep breath.

I wish Erica were here.

Ted flexed his hands and zipped in through the building's front door.

CHAPTER
3

Erica LaPlante felt the sun beaming down on her exposed midsection. While her eyes were closed beneath her designer sunglasses, she could still hear the sounds of the pool by her feet: children playing, the spring of the diving board and the lifeguard's whistle. The part of her that cared about teenage life told her to turn over to get a tan on her back as well. The part that wasn't in the 17-year-old mindset was itching for a bad guy to punch. Things had been quiet in Treasure since Ted hopped on that government plane. Too quiet for Erica's liking.

Erica turned her attention away from the blazing sun to her right. In the chair beside her, Natalie Dormer squirmed as she failed to relax in the beach chair. Her legs were too long to fit, and below her black bikini she proudly displayed a strip of white skin from her sports bra tan. Natalie noticed Erica's eyes and swung her body in that direction.

Erica suppressed her urge to mock the basketballer's discomfort. "Isn't this relaxing?"

"Yeah." Natalie rolled her eyes. "My favorite thing to do."

As a Treasure classmate passed by and looked them up and down, Erica had a sneaking feeling she was doing what everyone expected of her. In over a dozen lives, conformity was never her strong suit.

"Me too." She sat up and placed her sunglasses on a white, plastic table. "Race you 20 laps?"

Before Erica could blink, Natalie had leapt off the chair and into the lap lanes on the near side of the pool. Erica chuckled and dipped her toes in the chilly water. It sent a shiver through her body. The discomfort almost comforted her.

"Here goes."

Erica dove in and let the water cool off the heat she'd absorbed from the sun. It perked her right up, and she took one of the hairbands from her wrist and tucked her blonde mane back in a ponytail. By the time Erica began her swim, Natalie was already half a lap ahead.

As she started her crawl stroke, Erica flashed back to a previous life she'd lived on a tropical island. An evil force from another world was attempting to subjugate the community, and Erica inhabited the body of a fisherman's daughter to thwart the threat. The girl had practically lived in the water before her death, and Erica inherited every last aquatic muscle memory when she'd crossed over. As she blew by Natalie on lap five, Erica thought back to that simpler mission with a clear start and end. Things were much more complicated with a living soul/boyfriend in the mix. When she looked up at the end of 20 laps, Erica saw that Natalie was a full two laps behind.

Erica pulled herself up on the edge of the pool and waited for her opponent to arrive. When she did, Natalie leaned on the plastic lane divider to catch her breath.

"You... people... are the worst."

Erica smirked. "What do you mean, you people?"

The two girls laughed as Erica helped Natalie out of the pool. A few moments later, they washed the chlorine from their hair in the outdoor shower.

"When's the last time you heard from the anti-disaster task force?" Natalie tilted her head from side to side to get some water out.

"Six days." Erica lathered some shampoo between her hands and ran it through her locks. "Maybe a week."

Natalie turned off her showerhead and grabbed a towel. "Don't lie. I bet you know how long it's been to the minute."

Natalie was right. Erica could count the numbers of seconds it'd been since she'd talked to her boyfriend. And that gap was nearly the same as the one before that had been.

Erica forced a smile. "He's helping people. He's doing what a hero should."

Natalie tossed Erica a towel. "Are you trying to convince me or yourself?"

Erica wrinkled her nose and started drying off.

Natalie grumbled. "You know why you and all your other popular friends make me angry?"

Erica wasn't sure why, but pissing off Natalie brought her a certain kind of satisfaction. "Why's that?"

"You can scrunch up your face or bug out your eyes and you still look like a supermodel. If I do that, people call the police."

Erica laughed, which elicited another scowl.

"Even your laugh is cute. You're terrible."

Erica slipped on her sandals. "If my ever-present sexiness makes you so mad, why've you been hanging out with me all summer?"

"I guess I just hate myself." Natalie wrapped the towel over her bikini. Are you mad that Ted hasn't called more?"

"I'm just ready to fight what comes next." Erica pulled on a long t-shirt. "Hey, you wanna come to the caves with me?"

Natalie's mouth opened. "Really?"

"I feel like company." Erica took a few steps before turning back. "You comin'?"

Natalie gritted her teeth. "Sure. As long as you quit it with those runway turns."

Erica made a kissy face. "I'm just a natural, I guess."

"If you weren't already dead..."

The humidity of the caves made it harder to breath. Between the strain on her lungs and the darkness that surrounded her, Erica appreciated the challenge. It was only when Natalie had stumbled twice that she turned on her smartphone for some light.

The caves were a refuge from the perfection of the suburbs. The mustiness cleansed Erica's palette of the flower-filled lawns and power-washed sidewalks. The rocky terrain was the opposite of the foam protection that seemed to lie underneath every playground in Treasure. It almost felt like home.

About a half mile down the light-free passageway was a room with remarkable power. While Erica had never taken Ted to see the messages being sent between worlds, she had a feeling that Natalie should be there. What had once helped Nigel communicate with the dark souls was now Erica's only connection with Gan, Reena and the rest of the light soul army.

"This is way better." Natalie inched closer to Erica. "There's no way I'll get a sunburn in a cave."

Erica laughed until something else caught her attention. She shined the light as she spun in a slow circle. All she saw was rock and dark caverns, no matter which way she looked.

She swallowed. "I thought I heard something."

"And here I am, the one who's supposed to be scared. You know, I got stabbed in this cave. I should be the one freaking–"

Erica shushed Natalie and put her hand on her friend's shoulder. "Hold up."

Now the noise was becoming clearer. A low gurgling sound echoed throughout the cave.

"Okay." Natalie let out a short breath. "You said you wanted a fight. You should wish for better things."

Erica tried to grin, but the sound was starting to get louder. "Stay close to me."

"Man." Natalie placed her back against Erica's. "I knew I should've changed out of this. It's riding up on me something fierce."

The gurgling sound was right on top of them before it stopped. Erica flashed her light in the last direction of the noise, but she still couldn't see anything.

"Let's get out of—"

The crashing sound of rocks tumbling to the ground cut her off. The small bit of light coming from the entrance to the cave cut off completely. Erica grabbed Natalie's hand.

"This way."

They dashed through a wide passageway, with Erica pulling Natalie through the dark cavern with exact knowledge of where they needed to go. After a few minutes of running, they reached what was supposed to be an open entrance to the message room, but it was as blocked as the entrance had been. Erica's heart beat faster.

"This is bad." Erica took out her phone and attempted to dial. She prayed she'd be able to get a signal out.

"Erica, we've gotta hide or something. Calling a cave locksmith isn't gonna help."

Erica waved away Natalie's hand. "Look, if they know about the message room, they might know about other stuff, too." She had yet to hear a ring from the other side of the call. "Like the books. And the sword."

If Erica couldn't get through, there was a good chance the dark souls would get all they'd need to win the war.

CHAPTER
4

Dhiraj couldn't believe his luck. As he pulled his car into the Treasure High parking lot, Jennifer Norris was the epitome of cute in his passenger seat. Her licorice-black hair was pulled back into two braids, which seemed to match her knee-high pink socks and purple shorts. He had half a mind to pull through the lot and go straight to Wayne Park, but they had a mission today.

Jennifer seemed to be in her own little world when Dhiraj tapped her on the shoulder.

"Hey, Pippi Longstocking, we're here."

Jennifer blinked a few times and turned toward him. "Oh, sorry."

Dhiraj leaned over and kissed her on the lips. She gently returned the lip lock.

"You're cute when you're oblivious to your surroundings."

"You say I'm cute whenever I do anything."

Dhiraj kissed her again. "I've got this bad habit of telling the truth."

She shook her head. "I think you may actually have a silver tongue."

"It's an investment."

Jennifer laughed and grabbed up her duffel bag. She glanced at the sweet-smelling, white box that lay across the backseat. "You think today's going to be the day?"

Dhiraj took a deep breath. "You know from experience that I never give up."

Jennifer gave him a reassuring look. "I hope he's not too mean to you." She kissed him on the cheek and opened the door. "Bye, dollar."

"Bye, cents."

He watched her jog off to join the rest of the field hockey team.

A few minutes later, Dhiraj pulled into the Sheriff Department parking lot with the box of apple fritters in the back seat. He'd spent close to a hundred dollars on treats for the sheriff and his staff that summer, but he had yet to achieve his main objective: stopping the sheriff from giving him the cold shoulder. Jennifer had done her best to convince her father that Dhiraj had little to do with her pursuit of Deputy Daly five months prior. She'd even pointed out that Dhiraj had probably done more to keep her from doing something stupid than anybody else. The sheriff wasn't having it.

"Donuts didn't work. Donut holes didn't work. Let's give fritters a try."

Even though Dhiraj wasn't allowed in the house, at least he was still permitted to date Jennifer. And doing that was like a dream. With Ted gone and Natalie palling around with Erica, Dhiraj decided to shun an internship with his dad to spend all season with his lady friend. With the school year fast approaching, though, Dhiraj knew he'd have to get back on the sheriff's good side to get any afterschool Jennifer time whatsoever.

The inside of the Sheriff's Department had received a major makeover after Nigel and his gang escaped the previous year. The state diverted extra funding to the renovation, given the increased attention having a superhero around meant for the government. Dhiraj passed by a shiny bronze memorial to Grayson Riley and the other employees who'd fallen that day. He couldn't help but wonder how the last few months would've been different if Deputy Daly had suffered the same fate. The former deputy would be six-feet-under instead of behind bars, and he and Jennifer might still be just friends. Dhiraj spied Doris behind the counter. His favorite secretary looked like Natalie might in 20 years with 20 extra pounds of muscle. Dhiraj plopped the box on the partition between them.

"If it isn't the little money-miracle worker himself."

Dhiraj had a sneaking suspicion that Doris wanted to pinch his cheeks. "Hey, Doris. How's that new retirement account treating you?"

Her cheeks lit up with a creased smile. "You're a literal life saver, Dhiraj. What've we got here today?"

"Fritters. Is the big guy in?"

Her smile faded. "He is."

Dhiraj knew what that tone meant. While almost everyone in the office was pulling for him, few of them thought he had a chance. Sheriff Norris was a reasonable guy in all matters that didn't include his daughter.

Dhiraj placed one of the fritters on a paper plate. "Wish me luck."

Doris sighed. "I always do."

Dhiraj knocked on the half-open door to Sheriff Norris' office.

"Come in." The sheriff's tone was the happiest Dhiraj had heard in months. He hoped that this would be the day for forgiveness.

The room had a retro feel, obviously missing out on the renovation that had modernized the rest of the building. It was dim inside, causing the light from the hallway to cast harsh shadows on the sheriff's face.

The sheriff leaned forward into the light. When Dhiraj met the man's eyes, he felt the color drain out of the room.

"If it isn't my daughter's kidnapper."

Dhiraj smirked. "Technically, she kidnapped me, but let's not split hairs."

The sheriff let out a huff. "What do you want, Dhiraj?"

Dhiraj smiled as big as he could. "I brought some fritters for everyone to share. I thought it'd be a nice—"

"Leave it there." The sheriff gestured to the door. "I've got a lot of work to—"

"Sheriff, what do I have to do for you to forgive me? We used to go on ride-alongs. I still have my honorary deputy badge."

Sheriff Norris leaned back in his chair and into the shadow once again. He looked over his daughter's boyfriend from top to bottom. Dhiraj felt the anxiety wreaking havoc with his insides.

The sheriff cleared his throat. "Dhiraj, you violated my trust. That sort of thing takes time to get over."

Dhiraj wanted to hold his tongue, but he couldn't stand it any longer. "It's been five months. There's got to be something I can do to speed the–"

The ringing phone interrupted the exchange. Sheriff Norris put up his hand and answered. Dhiraj could feel a burst of anger building up inside of him. Even though the sheriff was Jennifer's father, the idea of anyone trying to keep him from the girl he loves was making him start to pace back and forth.

"Erica? I can barely hear– Are you sure?"

The sheriff's tone had changed once again. Now, instead of ire, it was thickly coated with worry.

"Alright, stay safe." The sheriff hung up the phone. "Dhiraj, you've gotta get out of here."

Before Dhiraj could reply, an otherworldly noise emerged from the parking lot. They bolted to the window to see the source. Beside the row of cars, a glowing, blue portal had opened up outside the Department. A green, scaly creature leapt out of the portal and landed on one of the cars in the lot. The lizard caught their eye and let out a gurgling scream. The sheriff drew the blinds.

All of Dhiraj's anger was replaced by utter terror. "What was that?"

The sheriff looked as pale as Dhiraj felt. "Erica's been attacked. She thinks... she thinks they're after the books and the sword."

The sheriff ran back behind his desk and flipped some kind of switch. An alarm sounded, accompanied by a red, flashing light that cut through the shadows.

As the sheriff ran out of his office, Dhiraj kept pace.

"This is the secret hiding place? Why would Erica leave them here?"

The sheriff continued to look straight ahead. "I guess she trusts me. You really should get out of here, Dhiraj."

Dhiraj scoffed. "No freaking way. Let me know how I can help."

They turned toward the front doors of the building, which the sheriff's switch had automatically locked. A loud thump shook through the floor as the doors seemed to bend inward. While they held from the first few efforts, Dhiraj wasn't sure they would last much longer.

"You want to be a part of this?" Sheriff Norris took out his gun and pointed it at the door. "Then you help me figure out how we're going to kill whatever comes through that door."

Dhiraj racked his brain for a plan to defeat a giant lizard-person. The first few ideas revolved around the presence of Ted.

The doors bulged again as the creature continued to smash ahead.

Dhiraj held his breath. "It sure would be great if we had a superhero right about now."

CHAPTER
5

Ted flew in through the front door of the hospital and landed in a puddle. At least, he thought it was a puddle, until he realized the entire ground floor of the building was now a six-inch-high wading pool. Vott and Harding had equipped him with waterproof boots, but the patients who remained inside weren't as lucky. Ted saw a nurse trudge through the water with a patient who didn't even have shoes on.

He should be wearing these, not me.

Ted flew over to the nurse. Her eyes widened, but her face relaxed when she recognized him.

"How many patients are left?" Ted put his shoulder under the man's other arm.

The nurse's voice was hoarse. "At least 20."

Ted looked down another hallway to see a doctor pushing a patient on a gurney as fast as he could while trying to hold onto the IV that led into the patient's arm. Ted watched another two patients coming from the other direction when the building creaked all around them. It was as if the hospital warned those inside to get out fast. Despite a summer of saving people from disasters, Ted felt a moment of panic.

We're not gonna make it.

The nurse must have noticed his facial assessment of the situation, because she pinched his wrist behind the patient's back. "Hey, we're gonna be fine. After all, you're here. You're not hiding like the politicians in some kind of bubble."

Ted nodded. That's when it hit him.

"Nurse, you're a lifesaver!" He paused. "Literally. In at least two ways." Ted tapped his earpiece. "Vott, Harding. You guys still there?"

"Yeah. Ted, you better—"

"I need somewhere in a three-mile radius where I can send about 20 injured people."

Vott didn't hesitate. Ted heard him tapping away on a nearby keyboard.

"There's a building we have secured and boarded up. You couldn't get in through the front."

Ted looked back to see the patients splashing their way to his position.

"Roof access?"

Vott made an affirmative noise. "What are you planning?"

"I'm gonna make a bubble."

Ted gathered all the patients and nurses in the lobby of the hospital emergency room. On the night of the prom, Ted floated the disguised Dhiraj and Jennifer through the air to lure the brainwashed mob away from their limo. Now, he was going to do the same with way more people, all while trying to protect them from the harsh effects of the storm. Ted explained his plan, but most of the looks he received back were dubious.

Nancy, the nurse he'd met, was the leader of the pack. She folded her arms in distrust. "Have you ever tried this before?"

He half-grinned. "Not really. But think of it as experimental surgery."

The nurse and the others didn't seem pleased at that line.

Ted shrugged. "One that works?"

The building uttered another large creaking noise and the ground seemed to move beneath them. A male patient in his 40s began crying, and an intern did her best to comfort him.

Ted straightened his spine. "Look, guys. I need to get you off the streets and somewhere safe. I don't know if this is going to work, but I'm here to help. Anybody who wants to take a chance with me, step forward."

Everyone in the lobby, from the patients to the doctors, stepped forward or did their best injured-version of the act.

Ted nodded. "Good. Everybody outside."

As they complied, Ted concentrated on blocking all wind and rain from coming into contact with the patients. It wasn't perfect and a few raindrops fell through, but to the naked eye, it looked like there was a clear glass box around the entire group.

The corner of the Nancy's lips turned upward as she nodded. "Okay. Okay, Super Ted."

Ted looked upward. "That's just part one. Vott, are your people in place?"

"Yes. On your cue."

Ted took a deep breath. Flying and moving objects were second nature to him now, but this was going to take all his facilities.

"Paint me a picture, Vott."

Off in the distance, through the raging storm, Ted could see a red flare fly high into the sky.

Ted locked onto all the patients, doctors and nurses and shifted them up two feet to ensure he had control. All of them moved as he intended, though even that small movement felt like he was lifting 100-pound dumbbells.

Ted tightened his face and muscles. "See you guys soon." With a hearty grunt, Ted lifted the entire group high into the air.

He heard several screams coming from the giant, invisible elevator he'd created. Ted had almost become numb to such pleas for help – the more shrieks of pain and fear he heard, the less his nervous system seemed to react. The group reached the same height as the top of the building, and Ted floated himself high into the air beside them to get a better view of the destination.

"Ready another flare."

"Alright, but it's the last one we've got."

Ted grumbled. "Next time, send your people to Costco to get 'em in bulk."

As he pushed the patients away from the hospital, the hardest part was keeping himself steady in the storm. The wind and rain beat against his face so hard, he could hardly feel it anymore. He was about to ask for the other flare when a giant gust of wind picked up his body and sent it flying. In his effort to regain control, he lost the protection around the bubble, though the group remained steady in the air.

Ted watched as the patients' paper gowns became drenched and the wind pushed the medical equipment every which way. He shuddered.

"Flare. Now!"

Ted thought the wind might rip the clothes from his body before Vott could comply. Thankfully, the red flare shot into the sky and Ted used all his energy to push the group to the rooftop as fast as possible. In the distance, Ted could barely see as they moved into position above the roof.

"Are they directly above?"

"Yes. Lower them. I'll let you know when to let go."

As Ted agreed, he heard something in his mind. Thoughts of fear and pain wafted through that he hadn't noticed before. He was reading the mind of a little girl – a girl who was still inside the hospital.

"Alright, you can let them go. Get out of there, Ted. The worst of the storm is coming your way."

Ted looked up at the clouds and saw a tint of orange begin to paint the sky. He shook his head. "Can't do it. There's someone still inside."

Ted zipped back down to ground level and went back in through the front. The rising water level on the ground had doubled through the almost deserted building.

"Ted, this is an order. Get out of there now!"

With his first step, Ted felt the liquid sloshing over the top of his waterproof boots. His socks were soaked.

"Are you gonna help me, or do I have to take out my earpiece like they do in the movies?"

Vott mumbled something to himself. "I'll help, but act quick."

The shuddering of the hospital had grown louder and Ted watched as several ceiling tiles and beams dropped to the ground. He searched his mind to find the girl. By pinpointing her thoughts, he detected her on the opposite side of the building. Ted's powers were somewhat weakened by his bubble rescue, but he used every last reserve to push himself to go faster. The girl's thoughts grew louder and louder until he walked into a room with several beds. There she was, standing on top of a pile of sheets in an effort to get away from the water.

A loud beam crashing down in the hallway caused her to squeal. Ted fought an urge to do the same and spoke like a parent.

"Hey, honey. I'm Ted."

The girl shivered and stared. "I'm Sophie."

"Good to meet you. Can I get you out of here, Sophie?"

The girl breathed so hard and fast, Ted feared she might hyperventilate. But through all that, the girl nodded her assent.

Ted wrapped his arm around her waist and flew the two of them out of the room. As he did, he heard a pipe burst in the distance and a flood of new water came pouring in. The water level was now up to Ted's knees. Sophie cried out and buried her head in Ted's chest.

"It's ok. We'll get out of—"

A beam came crashing down from the ceiling and hit Ted right in the back of the skull. He lost his hold of the girl and they both tumbled into the water. Ted's face made impact with the flood first. His eyes stung with whatever was floating around in the water. When he came back up for air, Sophie was nowhere to be seen. Ted felt his pulse race.

"Sophie?!"

He dove under the water. Ted looked in every direction but he couldn't see the girl. He felt his breath grow heavy. As Ted left the water, he saw something he never would've expected. In the middle of the crumbling building and the water, there was a blue portal hovering a few inches off the ground. Amidst the chaos, the shimmering light from whatever it was remained calm and steady. Sophie was right beside it, and though the water was up to her midsection, she waded toward the gateway.

"Sophie, no!"

Before Ted could stop her, the girl had disappeared through the blue portal. Ted ran toward the phenomenon, but it closed with a sound that reminded him of arcade Pac-Man. As he reached for where the portal had been, another series of beams fell to the ground and surrounded him.

"Ted, are you out of the building?"

Before Ted could respond, the rest of the hospital came down on top of him.

CHAPTER
6

With Erica on the phone, Natalie turned on the flashlight app on her cell phone. She saw a green slithering tail in the distance. Natalie growled.

Come to the cave, she said. It'll be fun, she said.

Erica tucked the phone away and bent her elbow in a stretch. "The line went dead, but I got through to Daly."

Natalie gave Erica a puzzled look. "And you asked for help, right?"

Erica bent over and touched her toes.

Natalie grabbed Erica by the shoulder. "Hey, Captain Flexibility. Did you ask for help?"

Erica took Natalie's wrist and removed her hand. "What, you think we can't handle this ourselves?"

Natalie threw her hands up in the air. "I guess we don't have much of a choice."

Natalie and Erica both shined their lights ahead, only to catch the lizard creature running toward them at full speed.

The beast swiped at them with its claws, but Natalie tucked and rolled out of the way. She looked back to see Erica finishing a backflip to avoid the attack.

"Show off." Natalie tossed her flashlight phone to the ground, which skidded against the stone. She formed her hands into fists.

The phone provided enough light to see the creature in its full form. Natalie figured it was about eight feet tall and wider than her and Erica put together. Not that being twice as wide as Erica would even qualify as a size 6.

The creature's gurgling noise bounced against the walls as it came for Erica. When it reached for her again, the protector did a split underneath the lizard. With a powerful punch, she nailed the beast directly in the crotch.

The creature howled in pain and fell backward onto the hard stone with a thump. Erica pushed herself up on the ground and joined Natalie by her side.

Natalie smirked. "What's with you and groins?"

Erica raised an eyebrow. "I was brainwashed and drunk. Are you ever gonna let that go?"

Natalie eyed the lizard squirming on the ground. "Nope."

Quicker than either of them expected, the creature sprung back to standing. He ran toward them so fast that Erica didn't have time to block the blow that sent her back-first into the wall. The lizard grabbed Natalie by the waist and lifted her into the air, ripping her shirt as its claws had grasped her. When she squirmed to get herself free, the scent of half-digested insects blew out at her from his mouth.

"From all that gurgling, I thought you'd be a mouthwash fan."

When the creature gave Natalie a confused look, she reared back her fist and connected with one of its eyes. Her knuckles stung against the lizard's orbital bone as the creature released his grip to cover its bleeding eye. Natalie looked to Erica, but she was missing from her previous spot.

As the stunned lizard tended to his sight, Erica ran and leapt from the other side of the room. She wrapped her legs around the creature's back and shot a blue wave of electricity between her hands. Erica moved her fingers to either side of the creature's head and let the lightning rip.

Natalie watched as the lizard fell chest-first and lifeless to the ground. Erica flashed her perfect prom queen smile. Natalie was grateful enough not to hate it for the time being.

"You couldn't have led with the brain zapping?" Natalie felt at the holes in her shirt.

Erica crouched down beside the lizard. "And take away all that fun we just had?"

"Your definition of fun is—"

The lizard gurgled himself awake. Natalie ran in to deliver the final blow, but Erica held her back.

"Just wait."

As the lizard got back to a standing position, his disposition had changed completely. His snarling face had relaxed itself to a vacant stare. He almost looked human, aside from being green and scaly.

"Great." Natalie folded her arms. "Now we have a lizard zombie. Just what I always wanted."

Erica rolled her eyes. "Hey buddy, can you help us get outta here?"

The lizard nodded and began walking toward the cave entrance. As the two of them followed, Erica tried her cell phone again.

"Damn."

Natalie gave Erica a sideways glance. "Calling animal control?"

Erica sighed. "I doubt our friend here is the only one in town."

As they reached the pile of rocks that blocked the entrance, the lizard started moving the rubble to the side.

Natalie scratched her head. "Why don't you ask him?"

Erica smiled. "Good idea. Hey lizard-breath, what's the grand plan?"

The creature began gurgling with a series of indiscernible grunts.

Erica cleared her throat. "In English, if it's not too much trouble."

The creature mimicked Erica's throat-clearing and began speaking with some difficulty. "The books. The sword. Gatekeeper."

As astounded as Natalie had been to see a giant lizard in the first place, she was even more impressed it could speak English.

"It can talk?"

"Draconfolk usually know multiple languages." Erica seemed preoccupied. "What did you mean by gatekeeper?"

The lizard continued to push the rocks out of the way as a sliver of light cut in from the outside world.

"Gatekeeper. Dark soul."

Erica joined in beside the lizard and started moving the stone away as well. "No, no, no, no, no."

Natalie did her best to help beside Erica. "What is it?"

"It's impossible."

"What's impossible?"

Erica ran her hands through her hair, causing small pebbles lodged in her curls to drop to the ground. "Gatekeepers control the flow of people between worlds. Their locations are secret and hidden. If one was turned into a dark soul, all the worlds could be in deep trouble."

All the otherworldly things Natalie had seen so far — the lizard, Mr. Redican's mind control, Nigel's gang of thugs — had been frightening, even to her. She had no desire to see what else the other worlds had to offer.

"What're we going to do?"

Erica and the lizard cleared a large enough hole for the three of them to escape the cave. She took Natalie by the shoulder.

"We kill her before she can do any damage. We need to get to the sheriff's right away."

Natalie felt the brightness of the sun burn her eyes after they'd spent so much time in the cave. They crawled out and walked to Natalie's car. The lizard followed closely behind Erica like a lost duckling.

Natalie gestured in the creature's direction. "What are we gonna do with him? No way he's gonna fit in my car."

Erica paused her momentary panic for a wide grin. "I think I've got an idea." She looked at Natalie. "You ever learn to ride a horse?"

CHAPTER

7

Dhiraj watched the top hinge of the door to the Sheriff's Department snap clean off and clank on the ground. He felt his heart skip a beat. Dhiraj looked over at the sheriff, who seemed to have forgotten about hating him for the time being.

He gestured to the hinge. "That does not inspire confidence."

The sheriff nodded. "Backup should be here any second."

As if on cue, a set of sirens blared through the parking lot. The sheriff got on the radio to the cars outside while Dhiraj scampered over to a window to watch.

"The creature at the door is extremely dangerous." The sheriff attempted to sound as assuring as he could. "You have a green light to fire. I repeat, a green light."

Dhiraj could see a few vehicles block off the entrance to the lot. Several deputies and officers came out with their guns drawn. While Dhiraj couldn't watch the creature from his vantage point, the terrified looks on the officers' faces clued him in that the lizard had turned his attention toward them.

"Fire!"

The sheriff's command roused the officers who began taking shots at the lizard. Dhiraj covered his ears from the noise and backed away from the window. He could feel his pulse racing as fast as the officers fired. While the first couple of shots elicited groans from the creature, the next set seemed to ricochet off him, like he'd toughened up his scales into armor. With bullets no longer working, they tossed two canisters of tear gas in the lizard's direction. A thick cloud of smoke blocked Dhiraj's vision. The sounds of gunfire and screaming had given way to silence. Several long beats of nothingness went by.

"I need a visual on the creature." Sheriff Norris had a growl to his voice. "Can someone give me eyes on that thing?"

An officer with a shaky voice replied. "That's a negative. Wait a second, I see something."

Dhiraj looked back at the window and saw the green creature emerging from the smoke. The roar it gave was so intense, one of the officers collapsed to the ground in fear. Dhiraj's nervous system considered forcing him to do the same. He gripped the windowsill and watched the creature approach the officers. The lizard put his claws underneath the front of one car and promptly flipped it over. It landed with a crash as glass scattered on the pavement.

The sheriff looked over at Dhiraj. "Alright, kidnapper, got any bright ideas?"

Dhiraj turned away from the mayhem in the parking lot. He wasn't a tactician; he was a businessman. But Dhiraj knew he'd have little chance to make his fortune if the two of them couldn't keep the creature at bay. He glanced at the box of apple fritters. An idea began to form in his head.

"You guys ever have to do any trapping in the woods?"

The sheriff caught Dhiraj's drift immediately and barked out orders to Doris, one of the only people in the office not cowering behind a desk.

"What else do you need?"

Dhiraj tried to visualize his plan as he looked around, ignoring the sounds of roaring and breaking glass from outside. "I need the books. And the sword."

The sheriff nodded and went into his office. When Dhiraj followed, he watched the man remove a family portrait from the wall and open a safe behind it. Inside, Dhiraj could see the five books encased in clear plastic, as well as the sword.

He took a deep breath. "Let's hope this goes better than my plan to start a women's fashion line."

A few minutes later, Dhiraj watched from behind a desk as the creature busted his way into the office. The wooden door scraped its way across the linoleum tiles and came to a stop in front of the service desk. While the office looked abandoned from the lizard's point of view, most of the men and women present were lying in wait as a backup plan if Dhiraj's idea failed.

It won't come to that. It's gonna work.

As the creature entered the room, Dhiraj could see it begin to sniff around. Up close, the monster looked like it'd jumped straight out of a comic book or the Cretaceous period. It was literally the color of money and it was terrifying. Dhiraj did what he could to slow and quiet his breathing as he watched the lizard move. It looked left and right before settling on the bait. In the center of the room was an apple fritter in the jaws of a bear trap. While the creature seemed to want to resist, it couldn't help but examine the prize. When it reached to grab the fritter, the trap sprung and clamped down on the creature's arm.

The scream mixed with a gurgle filled the building as the beast attempted to shake the trap off its arm. The sound was like nothing Dhiraj had ever heard, and he couldn't help but cover his ears. He looked over at Sheriff Norris.

From across the room, the sheriff cued Dhiraj for his part of the plan.

Dhiraj handled the special edition of *The Sound and the Fury* with care. He knew what happened to Ted when he'd grasped its cover at the Treasure Public Library. He hoped the same thing occurred with giant lizards. Dhiraj had put on a pair of black leather gloves to unwrap the book without damaging himself. When he was ready, he steeled his nerves and ran toward the creature.

"You wanted the book? Time to pay the price."

As the creature lunged at Dhiraj with his free hand, the teen tossed it directly into the beast's chest. When the book connected with the lizard, Dhiraj saw the magic in action.

The lights flickered as the creature flew backward into the nearest wall. Dhiraj could smell the aroma of powdered drywall wafting through the room after the beast left a lizard-shaped indentation in the wall. The impact seemed to have damaged one of the creature's legs, which now bent at an unnatural angle.

Dhiraj lifted his chin and looked over at the sheriff. "See, now that's what happens when two great friends put their minds—"

The creature sprung off the ground and gurgled loudly. Dhiraj froze and held his breath. Even though the beast only had one good leg, it was still agile enough to reach for Dhiraj. The creature snarled and made one last swipe before the sheriff used the sword to stab the lizard through the back.

Green blood pooled on the linoleum, and the creature collapsed. Steam rose up from where the sword had penetrated, and a foul odor emanated from the wound. While it was an unpleasant sight, Dhiraj figured it was worth it to keep the super items safe.

"You saved me from a dinosaur." Dhiraj tried to breathe out some of his adrenaline. "I owe you one."

The sheriff looked up at the ceiling and then back at Dhiraj. He sighed. "We're even, Dhiraj. About everything."

Dhiraj ran over and hugged the sheriff. "That makes me happier than a dead lizard."

The sheriff laughed. "Good. I don't understand why he didn't disappear, though."

A blue portal appeared near the wall, similar to the gateway Dhiraj had seen the lizard come out of. A white electric current seemed to run around the outside of the circle. The shimmering circle reminded Dhiraj of a movie special effect, but unlike a comic book's film adaptation, this was real.

A woman who somehow looked even stronger than Natalie exited the portal. She was stout and pale with an outfit that seemed to decry style for functional killing. At least, that's what Dhiraj assumed it was for, given the murderous look on the woman's face.

"He didn't disappear because he wasn't a dark soul."

Dhiraj had seen a lot in the past year. Magic portals and evil women from another world were new. He wasn't quite sure how to react.

"Now, give me the sword or I'll flay the skin off your disgusting human bodies."

CHAPTER

8

Ted looked up at the rubble above him. He was surprised he could see any of it until he noticed an emergency light built into his boots. Despite the weight of the building crashing down upon him, he'd been able to create a perfect protective dome around himself. If he hadn't done so, he would've been crushed for sure. In each direction he looked, all he could see was the remnants of the hospital.

If I ever tried to fake my death, this would be the time to do it.

Given the conditions of the city, it'd take the government days to search through the rubble. If he placed a little blood here and a piece of his outfit there, then he'd no longer be the subject of tabloids and tweets. He wouldn't have to make deals with the government to keep himself and his family safe. Faking his death would be the ultimate out, offering a relief he hadn't felt in months.

"Ted! Are you still in there, Ted?"

Agent Vott's voice brought Ted out of his thoughts. While the morbid idea of faking his death was in the front of his mind, Ted decided to save that trick for another day.

"I'm here. As soon as I can figure out how to leave without crushing myself, I'll meet you at the rendezvous."

Vott breathed a sigh of relief. "And the girl?"

Ted saw the portal again in his mind. He'd seen some odd stuff, but never anything as strange as the girl walking into the otherworldly portal. Ted didn't know how to explain it, so he opted to leave a few items out. "I lost track of her. I'm not sure she made it."

"I'm sorry."

"Me too. I'll see you guys in a little bit."

Ted tried to move the pocket of air closer to the exit. As he moved to the left, a piece of ceiling tile slipped into his protective bubble and landed beside his feet. When he tried moving to the right, one side of a metal beam came within inches of slamming into his shoulder. He looked straight above him.

"Onward and upward then."

Ted lifted off the ground and moved the pocket up as he pushed his way through the rubble. He could hear the sounds of broken wood and metal clearing his way as he moved through what used to be a building. After a minute of pushing, he found he way to the surface, where the Hurricane Winston continued to rage. He blasted through the air and made it to the rendezvous point within minutes.

Ted tapped his foot on the ground at a rapid clip. Nobody seemed to notice his anxiety as the rest of the agents focused on Vott. Ted had changed out of his wet clothes, and he'd been given a few minutes to recover before being pulled back into bureaucracy. Every mission he'd gone on that summer was immediately followed by a debriefing session. Ted dreaded them all and wished he could simply do the hero work and then take a well-deserved nap. But no such luck. Vott's words melded together, and for all Ted knew, the man was talking about the birds and the bees instead of their latest mission.

As Ted's mind wandered away from the discussion, all he could think about was the portal and Sophie. A tap on the shoulder extracted Ted from his guilt and confusion.

Ted looked over at the tapper to see a female agent in her early 20s. The blond beauty must've been straight out of college, because Ted wouldn't have been too surprised to see her roaming the hallways of Treasure High.

"Hey, you did great out there."

The agent's soothing voice may have been exactly what Ted needed.

He nodded. "Thanks, agent—"

"Just call me Allison."

Ted extended his hand. "Ted."

She giggled. "As if anyone in the world doesn't know your name by now."

Ted gripped Allison's hand. "For better or worse."

Agent Vott cleared his throat and stared right at the two of them. When Allison rolled her eyes, Ted laughed for the first time in a long while. A summer of helping people out of burning buildings didn't exactly promote comedic situations.

When Allison turned her attention back to Vott, Ted checked his phone. Whether it was the cement walls or the storm, Ted had no signal whatsoever. He desperately wanted to talk to Erica and see what she'd say about this portal business. Given the lack of action in Treasure most of the summer, he was certain she'd want to discuss it in depth. She certainly didn't seem to want to talk about their relationship during the last few phone calls.

"Lastly," Vott said, "we need to thank Ted Finley for his service on this mission. He saved more than two dozen people and we're all thankful for his efforts."

Allison and the rest of the agents turned toward Ted and began clapping. He scanned their minds as they looked his way. Their thoughts of praise matched their applause for the most part, and he welcomed the positivity. When the meeting concluded, Ted made sure he was the first one out of the room. After all, if he stayed there even for a second, he'd have to go through at least 45 minutes of handshakes and conversations that couldn't have interested him less.

As he walked through the hall, Ted tried to find an area with a signal. He passed by a TV that displayed a report of Ted's heroics, along with an image of Sophie's parents crying when they heard the news. Ted wasn't sure where the portal led, but he had to hold onto some hope that the girl was still alive. Otherwise, he'd lose it right then and there.

After a few seconds, Ted found the signal he needed to get a call through. Before he could dial Erica's number, he received a series of text messages.

The first came from Dhiraj, telling him that the Sheriff's Department was under attack. The next one was from Erica, describing a similar situation at the caves. The third came from Natalie, and it displayed an image that looked Photoshopped. It was a selfie, with Natalie and Erica riding on the back of what looked like a miniature Godzilla.

"What in the hell?"

Ted passed the TV one more time and went back into the room where Vott, Harding and several others were discussing the day's mission.

Vott smiled and pointed at Ted as he came back in. "There he is! The man of the hour."

Ted tried to build up his resolve. "I need to go back to Treasure."

Vott's face went from happy to annoyed in a hurry. "As I told you last time, the only reason you can go is—"

Ted pulled up the picture. "If my town comes under attack from otherworldly creatures?"

Vott pulled the phone closer. "What is that thing? A freakin' dinosaur?"

Harding piped up. "Can you forward me that picture? My niece would love that. She's really into science right now."

Vott glared at his partner. "Ted, there are things left to figure out here. Relief efforts."

Ted rubbed at his chin. "None of which you need me for."

Vott took a step toward him. "We can't spare the resources to fly you—"

"Not a problem. Just give me permission to go."

Vott put his arm around Ted's shoulder and led him away from the other agents. "Ted, do you really want to fly up the entire East Coast? Just wait a day."

Ted shook his head and stared right into Vott's eyes. "We had a deal."

Vott flared his nostrils. "Fine. Take some goggles at least."

Ted wrapped his arms around Vott for a hug. "Thanks, man. I mean, agent man."

Vott laughed. "Don't mention it. Let us know when you get there."

Ted let go of the hug and nodded. He waved to Harding, Allison and the other agents before speeding over to a supply closet for some goggles. He sent a group text to the gang and said he was on his way before opening a window and flying out.

It took Ted a moment to get his cardinal directions right, but once he did, he flew due north and tried to pick up as much speed as possible. He'd flown fast before, but he'd never tried hopping over several states at a time. The air was cold against his skin, so he formed a protective barrier around himself. It seemed to help, though he wasn't sure he had enough speed. It was nearly impossible to gauge until he came up upon a commercial airplane.

Ted felt a competitive spirit bubble to the top.

Let's see what this body can do.

Ted pushed himself to zip past the plane, waving as he went. At this rate, he'd get to Treasure in under an hour. He hoped that Erica and the gang would be able to hold off the threat until then.

CHAPTER
9

Senator Kable kept his smile wide as the makeup artist placed some powder on his cheeks. He'd learned a long time ago that a positive demeanor made a major impact on the people around him. His campaign runner, Terry, often made notes about how his pearly whites had won him the heart of America. Kable's poll numbers showed otherwise.

Once the makeup session had concluded, a local Florida producer gave him the two-minute heads up. Some of Kable's staff members thought it was distasteful to go on the air with the hurricane still raging. He'd told them nothing was off the table until he was the one sitting in the White House.

When he got the cue for the last five seconds, he adjusted his earpiece and prepared himself for the painful sounds of Rudy Bolger's voice.

"Today, I have Presidential candidate Senator Kit Kable live from Florida. Senator, thanks for being here."

Kable traded out his grin for a respectful frown. There would be a place and time to display happiness. This was not one of them.

"Thanks for having me, Rudy."

Bolger took on his fake sympathetic tone and pressed on. "What's it like down there?"

"As during any disaster, there are hardworking Americans trying to keep their neighbors safe and secure. They've taken action into their own hands, and it's a good thing, too, because action isn't on everybody's mind these days."

Kable could hear the sly smile forming on Bolger's face.

"Are you referring to someone in particular?"

Kable psyched himself up to be as authoritative as possible. "I am, Rudy. President Blake knew this hurricane would be brutal, and yet he didn't encourage evacuation until it was too late. Instead, he sends in superhero Ted Finley to clean up his mistakes. It wasn't enough for some innocent Floridians, like Sophie Kent."

Bolger made a grunt of assent. "Here at YNN, we offer our condolences for any of the families who have suffered losses during the storm. Senator, are you saying you wouldn't have sent Ted to Florida?"

Kable loved interviews with Bolger. The rat was prone to serve up big fat meatballs of questions that Kable was much obliged to devour.

"I wish Blake had sent leadership down to Florida. I recently met Ted Finley, and he's a good kid, but we can't rely on him to bail us out of problems caused by the White House."

Bolger's smile came out in his voice again, and Kable assumed the rodent was counting the number of times that quote would be replayed on the other networks.

"Senator, do you have a message for the people of Florida?"

Kable sat up a little bit straighter. "I do, Rudy. People of Florida, it will be a rebuilding process to fix up your homes and businesses. I'm already here and ready to help. Let me guide you through this challenge for the next four years."

After Bolger transitioned to commercial, he became a completely different person.

"Kit, Kit, Kit. You are something else. It's like you're out of some ratings fever dream I had after too much lobster and scotch."

Kable chuckled. "After I get elected, you'll have to have me over for some of that lobster."

Bolger laughed as if it was the funniest thing he'd ever heard. "Oh, man. As long as you treat me to cheesesteaks in the Oval Office."

Kable suppressed the urge to roll his eyes. "It's a deal. Good luck with the election coverage."

"Make up the five points. Give us something to get excited about."

"We're on it. Bye for now."

When Kable took off his earpiece and got the all-clear, Terry led the rest of the room in a round of applause. After his makeup was wiped off, the group gathered in the next room over. It was dull beige from top to bottom and the staff crammed in around a long cafeteria table.

"This was a turning point, ladies and gentlemen." Terry's eyes twinkled. "And you have your fearless leader to thank."

Kable watched his staff members as they grinned like idiots. Most of them were young, in their 20s and full of life. They laughed and held conversations underneath the noise of another round of applause. Many wanted to be right where he was sitting in a few decades. These people had devoted much of their time to him and his cause without really knowing what it was, and Kable didn't plan to reveal that until inauguration day.

"Please, Terry. I couldn't have done this without you. It's been one heck of a day." Kable let his shoulders relax to appear more down-to-earth. "What's say we take the rest of the night off and get ready for the next step tomorrow?"

This brought about a small cheer, which echoed against the walls of the room. After countless long days in a row, he hoped the full night's sleep would energize his staff for what lay ahead. Before long, Terry was the only other person left in the room.

"Senator, do you want me to send you updates for any polling numbers after the interview?"

Kable put his hand on Terry's shoulder. The man was willing and able to work 20 hours a day if he had to.

"Terry, you're incredible. You won't get much sleep for the next three months, so I would take a night now if I were you."

Terry took the hint, though he felt the need to offer his hand for a high five first. Kable slapped his hand and watched him exit the door. As soon as it closed behind him, a shimmering portal opened up on the other side of the room. Cal Fortbright stepped out of it before sitting down and crossing his legs.

"I thought they would never leave."

Kable walked over toward Cal and took the seat next to him.

"They're very excited. You can't blame them."

Cal laughed. "Do you think they'd still be as excited if they knew you caused the hospital to collapse?"

Kable pondered the question. "You know, half of them would probably stay on the campaign. Scruples don't win elections."

Cal sighed and leaned forward in his chair. "What does win elections?"

Kable imagined what he would have said had the question been posed on Bolger's show. That answer would've been the exact opposite of the truth.

"Fear. Delivered in just the right way to the right people."

Kable stood up and looked out the window. The storm was starting to lose its power as it moved further out to land. Though the meteorologists didn't realize it, another kind of storm was about to begin.

"And together, we're going to deliver a whole lot of fear."

CHAPTER
10

Dhiraj felt significantly more tongue-tied than usual as he looked at the woman who'd just come through the portal. He prided himself on being able to talk his way out of any situation, but this might be the biggest challenge of his life. After all, he didn't even know what species she was.

The woman reached back toward the portal and it closed behind her. "I imagine it's breathtaking to see a creature from another world in your presence, but there's really no time for delay. Hand over the sword and the books."

Dhiraj looked over at the sheriff. He seemed to be as speechless as Dhiraj was. The sword in the sheriff's hands continued to drip the green blood of the fallen creature. The sheriff didn't seem to mind the putrid smell; his eyes were focused on the mysterious woman.

"This is the property of the living soul." The sheriff took a step back. "Taking it could make him very angry."

"Yeah!" Dhiraj felt the pit in his stomach grow. "You wouldn't like him when he's angry."

The gatekeeper guffawed and held her belly as if it were about to burst. "Humans. Even before I saw the dark, I never understood why we valued you so much."

The woman took a long metal staff out of a holster on her back. The weapon made a ringing sound as it emerged. Dhiraj noticed ancient writing from top to bottom of the staff. The sight of it didn't help to settle his stomach.

"We're really good at talking things out." Dhiraj felt a buzz in his pocket. "In fact, why don't we just have a nice conversation over some delicious apple fritters?"

The woman's smile turned sour. "You're stalling. I think I'll take the sword. And the pastries." With a swift motion, the woman swung the end of the staff into the ground. With that, a portal began to form underneath Dhiraj and the sheriff. Dhiraj looked down and watched as a blue dot the size of a pin swelled to the dimensions of a manhole and continued to expand. The portal was mesmerizing and terrifying all at the same time. It seemed to compel Dhiraj to keep his feet planted and let himself be sucked inside.

The sheriff grabbed him by the waist and pulled him away from the opening. As they leaned up against the wall, the blue hole grew continued to expand, sucking in a wastebasket and a few papers that had fallen to the ground in the attack.

Dhiraj turned his attention from the hole back to the woman with the staff. "That's quite a trick. I guess you make holes for a living. I'm going to college soon, so what classes should I take to get into this enterprising new field?"

The woman gestured to the portal, making it expand at double its rate.

"You know, I've always had this power." The woman moved like water with each fluid step. "I can see between worlds. I can travel to any of the realms at any time. Before, I couldn't use that power for myself."

Dhiraj and the sheriff continued to move along the wall, as the portal sucked in a small desk and the deceased creature's body. They reached a dead end next to a large metal storage cabinet.

The woman's eyes looked as wide as the portal growing beside them. "Now that I'm free, there's nothing I can't do."

Dhiraj looked down into the portal. Through the glowing blue, he could see down for what seemed like miles. There was no telling what was at the end of that tunnel, or if he and the sheriff would survive the trip.

Just then, something caught Dhiraj's eye on the other side of the room.

He tossed a smile in the woman's direction. "I can think of one thing you don't have."

The woman wrinkled her forehead. "What's that, mortal?"

"Eyes in the back of your head."

With a gurgling battle cry, another eight-foot-tall lizard creature came dashing into the office. It was on a collision course with the woman in the center of the room. Dhiraj watched as Natalie and Erica dove off the beast and rolled to the side. The creature lowered its head and rammed right into the woman's midsection. As she flew through the air, the staff bounced out of her hands and the portal beside Dhiraj closed in an instant.

He smirked at the sheriff. "Remind me never to go cliff diving."

The sheriff shook his head before pulling Dhiraj toward Erica and Natalie.

"You guys okay?" Erica trained her eyes on the woman across the room.

"Sure." Dhiraj felt his heart rate come down slightly. "Every day I don't fall into a blue death hole is a miracle." Dhiraj noticed that Natalie's hand was tinted green. "You teach that lizard to play nice?"

Natalie gave Dhiraj the stink-eye. "You know I have a way with animals. Who's the chick?"

The woman stood up. She looked as if she'd almost enjoyed being slammed into by a giant lizard. She then looked Erica square in the eyes.

"Protector. You shouldn't have come."

Erica put her hands on her hips. "What? And miss this inter-dimensional party?"

The lizard had been catching its breath in the corner, but after a full recovery, it made another charge at the woman. All in one sweeping motion, she accelerated rapidly across the room, rolled over to her fallen metal staff and slammed the end on the ground. Another portal opened up in mid-air, and the lizard ran right into it. With another tap of the staff, the portal and the creature were gone.

Dhiraj's shoulders slumped. "Never send a lizard to do a man's—"

Before he could finish, Erica had rushed over to the woman and kicked her in the back. When the woman turned and swung her staff, Erica roundhouse kicked it out of her hands. It clanged against the ground.

"Protector. You have no idea what's coming."

Erica tossed her hair. "Gatekeeper. Shut up and fight."

The woman grinned at the barb and started to swing her fists at Erica. Erica blocked the first two blows easily, but a third one surprised her with a whap to the side of the head. Erica shook it off and went on the offensive with three punches of her own, one of which landed in the gatekeeper's gut. As the gatekeeper started another volley of blows, Dhiraj watched as the fight moved away from the metal staff.

"We've got to keep that from the crazy woman."

Natalie nodded. "I'm on it."

As the athlete ran toward the staff, the gatekeeper sent Erica smashing into the wall with a powerful kick. Before Natalie could reach the weapon, the gatekeeper moved so fast that Dhiraj lost track of her for a split second.

The woman grabbed one end of the staff while Natalie gripped the other. She yanked hard, but Natalie wouldn't give up her position.

Sela scowled. "Kids shouldn't play with toys that don't belong to them."

Natalie returned the look. "You should learn how to share."

The tug of war ended when the gatekeeper lowered her shoulder and slammed into Natalie's chest. Natalie flew backward and landed hard on the ground.

The gatekeeper took the staff back in two hands and held it above her head.

"You made a valiant effort. For your troubles, I'll try to send you somewhere nice."

The gatekeeper slammed the staff back into the ground and opened up a wide portal on the wall nearest Natalie. Dhiraj held his breath, and the power in the building went out. As the room became dim, the blue portal continued to cast a pale blue light in the area around it. Dhiraj could see the woman's blue-tinted face smiling.

"Too bad I'm not afraid of the dark. Show yourself!"

Something sent the gatekeeper to the ground with a "thwap." She grunted with pain, but before she could get up, the figure behind her sent a series of kicks into her body. The attacker was silent and continued to pepper the gatekeeper with punches and kicks on the ground. Dhiraj took the opportunity to run over to Natalie's side.

"Are you alright?"

Dhiraj could barely detect Natalie's nod in the dark. "Is that Ted?"

He couldn't tell, but whatever it was, it now had the gatekeeper above its head. The woman let out a primal yell as the figure tossed the gatekeeper, staff and all, into the blue portal on the wall. As the echo of screams stopped, the portal closed up completely.

Dhiraj fumbled for his cell phone to turn on the flashlight feature. He expected to see a big smile from his superhero best friend Ted Finley. Instead, he saw a person he didn't recognize in the slightest. A Japanese man in his early 40s walked over to help Erica to her feet. While the man looked straight out of an old samurai movie, he spoke perfect English.

"Hello, my old friend."

Her pained expression turned into one of recognition. "Yoshi?!"

PART TWO

CHAPTER
11

A wave of emotions hit Ted as he grew tired in the last half hour of flying. Between moving two-dozen people through the sky in a protective bubble and trying to get to Treasure in record time, his lack of endurance was beginning to get to him. Through his pounding heart, he wondered if he'd made a mistake choosing the government over a summer of training with Erica. He'd saved people's lives throughout the U.S., but that would mean nothing to him if his friends were lost in the process.

They attacked because I wasn't there. I let her down.

Ted knew that Erica had kept things from him and that she might never be completely honest, but he still wanted her approval. He hoped the summer away hadn't caused irreparable damage to their relationship.

From takeoff to landing, it took Ted exactly 32 minutes to plant his feet on the front steps of the Sheriff's Department. As his body readjusted to being on the ground, he could feel just how fast his heart was going. Part of him wondered if it would burst. Ted shook off the worry, clenched his fists and walked into the building.

The doors were marred, battered and lying on the ground. There were multiple cracks in the walls from bodily impact. Ted also spied a puddle of green blood before Dhiraj came running up to greet him.

"Ted! You just missed the party."

The others in the room – Sherriff Norris, Natalie, Erica and someone he didn't recognize – all perked up at the mention of his name. Ted felt the room begin to spin. He steadied himself on Dhiraj's shoulder.

"Thanks, I–"

The spinning grew faster and faster until Ted felt himself slip away from consciousness. A wave of darkness came over him. Images flashed before him from his last year as a hero. He saw himself in the Treasure High gym while the dark soul version of Sandra threatened him and Dhiraj. He watched as he and Natalie ran from the terror of former substitute teacher and brainwasher Mr. Redican. He saw the night of the prom and his slow dance with Erica LaPlante. Ted felt a mix of peace and anxiety as the images left him, replaced by what he saw when his eyelids fluttered open.

For the first time in three months, Erica's face was before him. There was no laptop or tablet screen distorting the image, nor were there thousands of miles between them. It was her, and despite everything that had happened, all Ted wanted to do in the world was kiss her.

"Hey."

Erica took his hand and smiled. "Hey. You sure know how to make an entrance."

Ted's eyes adjusted to the light in the room as he got his bearings. The dark, gray walls clued him in that they were inside a vacant cell in the Sheriff's Department building. Scratched into the walls were poorly thought out sentences and crude drawings. Erica's minty shampoo was almost overcome by the scent of mildew. She knelt on the ground beside the uncomfortable prison bed.

Ted laughed, which sent a sharp pain through his ribs. He figured he must have landed right on them when he collapsed. "I flew here from Florida in half an hour."

Erica pursed her lips and nodded. "I'd be more impressed if you hadn't passed out right after."

Ted lifted his hand to Erica's face. Her skin was smooth and warm. He watched her close her eyes and take a deep breath. She moved her face toward his.

"I missed you, Ted Finley."

Ted felt the warmth from her touch radiate down his arm and spread through his chest.

"The feeling is mutual."

Erica leaned down and placed her lips on his. Ted kissed back and let the magic of her taste bring him back to all the time they'd spent together. Holding each other, training and saving the world. It was all in that kiss. Erica leaned against him and Ted put his arms around her. He couldn't resist the impulse to smile as he kissed her. His heart was filled with pure joy. From the relaxed look on Erica's face, Ted imagined she felt the same way.

Erica laughed and wiped one of her eyes. "I know the light souls didn't choose you because you were a good kisser. But they really could have."

Erica lay down on the prison bed beside him and intertwined their legs. They shared another short kiss before she touched her nose to his.

"I heard you fought a hurricane."

Ted tried not to think about the portal and Sophie Kent.

He scrunched his nose. "I heard you rode a dinosaur."

Erica laughed. "We have a lot to catch up on. With business—" she locked her fingers in his, "—and pleasure."

The sound of a throat clearing outside the cell startled both of them. Erica sat up and scooted away from Ted as if her parents had caught them making out in the basement. Ted looked up at the Japanese man he hadn't recognized earlier. The man wore tight-fitting athletic clothes. He might be as old as 40, though he appeared to be in the shape of a 20-year-old. The veins popping out of his muscles made Ted jealous.

"Ted. My name is Yoshi, and it's an honor to meet the living soul."

Ted looked over at Erica before accepting the man's hand. Even the media didn't know him by that term. From his experience, the only ones who knew what "living soul" meant were his closest friends or his greatest enemies.

"Good to meet you, Yoshi." Ted took the man's hand and felt the squeeze of immense wrist strength. "Nice, firm grip."

Yoshi nodded. "Grip is very helpful in battle. That's one of the many things the elders taught us in the Academy."

Ted nodded.

Elders? Academy? Who is this guy?

While Ted was the one with the ability to read thoughts, Erica seemed to pull all the questions from his mind.

"Yoshi is one of the grand masters from the Academy, a school in Japan that trains warriors to fight against the dark souls."

Ted recalled Erica mentioning the facility as a place where they train potential living souls. Ted could see why the light souls might consider Yoshi a strong candidate.

He got off the bed. Yoshi was taller and his eye contact was as firm as his handshake had been.

Ted tried to step out of the samurai's gaze. "That's cool. I'll have to go there sometime. What brings you here?"

Yoshi's mouth nearly formed a smile. "The elders sent me here to help you and the protector."

Erica put her hand on Yoshi's shoulder. "Just in the nick of time, too. He saved us from the gatekeeper."

A pang of nervousness went through Ted's chest when Erica touched Yoshi's shoulder. He shook it off and looked at Erica. "Gatekeeper?"

Erica took her hand off Yoshi and locked arms with Ted. "There's a lot to explain. Yoshi, if you'll excuse us."

Yoshi bowed and moved away.

Ted and Erica walked down the hallway of cells together, the mildew stench now overpowering any other scent.

Ted pulled his arm around Erica's more tightly. "You know that guy. From before. Don't you?"

Erica kept her eyes straight ahead. "In another life, we were good friends. I was in the body of a student at the Academy."

Ted narrowed his eyes. "So girls and boys both train there?"

"No."

Before Ted could let that answer sink in, the two of them had moved back into the main lobby.

Now that Ted wasn't about to pass out, he could see the disaster the Sheriff Department lobby had become. One officer had a mop and a water bucket and tried his best to soak up the green pool of blood. Another swept up bits of drywall from the multiple structural collisions.

Natalie was the first to see Ted. For some reason, he flashed back to the dance they shared at prom.

"Hey." Natalie wrapped her arms around him. "I'll try not to hug you so hard that you pass out again."

Ted hugged her back. It felt so good to hear Natalie's voice again, too.

"I'm going to get made fun of a lot for this, aren't I?"

Dhiraj ran over and patted Ted on the back.

"Well, if it isn't our little southern belle." He mimed the action of waving a fan in front of his face and did his best southern accent. "I do declare, I was so overwhelmed by seeing my best friend Dhiraj that I up and lost consciousness."

Ted made sure to return the back slap with twice as much force. "Good to see you, too, Dhiraj. Where's Jen?"

Ted knew his friend well enough that it wouldn't be hard to get the subject changed from his fainting spell.

"Field hockey camp. Can you believe they start two weeks before school? Although, it does give me the chance to give more foot rubs."

Ted felt his strength start to return as he surrounded himself with friends. Sheriff Norris gave a nod from the other side of the room as he took care of the business of cleaning up the department. Ted noticed Yoshi sitting far across from them and out of earshot. He was watching the four of them interact.

"I want to know more about this gatekeeper and about this Yoshi guy." Ted smiled at the samurai before turning back to the gang with a neutral look. "Can we trust him?"

Erica looked surprised. "With our lives, Ted. He's been fighting for the cause a lot longer than you have."

Ted looked back over at Yoshi and wondered if he'd had the same lack of choice in the matter. Ted furrowed his brow and tried to read the man's thoughts. For the first time since he'd learned about the power, he couldn't detect a single emotion, memory or short-term thought. The lack of information was unsettling.

"I'm sure you're right." Ted put his arms around Dhiraj and Erica, trying to hide his line of conversation from the samurai. "I've just got a bad feeling about him. Let's hope I'm wrong."

CHAPTER

12

Jennifer laid out her field hockey uniform on her bedspread. Unlike previous years, her top had a red C stitched on the front for captain. Natalie had quit the team to focus all her attention on basketball and recruiting. While Jennifer's skills paled in comparison to Natalie's, she was a senior, and Coach Fowler knew she'd do anything to win.

She looked down at the outfit and thought about how little the captainship meant. How little the team meant. A dark soul that could cross between worlds had attacked the Sheriff's Department and put both her father and Dhiraj at risk. She sighed.

And what was I doing? Running sprints?

Jennifer knew she couldn't have done anything to stop the gatekeeper or the giant lizard creatures, but she felt like she should have been there nonetheless. Field hockey was fun and she'd been playing it her whole life, · but she had a new team now.

But what position should I be playing?

Jennifer felt empty. For the past decade, whenever she felt that way, she looked through her pictures. Lately, she'd shunned her collection of Polaroids and yearbooks for the Deputy Daly binder.

Jennifer flipped through the familiar pages detailing Daly's disappearance after he'd nearly killed Erica a second time. She recalled how her blood used to boil upon seeing his pearly whites in the article photos. The last few pages in the binder were the ones that made her smile. After she and Dhiraj had hunted Daly down, he'd been sent to prison on a host of charges. She regretted that he couldn't be tried for murder, since to most people's knowledge, Erica LaPlante was alive and well. But he'd still be locked up for over 20 years.

Jennifer had cut out and read the article from the local paper more than a dozen times. The black and white picture of Daly in his prison jumpsuit made her squeal with glee the first time she saw it. While it still made her feel warm to see his suffering, the joyful sensation diminished with each read. He'd been her obsession. Catching him had become her entire life. She'd been surprised to find that the realization of her revenge had failed to fully satisfy her for more than a couple of weeks.

Jennifer closed the binder, changed into her uniform, and drove her car a few blocks out of her way to pick up a teammate. Jeannie Moss was a hotshot freshman who would probably play varsity. She looked closer to 20 than her 14 years, and her skills spoke as loudly as her entitlement. Coach Fowler had told Jennifer to look after her. She reluctantly agreed.

Jeannie slammed her duffle bag on top of Jennifer's in the back and hopped into the front seat.

"Hey, Captain Norris. You still slow as hell?"

Throughout training camp, Jeannie had destroyed Jennifer in their three-mile runs. Jeannie had the delightful habit of gloating in the face of each captain she'd beaten.

Jennifer made a face at her passenger. "I don't know. Are you still terrible company?"

Jeannie crossed her arms and stared straight ahead. "You're just mad 'cuz your boyfriend cares more about money than you."

Jennifer glanced over at the hateful girl beside her. She could tell why Jeannie was one of the most popular girls in the freshman class. She was smoking hot with perfect proportions, and most of the guys she spent her time with didn't seem to care much about the bile that frequently spilled out of her mouth.

Jennifer smiled. "You've got me there, Jeannie. I'm sure your relationships are much more substantial."

Sometimes the subtle insults are the ones that cut the deepest, and Jeannie's lack of response showed it. There were a few minutes of silence before either of them piped back up again.

"You're pretty." Jeannie's eye twitched at the complement. "It's not like you couldn't do better than Mr. Moneybags."

Jennifer took in a deep breath. "Dhiraj is hot in his own way."

Jeannie smirked. "The kind of way that doesn't register on film?"

Jennifer ignored her. "I've dated some hot guys in my time." She glanced over at Jeannie. "Guys even you'd be jealous of. But it's totally different when a person likes you for something deeper. Dhiraj would like me even if I was as butt-ugly as you."

Jeannie's stink eye made Jennifer chuckle.

"You suck."

"I learn from the best." Jennifer pulled the car into the Treasure High backlot. "You ready?"

"More than you'll ever be."

For all her terribleness, Jeannie was right about the last point. About halfway through the exhibition, Treasure High was up by two goals. Jeannie had scored one and assisted on the other. Jennifer couldn't believe how fast the girl could move. The only person she'd seen run that quickly on the field was Natalie. Maybe Jeannie would be the former captain's heir apparent.

Jennifer was playing on the opposite side as Jeannie when the freshman got another breakaway. Her ponytail oscillated back and forth as she ran, with Jennifer doing her best to catch up to the action. Jennifer could feel her heart pounding. Jeannie had just one defender to beat and was about to juke her out. The defender took a frustrated swipe, slamming her stick directly into Jeannie's knee. The hotshot freshman fell face-first into the ground, a scream of pain filling the field. As the girl lifted her head, the onlookers could see a mouthful of blood from where her teeth had clamped down on her lip.

Jennifer continued running despite dimly hearing the whistle blow. Even though she saw Jeannie writhing in pain before her, her mind had gone elsewhere.

Natalie was on the ground in the middle of the caves. Jennifer could see her and Dhiraj beside the former team captain as blood poured out from her stab wound. She remembered Mr. Faraday with his arm around her neck, threatening to kill her and bring her back as a dark soul. Then Jennifer pictured herself pointing a gun at Daly just after she'd fired a round into his ear, the blood pooling on the off-white carpet.

When she reached the spot of the foul, there was nothing left inside her but rage. Jennifer leapt off the ground and tackled the offending opponent to the ground. Amid the cries of pain from Jeannie to her left, the team captain took a swing and connected with the defender's cheek. She slammed a second fist into the girl's nose, causing a steady drip of blood to seep out. Jennifer felt nothing as she let a third and final blow rip, connecting with the girl's eye socket. She wasn't sure if the referee or a coach pulled her away, and she didn't know the source of the primal yell she let out, either. All she knew was that nobody was going to hurt her or her team ever again.

CHAPTER
13

A few days after Ted's return, Natalie dribbled a basketball between her legs on the edge of her bed. A year earlier, she would've been nursing the pain of a long day of field hockey camp. After a recommendation from Coach Fowler, she opted to quit her secondary sport to focus on training and recruitment. The latter had taken up way more time than she'd expected.

Natalie palmed the ball and looked at the overflowing box of letters. Dhiraj and Jennifer had helped her sift out all the Division II and III offers, but the number of letters from Division I alone was staggering. She let the ball roll into her closet and dumped the envelopes on her bed. All the big schools were there, and many of the teams were the ones she'd followed growing up. She'd done her best to avoid thinking about where she'd visit or commit.

Earlier that summer, Dhiraj held a get-together at his house to discuss the next step for Ted Finley LLC. Natalie didn't give two craps about the company, but she'd been isolated ever since Ted hopped a plane to DC. When Dhiraj left the room to get snacks, she, Jennifer and Erica changed the conversation quickly.

Natalie leaned her head back and sighed. "Do any of you actually care about Dhiraj's enterprise?"

Erica shook her head and laughed. "If I hear the word synergy one more time, I'm going to throw Dhiraj through a wall."

The two of them looked at Jennifer.

She forced a smile. "I want Dhiraj to be happy, but I don't care either."

Natalie smiled. "Good. Ugh, my social life this summer is gonna be nonexistent."

Erica groaned. "I know, right? The whole reason I'm here is in a government straight jacket."

An idea formed in Natalie's head. "Wait. You're supposed to be training him, right?"

Erica nodded.

Natalie leaned forward in her chair. "Train me instead." Her smile grew wide. "I'm gonna be training anyway. The lovebirds are gonna be off talking dividends."

Jennifer suppressed a giggle. "You're probably right."

"So, you can train me. Get me a leg up before I get recruited."

Erica's eyes changed. She'd gone from bored to purposeful in a hurry. "I like it. Besides, I'd like to see how far I can push a human body."

Natalie raised an eyebrow. "Good. I think."

Dhiraj returned to the conversation with a plateful of cookies. Natalie couldn't believe the way they were shaped.

"Um, did you seriously make cookies with an 'LLC' cookie cutter?"

Dhiraj looked at Jennifer and smiled. "I did."

Jennifer cleared her throat. "It was a three-month-iversary present."

Natalie and Erica groaned in unison.

The last three months had been grueling. Five-mile runs and weightlifting followed by hand-to-hand combat and time on the court. Even though Erica was stuck in a cheerleader body, her enhanced strength and speed made her an incredible basketball defender. Natalie developed some new low-post moves and increased her vertical three inches during her intense training with her unlikely friend. Now that bad guys were back in the picture and Ted was in need of Erica's full attention, Natalie would have to take the training baton from here.

Natalie organized the letters into her top 68 picks and seeded them based on stats like climate, academic reputation and number of NCAA championships. Over the next couple of hours, she held a tournament among the different schools to come up with her own "excellent eight" of places to visit. It took longer than she expected, but after debating the merits of all the universities, she was able to narrow them down. It took her a moment to realize that one of the schools, Southern Ohio, was where Ted's sister Christina had a scholarship to play softball. She made a mental note to room with her when she made her visit. After admiring her choices and tacking the letters to the wall, an alarm on Natalie's phone went off. A smile crept over her face as she silenced the ringer and threw on a hoodie.

A light breeze brushed against her face as she snuck out the back door of the house and eased herself through the gap in the fence. She looked across the street to see a pair of unlit but familiar headlights. Natalie had told him to keep his lights off because it would attract less attention. She looked both ways before crossing and walked around to the passenger side. Natalie entered and plopped down on the leather seat.

"You're sure you weren't followed?"

The driver was tall and muscular like Natalie. He gave his passenger a disapproving look. "Have I ever been?"

Natalie ignored the insolence and leaned over to his seat. He met her halfway and they kissed deeply. Natalie took in his grungy aroma, which smelled like he'd been working on an engine all day. At first, it was a turnoff, but now it was all tied into the experience of being with him – an experience she found herself having more and more often. Natalie wanted to kiss every part of his body from head to toe.

He pulled away from her kiss and put his hand on her shoulder. "I wanted to ask you something."

She tried to move back toward him for a second round, but he kept her back with his hand. She grumbled. "Fine."

He mimicked her grumble. "I know that telling people I'm dating you will kill my reputation."

Natalie folded her arms. "Uh-huh."

"But school's coming. It's gonna be tough seeing you unless this thing goes public."

Natalie leaned back and opened the car door.

He reached across the console and put his hand on her leg. When she turned back toward him, he had a massive grin on his face.

"Come on. Do you really hate me that much?"

Natalie moved her tongue around in her mouth. She wanted to taste his lips again, but she knew he'd be resistant unless she responded.

"It's complicated."

"It's complicated for me, too." He sighed and looked around as if someone was watching him. "I just want this, okay?"

As much as it pained her, she wanted it, too.

"Fine."

He raised one eyebrow. "Really?"

She rolled her eyes. "Really. Now shut up and kiss me."

Natalie allowed him to do all the work reaching her this time.

He smiled as he kissed her before resting his head on hers. "I think your friends'll be happy for you. Even Dhiraj."

Natalie gave him a playful slap in the head. "Don't be an idiot, Travis. You tried to punch him in the face."

CHAPTER
14

Kikuchiyo's body was in the midst of a ritual funeral when Erica had crossed over into it. The Academy understood the meaning of the young boy's resurrection immediately. It meant that something was coming and the boy was there to save their lives.

The beauty of the small, isolated school amazed the new Kikuchiyo. Cherry blossom trees and buildings that had stood for hundreds of years dotted the mountainside. The protector felt like he'd been transported far into the past, and his heart ached for time gone by.

After experiencing his vision and acclimating to his new body, Kikuchiyo failed in his first efforts to connect with Yoshi, the boy's best friend before Kikuchiyo's untimely passing. Yoshi cursed the light souls and said the one who died should have been him. It took weeks for Kikuchiyo to convince Yoshi that the boy's memories would always be a part of the protector for generations to come. As a result, Kikuchiyo would live longer than most of humanity.

Yoshi warmed up to Kikuchiyo just in the nick of time. An ancient spirit older than the light and dark souls had targeted the school and its students. The embodiment of the evil spirit was eight feet tall and covered from head to toe in flames. After it slaughtered several of the elders, Kikuchiyo told the students to stand back. Only Yoshi stayed by his side.

They flushed the spirit onto a narrow cliff, wielding weapons that had been charmed with an incantation that made the blades colder than ice. The creature swung for Kikuchiyo. Even though he evaded direct contact, his neck had been singed, exposing burned flesh to the heavy wind of the mountaintop. Before the spirit could strike Kikuchiyo again, Yoshi seemed to fly through the air, slicing off its arm. The sound that left the spirit's mouth made their ears bleed as the appendage disappeared in a puff of smoke on the rocks.

The creature became twice as determined and seemed to move faster despite the injury. A swift kick set Yoshi's clothing aflame while a painful slap left charred burns on Kikuchiyo's face. The creature laughed and seemed to grow taller and thicker with fire.

Kikuchiyo watched his friend. He knew Yoshi would be willing to give his life to save the school and his friend. But Kikuchiyo was the one with lives to spare.

He smiled. "Go for the head."

"What?! He's too fast."

"Goodbye, my friend."

With that, Kikuchiyo ran at full speed for the belly of the beast. He dodged the spirit's attempts to grab him and ran his sword through its stomach. The beast howled again and wrapped its flame-coated arms around the protector. Yoshi screamed as pain exploded in every cell in Kikuchiyo's body. He was halfway to death when Yoshi swung his blade into the neck of the occupied spirit. The head slid off its body and exploded on the rocks. The flames surrounding Kikuchiyo disappeared, along with the spirit itself.

Kikuchiyo crumpled to the ground, his body burned on every visible inch. He did his best to remain conscious as the agony coursed through him.

Yoshi seemed to be doing everything he could to remain stoic. He ran his hands through his friend's hair. "I don't want to lose you again. It's more painful the second time."

Kikuchiyo forced a smile through his charred face. "I'll never be lost, my friend. I... I'll return in another form."

Despite the heat that had worked its way through his body, Kikuchiyo began to feel cold and weak.

Yoshi nodded. "I will find you. I will be chosen and together we'll save the world."

Kikuchiyo felt the life draining out of him. "We already have."

That was the last time Erica had seen Yoshi, until he tossed the gatekeeper back through the portal. She tapped a pencil absently on her new notebook for senior year. She was supposed to be taking notes on one of her summer reading books. After an hour passed with only a paragraph to show for it, she dialed up Ted.

"Hey."

Ted sounded groggy on the other end. "Hey. We still meeting at 7?"

Erica glanced at her bed. She pictured Ted lying between the ruffled sheets. It was a good distraction from her memories of battle and death.

"Wanna move it up two hours?"

Ted yawned. "More time with you? I knew I was having a lucky day."

Erica giggled. "See you soon."

Erica had her arm around Ted's waist as they walked by the pond. In the midst of the suburbs, the nature walk behind Ted's house was a microcosm of the seasons. They had trudged through ice and snow in the winter and lush, green grass in the spring. The summer brought dry, brown plants and a water level that was much lower than usual. No matter what the season, the connection to the earth made Erica feel energized. The trail went for several miles behind a few housing developments, and they'd already made a full loop of walking and talking.

After Ted launched into a conversation about Sophie Kent and Erica countered with her adventures in Japan, they both opted to discuss only positive things for the rest of the walk.

"So, you and Natalie are BFFs now?"

Erica could see through Ted's nonchalance. "Yes. And we talked about you the whole time."

Ted let out a grunt and kissed Erica on the neck. A faint hint of stubble tickled her skin and sent a shiver through her body. She let out a girlish yelp.

Ted laughed. "That's not what I meant. I'm just glad you two are getting along."

Erica tightened her grip around Ted. "She loves to win. She also likes keeping her secrets."

Ted's tongue slid along his upper lip. "What do you know?"

Erica tousled the back of his hair. "We're BFFs now. I couldn't possibly divulge that information."

Ted spun around and caught Erica by the waist. "I swear, I'll kiss you until you tell me everything."

Erica could feel the anticipation grow in her chest. She couldn't believe how great it was to have him back. She put on a fake stern look. "I will never submit."

With that, Ted used his grip to roll Erica onto the grass beside the pond. She squealed and pretended to fight back against his hold. If she'd really wanted to escape, a few well-placed blows to the stomach and groin would get her out in an instant – but there was nothing she wanted to do less. After a few rotations, Ted lay on top of Erica and pressed his lips onto her cheek and neck. The tickling layer of hair on his face forced the laughter right out of her.

He pulled away for a split second. "Tell me!"

She could barely speak through her heaving belly laughs. "Holy crap. You... need a shave... so bad."

Ted went back to his kissing game and Erica's chest burned from too much laughter. She couldn't remember the last time she'd been so happy, in this life or any of the others.

Ted rested his hips on hers and straightened his arms beside her to look straight down into her eyes. "This is your last warning. If you don't tell me all the rumors, I'm going to kiss you on the lips."

Erica felt twitchy with sensitivity, as if any part of his skin touching her would send her into another giggle attack. She took in a deep breath and let it out with a half-chuckle. "Do your worst."

As he pressed his lips into hers, Erica let everything go. Thoughts about training Ted, killing the gatekeeper and thwarting evil with Yoshi all fluttered away. There was only Ted and his mouth against hers. Erica closed her eyes and kissed him deeper. For all she cared, they could've been the only two people in the world as the sun began to set.

The sky was much darker an hour later when they lay beside each other and looked toward the stars. Erica felt light inside, as if the only things tethering her to the ground were her fingers intertwined with Ted's.

Ted broke the endless silence. "If I weren't a hero, would it be like this all the time?"

Erica almost couldn't bear Ted's cuteness. "A few things might be different."

"I know." Ted bit his lip. "You wouldn't be here. I might still be a dork."

Erica tickled Ted's thigh. "You are still a dork."

Ted re-gripped her hand. "I'm just staying, sometimes I wish... we could have fewer nights training and fighting evil, and more like this."

Erica shifted onto her side to face Ted and he did the same toward her. She spied the pain in Ted's eyes and locked his other hand in hers.

"You're back. That's what's important. I'm going to teach you your other powers. If the gatekeeper comes back, we'll find a way to stop her together." Erica leaned her neck in and kissed Ted on the cheek. "And after we do, we can celebrate with another night like this."

Most of the pain left Ted's look as he reached around Erica and pulled her close. Erica didn't want to tell him, but she wished she could take a break, too. Feeling his warm body pressed against hers almost made her forget they were in the middle of a war.

The pair walked back to Ted's house, arm-in-arm. The motion-sensing lights kicked in, which brought a black SUV into view in the Finley's driveway.

Erica's lightness gave way to a sense of dread. Her stomach squeezed. "Your friends are here."

Ted let out a deep breath. "I guess the government doesn't call ahead."

As they approached the vehicle, the door closest to them opened up. Erica recognized Vott and Harding right away.

"You two should come with us." Vott motioned the two of them forward. "We think we may be able to predict the next attack."

CHAPTER
15

Senator Kable sat at the head of a long table as his campaign manager prepared a series of slides on his laptop. There'd been hints of good news online, but Kable would only trust the hard evidence Terry presented to his staffers. His fingers tapped against the table.

"Ladies and gentlemen, we've got some great numbers today." Terry's grin boosted the mood in the room. "Let's take a look at Florida."

Kable clamped his hands together and leaned forward. Terry displayed a slide of polling numbers in the Sunshine State.

"Two weeks ago, Blake had a five-point lead." He pressed the button in his hand to shift to a new slide. "As of yesterday, the state is a complete toss up."

Joy filled the room. The state of Florida had been close in previous elections, but Blake's pull among the older population was set to make it a lock. Kable wondered if the polling would've been even more in his favor if he'd taken down the hospital with the patients still inside. He pushed aside the thought and clapped loudly.

"It's all because of you." Kable conjured a few tears. "I'm absolutely blessed to have all of you on board. You've made me a very happy man."

Kable watched as two staffers held each other while watching the tender moment he was faking. He wondered how often President Blake had fake-cried behind closed doors to rally the troops.

"Mr. Senator." Terry's grin had doubled in size. "We've got a surprise for you, too."

"Terry, if you make me happier than I am in this very moment, my heart might burst."

The staffers in the room laughed at that.

"We're just going to have to risk that, sir. Do you remember when you took pictures with patients a couple of days before the storm?"

Kable did his best to seem like he didn't understand. "Sure. I remember."

Terry clicked forward.

The next slide displayed Kable with his arm around a little girl – Sophie Kent. Two of the staffers gasped.

"We didn't know this at the time, but one of those pictures was with Sophie Kent. After it picked up some social traffic, we refashioned it into an ad." Terry pressed the button once again.

The picture now displayed text that read, "Because He Cares. Vote Kable to Keep Your Children Safe."

Kable nodded. "How much traffic has it gotten?"

Terry beamed. "It's been shared 250,000 times and counting."

The ovations in the room grew so loud that Kable could barely hear his phone when it rang. The caller ID told him it was his wife.

The senator held up his hand. "Please, don't stop celebrating on my part! Marriage calls."

Kable received a thumbs-up before he stepped out of the room. "Hello, dear."

"Are you at a bar? If so, I'm jealous."

Kable laughed. Even through the door it sounded as if he'd already won the election, despite the reality of being several states short.

"Just some happy news, darling. Can't wait to share it with you tonight."

Mrs. Kable let out a girlish giggle. His staffers had questioned him marrying a younger woman so close to the election, but he told them they'd made it work for the campaign.

"I'm so glad to hear that. I wanted to tell you I've got something special for tonight. You'll be home for dinner?"

Kable knew he finally had the life he deserved. "Of course. Anything for you."

"Good, then I'll see your sexy face later."

Kable laughed as a warm feeling came over him. "Until then, love."

The room had settled a bit when Kable re-entered. All the big news of Terry's presentation had been given at the top. Kable let himself daydream a bit and think about what his wife might have in store. As Terry's talk ended, he left the floor open for questions. Kable let several staffers have their moment in the sun before he put the next step of his plan into motion.

"Terry, how would you describe our bases of operation in Ohio and North Carolina?"

Terry's smile faded. "I'm not going to lie to you, sir. They could be way better."

Kable had predicted that would be the answer. "That's fine, Terry. Let's take a few folks out of our lock states and move them there. I want twice as many people on the ground as Blake."

The people beside him at the table seemed confused. They had good reason to be. While Ohio and North Carolina were two other so-called purple states, swinging either red or blue depending on the year, both were headed in Blake's direction.

"Sir, if you don't mind my asking—"

Kable gave a flashy smile. "Your questions make me a better man, Terry. Go ahead."

The compliment seemed to settle Terry's nerves. "Don't you think our resources could be allocated better elsewhere?"

Kable stood up. "Terry, you've got a good point, but I have a gut feeling about this." He looked around the room, addressing different staffers at the end of each phrase. "We've got Blake on the ropes in Florida, but that alone isn't going to win this election. We've got to trust ourselves and trust that we can pull this thing out. There are a lot of long nights ahead, everybody, but I promise you, if we work together on this and go with our gut, we're bound to find ourselves in the White House in January."

After a moment of silence, Terry began clapping. The rest of the room joined in with several hollers and whistles accompanying the applause. A chant of "Kable! Kable!" effectively ended the meeting.

As Kable got in his car to drive home, he noticed a shimmer of blue in the backseat. By the time he glanced in his rear-view mirror, a pale woman with jet-black hair appeared and stared right back into his eyes. The gatekeeper looked sullen.

"Sela, my dear." Kable started the car and pulled out onto the road. "We'll have to make this quick – my wife is expecting me any minute."

Kable watched as Sela nursed a wound on her shoulder.

"I wasn't able to get the sword. Or the books."

Kable's loud laugh startled Sela, causing her to jump a few inches in her seat.

"My poor gatekeeper. It was never my intention for you to succeed."

Sela's confusion amused Kable. It was almost as fun as hearing about his rising poll numbers.

"You wanted me to fail."

"It's all part of the plan. I'm sorry I didn't tell you earlier."

Sela seethed with anger. He watched as her chest began to heave faster and faster.

"Do you know how easy it would be to put a portal right under your car? I could send you to a world that's deeper and darker than anything you've ever seen. You would burn. Forever."

Kable liked the confrontation. It allowed him to feel something he hadn't felt for quite a while: the hint of a real battle.

"Sela, you can't know every part of the plan. It's just how it is. You'll still have the role we discussed when everything falls into place."

The statement seemed to pacify the backseat passenger for a moment. She dragged her nails across the leather. "I don't see why we can't just lead an army in and take the place over."

Kable nodded. "I know it seems like that would be the best plan, but there's an easier way. If we go about it diplomatically, we may be able to take this world without losing a single soldier."

Sela laughed. Kable found the sound creepy coming from such a serious warrior.

"I wasn't aware of your deep desire to preserve life."

Kable pulled into his driveway and parked the car. He turned around to view the gatekeeper head on.

"Just our own lives, Ms. Fortbright. Just our own. I'll contact you soon about the next step. Now, if you'll excuse me, I have a dinner date."

Sela assented and disappeared from the back in a flash of blue light.

The aroma of savory meat and spices hit Kable as soon as he walked in. He glanced the delicious-looking spread on the table and noticed two open bottles of wine on the kitchen counter. In the midst of it all was his wife. Her long black hair couldn't have been more different-looking from when he'd met her, and she also wore makeup that made her look more mature than her actual age. Her hair and makeup weren't what caught the bulk of his attention, though. The low-cut black dress with an apron tied around the waist made him feel like he'd just walked into heaven.

"Honey, I'm home."

Mrs. Kable moved across the room as if she were gliding. She wrapped her hands around his midsection and kissed him on the lips.

"I can see that." She gestured back to the food and wine. "What do you think of this spread?"

Kable smiled and shook his head. "You've outdone yourself. It's a good thing I married someone who knows her way around a kitchen."

She undid the apron and let it fall to the ground. Her dress was stunning as it hugged every curve on her body.

"And I'm glad I married a man who likes to eat." She patted his stomach.

Before she could pull her hand away, Kable took hold over her wrist. He rubbed his fingers on the top of her hand and felt the thin layer of makeup. She smiled devilishly at him as he scratched through the concealer to reveal one wing of a rainbow-colored butterfly tattoo.

She used her free hand to tuck her hair behind her ear. "Do you miss the old me?"

Kable took his attention off her hand and brought it back to her eyes. "Nothing in the world will ever change who you are on the inside, Sandra."

CHAPTER
16

Agents Vott and Harding took Ted and Erica just outside of town. They drove past Wayne Park, a popular place for the area's teens to park, and came upon what looked like an abandoned power station. The car stopped and the agents ushered the high schoolers out. Ted gripped Erica's hand as they passed through an open gate of a fenced-off area. The warning signs on the outside looked as though they'd been posted at least 50 years ago.

An elevator dropped them down for several minutes until the unassuming location gave way to a secret underground facility. The doors opened to reveal a massive compound. Ted felt like he was in some kind of spy movie. The main area was all shiny metal with touch screens, computers and panels in every direction. It reminded him of the GHA headquarters, though this was much more impressive.

Vott interrupted Ted's self-guided tour with a pat on the back. "We're sorry we interrupted your date."

Erica coughed. "That's okay. It's always been my dream to end a date by going into a creepy unmarked vehicle."

Harding sported a crooked grin. "If it's any consolation, I missed the end of a really great Nats game on TV."

Ted and Erica shared a glance. "It's not," they said in unison.

Vott and Harding led them through the compound. Of the 50 people Ted saw working there, only one or two seemed to notice them.

What are they doing? And why are they doing it here?

Agent Vott opened a door and gestured for them to sit down in a conference room not much larger than Sheriff Norris' detention cell. They took two chairs next to each other and Ted looked up at his former handlers.

"So. What's this about, guys?"

Harding switched off a light and flipped on the controls for a holographic interface. It took Ted's eyes a moment to adjust to the display, but once they did, he could see a green map of the United States. There were red dots in certain parts of the map. Most of them were concentrated in Treasure, but there were others in Colorado, California, Florida and some of the other places Ted had visited during the summer.

Vott paced the length of the room, his loafers tapping with each step. "While we appreciated your service with the government this summer, we must admit, having you save lives wasn't the only reason we brought you to work with us."

Erica let out a huff. "What? The government keeping secrets? I thought you had a 100% transparency policy."

Harding leaned forward. "Actually, the government doesn't have an official position on—"

Vott squeezed his partner's shoulder. "She's kidding, Harding." He focused back on Ted and Erica. "Our scientists have been working overtime to learn more about your powers. In the process, we've developed a system that tracks when you've accessed them."

Ted understood the map even better now. It wasn't just a collection of all the places he'd visited. It was measuring all the otherworldly energy present in the U.S. Ted heard Erica's breath quicken beside him. He placed his hand on her leg and she gripped it.

"We detected several traces of this kind of energy while Ted was out of town." Vott locked eyes with Erica. "And we've traced that power back to you, Ms. LaPlante."

Harding pointed in her direction. "If that's who you really are!"

Vott rolled his eyes. "Shut up, Harding."

Harding pouted. "I thought... I mean, we don't really know who she is."

Ted felt his heartbeat speed up. The world had more or less embraced him, but it was more difficult to explain who Erica was and why she was there. What would the government think if they knew she was part of a war that placed Earth right in the middle?

Vott turned the light back on and sat across from Ted and Erica. He pulled out a notepad and a pencil. "We know you disappeared for about a month and you returned on the day Ted fought Nigel and the other... beings. We also know that Stucky Crane died two days later and seemingly came back from the dead with enhanced abilities." Vott took the pencil in his hands and placed the point on the notebook. "This picture is half-painted, Ms. LaPlante. Paint the rest of it for me."

Ted's eyes grew wide as he looked at Erica once again. He'd known her long enough to guess the two options she was playing over in her head. One possibility was to fight off Vott and Harding before escaping the facility and living in hiding the rest of her mission. The other would be to share part, but not all, of the story. When she let out a breath of relief, Ted assumed she'd take the later path.

"I was sent here to protect Ted by the same people who gave him his powers."

Vott took down a note or two and leaned forward in his chair. "Are these the same people who gave Nigel his powers? Or Albert Redican?"

Ted knew that Erica was the one on the spot here, but he couldn't help but feel the anxiety coursing through his body as well. The heel of his foot bounced up and down against the floor.

Erica smiled. "No. I'm one of the good guys. We're on the same side, Vott."

Vott took down another note and leaned even closer. "Do the good guys have a command structure?"

Erica nodded. "Yes."

"Are you at the top of that structure?"

"No."

Vott was holding his pencil so tightly, Ted thought he might break it. "Then, we'd like to talk to your superiors."

Erica leaned closer to Vott. "That's not possible."

Vott pushed away from the desk and flipped the light back off. He pointed back to the map.

"Ms. LaPlante, we've detected signatures in multiple locations. Places where you and Ted haven't even been. Something is using these powers, and we need to know if this is part of another attack or if it's your 'friends' in action."

Ted watched as Erica stood up to get a closer look at the map. He followed suit. There were signatures in the Midwest and the Southeast in locations he'd never been.

Is there gonna be another attack?

"I had one way to communicate with my people, but it was destroyed during the attacks in Treasure." Erica's tone progressed from annoyed to angry. "I couldn't reach them if I wanted to."

"That's awfully convenient," Harding said.

Vott's pencil finally did snap as his eyes darted back to his partner. "Shut up, Harding!" He focused on Erica again. "That's awfully convenient, Ms. LaPlante."

Erica rested her hands on the desk. "If your world was ready to know about everything there is out there, we'd gladly share it. But it's not."

Vott brought his hands together over the map to zoom in on the state of North Carolina. "We're sending a team to investigate these signatures in three days. I've been asked to invite both of you to join us, but unless you tell us the truth, Erica, we'll have to protect Ted for you."

Ted could sense that Erica was about to burst. If she threw the table across the room or lashed out at the agents, Ted didn't know what the consequences could be. He stepped in between the staring contest that had begun between Vott and Erica.

"Hey." Ted put his hands on Erica's shoulder. He could feel heat radiating off her, as if Vott had caused Erica to catch on fire. "Hey. He's just trying to rile you up, okay?"

Erica flared her nostrils. "It's working."

Ted tried to calm her with his eyes. She looked through him like he was transparent. Ted turned back over his shoulder. "Can we have a minute to discuss this alone?"

Vott blinked before nodding. The agents turned the lights back on as they exited the room. As soon as they left, Erica pushed Ted out of her way, sending him flying against the wall. Ted's shoulder took most of the blow. She flipped the table over with a yell and the loud crash that ensued reverberated throughout the small room. Ted waited a moment for Erica to get some deep breaths in before he walked back over.

"You know, you get this cute little vein over your eye when you get angry."

Erica gave one last exhale before she rested her back against the wall and slid to the ground. "These are things they're not supposed to know, Ted."

Ted crouched down beside her. He watched Erica's arms began to shake.

Ted put an arm around her shoulder. "They already knew about me. It was bound to happen eventually."

Erica relaxed a bit and looked into Ted's eyes. He wished they were still beside the pond. Ted didn't want to be a hero anymore. He just wanted to be a boyfriend.

"I can't give them what they want, Ted."

Ted leaned his face close to hers. "Then I won't go with their team to North Carolina. Besides, I was really looking forward to speech and debate class this semes—"

"It's not that simple." Erica took Ted's hand. "If something's going to happen down there, you need to be ready to stop it."

Ted shook his head. "But I just got back. We were going to do this together."

"I know. It sucks. But, we'll help you from this end. At least we'll be working toward the same goal."

Ted scratched the back of his neck. "I guess. What am I going to tell them?"

Erica kissed Ted's forehead and pulled herself back. Even with the tears in her eyes, she was as beautiful as ever.

"Tell them you're in, because you're here to protect the world."

CHAPTER
17

Dhiraj awoke to his alarm clock with a smile. He wasn't sure if he'd ever been more fired up for a school year. After years of getting up at the crack of dawn to work harder than anyone else at Treasure High, he had the grades and test scores he needed to get into his top school, as well as the money to pay for it. His business dealings with Ted Finley LLC had earned him more than enough to pay for undergrad and up to two graduate degrees. Now that everything was lined up perfectly, he was prepared to live out his dream senior year.

After a few hours of giving his army of outsourced overseas workers their tasks for the day, he pulled on a white button-down shirt and looked himself in the mirror.

"You've put in all the hard work. Now it's time to reap the rewards, you handsome, wealthy devil."

Dhiraj turned on some classic rock and shook his hips as he donned the rest of his outfit. The music was still playing when the horn honked in his driveway. He looked back in the mirror.

"Sorry, Dhiraj, I've gotta go. My dream girl is driving me to school today."

Dhiraj shut the door to his room and shimmied down the stairs. He tossed his backpack into Jennifer's car and strapped himself into the passenger seat. Jennifer wore a light top and purple jeans. With her hair tied back in a ponytail and sporting a necklace Dhiraj had given her as a birthday gift, she was absolutely beautiful.

And I'm the one who gets to kiss her.

Dhiraj leaned over, and she kissed him. He let himself linger in front of her mouth for a moment.

"Hi." Dhiraj felt the happiness wash over him.

"Hi." Jennifer closed her eyes and moved forward for another kiss.

Dhiraj gladly obliged before leaning back in his seat.

After a few minutes of discussing Ted Finley LLC business, including merchandising rights for Super Ted action figures and a Saturday morning cartoon show, the car pulled into the Treasure High lot. Dhiraj had worked his administrative magic to get them one of the best spots in the entire school. All he'd had to do was balance the district budget, which only took a few hours of his spare time.

Dhiraj was about to open his door when he noticed Jennifer staring straight ahead at the school. The gloss glistened off her lips and a peach aroma wafted over.

"Can you believe it?" Jen's eyes were as wide as silver dollars. "We're seniors. I wasn't even sure we were gonna live through junior year."

Dhiraj took Jennifer's hand and rested it on the gearshift. "It's like a dream, Jen. We get to run this school. A field hockey captain and a current business leader of America."

Jennifer's face twitched. Dhiraj had read countless books on body language, but he wasn't sure what the tick meant.

He put his hand on her shoulder. "You okay?"

She let out a sigh and the look disappeared. "Of course. I'm just nervous, I guess."

Dhiraj grinned. "We got this." He took her hand. "Right, cents?"

Jennifer undid her seatbelt. "Right, dollar." She turned toward him and leaned in for another smooch.

Can it possibly get better than this?

The familiar scent of floor polish struck Dhiraj as he held open the front door for his girlfriend. In past years, he'd associated the smell with bullies and homework and lectures that wouldn't end. Now it was the aroma of superiority.

After bidding adieu to Jennifer at her locker, Dhiraj walked the halls like the top dog in town. He got a few high fives from classmates and several awe-filled stares from lower classmen. He knew the younger kids wished they could rule the school like him and Jennifer, but it was the seniors' time for sure. Dhiraj planted his books at his homeroom desk and walked over to Ted, who appeared to be moping in the direction of a wall.

"Hey, buddy, your face is longer than usual." Ted moved his eyes off the wall and toward Dhiraj's face.

"Hey, man. I can't believe I only get one more day of this before I have to go."

Dhiraj felt for his friend, but he wasn't about to let anything mess with his vibe. He gave Ted a playful tap on the cheek.

"Soak it up while it lasts, my man. Whether it's a day or eight months, senior year is a temporary state of mind. Love everything as long as you can."

Ted's glum demeanor brightened slightly. "You're like a cross between a hippie and a self-help guru right now."

Dhiraj turned his open hand into a fist and presented it for Ted. "I can dig it."

Ted looked away before giving into the fist bump.

When the next bell rang, Dhiraj and Ted headed to first period calculus. Ted's mood had perked up slightly, but Dhiraj wanted to take it all the way to joy.

"Do a favor for me, buddy. Close your eyes and breathe in the senior superiority. It'll help you feel better."

"Fine."

Ted closed his eyes and Dhiraj followed suit. He took in a deep breath and thought about how fulfilling this year would be. As they both exhaled, Dhiraj opened his eyes. The image before him didn't seem to make sense. He blinked several times just to make sure.

"No freakin' way." Dhiraj turned to Ted and saw the same shock and awe on his face as well. He turned back ahead to see Natalie and Travis walking toward them, and they were definitely holding hands. Dhiraj's cloud nine had evaporated, and he landed with a thud back on solid ground.

Travis looked smug as he nodded in their direction. "Ted. Moneybags."

"Hey guys." Natalie wore a strained smile. "Travis is my boyfriend now. Deal with it."

CHAPTER
18

Sela and Cal Fortbright sat on the top of a church tower overlooking the bustling main street. Behind them lay the fresh green grass and tall brick buildings of the university. In front of them, students and residents moved from shop to shop, unaware of what was coming their way.

Sela felt strange next to her brother. Even though they'd both died and come back as dark souls, there was still a part of them that remained family. And yet, Cal could barely talk at the time she was taken away for her training.

They watched a mother and father pass by below. The father pushed a large stroller in front of him, as their infant's legs kicked forward at an odd angle. The mother led a toddler by the hand as they continued at a slow pace toward the busiest part of the strip.

"How do you think things would've been different if you'd stayed?" Cal ducked his head in an effort to reach Sela's downturned eyes.

She continued to look more at the passersby than her brother. "We probably wouldn't be at the top of a tower together on Earth."

Cal sighed with his entire body. "You know that's not what I mean."

Sela let her eyes drift to her left. Cal looked like the rest of her family, but aside from a similar nose and complexion, most people wouldn't have pegged them as related. "Look, Cal." Sela turned her body completely toward him. "They thought I could be something great. And I was." She put her hand on Cal's leg. "But I was also lonely. And I wasn't even allowed to do most of the stuff I learned."

Cal's eyes softened. "That's the most I've heard you say… well, ever."

Sela grinned. "I'm half the girl I used to be." She reached behind her to take the metal staff from the holster on her back. "Do you want to help me do this?"

Cal's face went from quiet grin to goofy chuckle in a hurry. Sela felt like the look gave her a peek into her brother's adolescence, and she was grateful for it. She offered part of the staff to him, and he touched it lightly, as if it were a piece of artwork he was worried would break.

"How do I do it?"

Sela clasped her brother's hands around the very edge of the staff. She gripped just beneath his.

"I'm going to concentrate on the middle of the street there." A thought washed over her of what it would've been like to teach Cal to string his first bow or set his first trap. "Once you're focused on it, we're going to tap the other end of the staff against the building."

Cal looked down at the street so intently, Sela thought he might burn a hole in one of the vehicles passing by. She followed suit and focused in the very middle of the intersection just across from a post office. "Are you ready?"

Cal nodded. "I'm ready, sister."

Sela felt a calmness take her body as they tapped the staff against the building. A stream of energy zipped through Sela's body and out through the weapon. She watched as a portal began to open on the street below. A car making a turn onto the road was almost right above the gateway as it expanded. The vehicle's front wheel dipped immediately. Soon, it titled deep into the portal. Sela continued to concentrate on growing the gateway, ignoring the screams of the people on the sidewalk. Two students rushed to the car in an effort to save the vehicles' passengers. As the portal grew and grew, the entire car and its rescuers fell inside, disappearing into the blue unknown.

Sela smiled and looked away from the street. "Okay, we did it."

Cal's body vibrated with energy. "That was amazing, Sela!"

He pulled his hands from the staff and wrapped his arms around his sister. She felt lucky to have a second chance with her family. Sharing her power made it feel like an infinitely more impressive accomplishment.

"You did great, brother." Sela looked down to see the street dwellers who hadn't run in terror attempting to look down into the portal. "Now comes the fun part."

A growling noise from the other side of the gateway was loud enough to reach them all the way at the top of the tower. It sent most of the people below running for their lives. When the snarling noise stopped, the car that had gone through the portal shot into the air much higher than the adjacent buildings and came crashing down on the sidewalk. The driver and passenger were gone. In their place was a trail of broken glass and a streak of dark red. The good Samaritans who tried to rescue the car were nowhere to be seen, either.

After a moment or two of stunned silence, three hairy beasts emerged from the portal. As tall as the Draconfolk but twice as intimidating, the wolf-like creatures looked like they were all fur and teeth, though the latter part was what did most of the scaring. The blood from their afternoon snack trickled from their mouths. The three monsters surveyed their surroundings and let out a street-shaking howl in unison.

"Wow!" Cal's mouth was wide open. "I've never seen a Lychos up close."

Sela tapped her brother on the chest. "I wouldn't recommend it. I still have a scar from the last time I did."

As the siblings spoke far above the ground, the Lychos had done enough howling. All three dashed in different directions. For creatures of such size, their speed was impressive. One Lychos snatched up a short-skirted sorority girl from a pack of her friends. Another took an older man who couldn't get away fast enough. The third one took the father of the family the Fortbrights had watched earlier. The girl screamed the loudest of the three, though it was difficult to hear through the rest of the havoc. Once the Lychos had their prey, they ran off together toward the wooded side of the street and dashed into the forest.

"They make quick work." Cal put his hand back on the staff. "Should we let out any more?"

Sela shook her head and reached toward the portal. The gateway made the sound of electricity running through a circuit as it closed in on itself. It only took a couple of seconds for the car-sized hole to disappear, leaving a pristine street beneath it.

"That's all he wants," Sela said. "Enough to make the news, but not enough to destroy a town."

She tapped the staff into the church one more time. Sela concentrated on the air beneath them and a portal big enough for two opened by their feet.

"Was it worth it?" Cal's eyes were fixed on the blue hole below. "Learning how to do this? To create portals between worlds?"

Sela looked down to see the mother holding her toddler, both of them sobbing.

"It's been a gift and a curse." She took her brother's hand. "But now that we're back together – now that we're a family again – I think it was a good tradeoff."

Her brother grinned. "Race you to the hole."

Before Sela could react, her brother had already leapt inside.

She shook her head. "Little brothers."

Sela placed her staff back into place and let herself fall inside the portal. High above the terrorized streets, the blue gateway closed into nothingness.

CHAPTER
19

Erica watched as Ted scribbled notes feverishly during the last half of English class. It wasn't that the teacher's lecture was all that interesting. The period had been typical first-day stuff with a reading list, what activities made up the final grade and general getting-to-know-each-other activities. Ted pushed his pencil so hard against his notebook that Erica wondered if it would leave a mark on the desk below. Part of her wanted to reach over and stop him. She didn't like the look in his eyes of half anger and half fear. It couldn't be healthy, but she needed to let him have this. She'd been to school several times over in her lifetimes. Unless he took a similar path as her, he'd only get to do this once.

Ted continued to scribble down notes when the bell rang. By the time all the students had packed up their bags and left, Ted put the final period on the lecture. He looked around and squinted his eyes.

"Where did everybody go?"

Erica put her hand on his shoulder. "Even Ms. Adler left, Ted. It's time to move on."

He threw his pencil onto the ground and rubbed at his cheeks. "I'm not ready." He looked up at her. "Why'd the light souls have to pick me?"

Erica had gone through the same phase when she was a living soul. It just surprised her how long it took Ted to ask the same question she had.

Erica pulled up a chair next to him. "Because you're strong on the inside. Because you're a good person. I mean, look at what you've done already."

Erica could tell her words weren't reaching him. She opted to let him talk it out instead.

Ted scrunched up his face before relaxing his features. "I could've run away, you know. I had a chance to fake my death in Florida. Maybe I could've gone somewhere where nobody would know me."

Erica ignored the anger that bubbled up. Confronting him about this new piece of information wouldn't make the situation any better. She rubbed his back. "I'm glad you didn't."

Ted's voice broke. "I could make everyone forget. Just change everybody's brain so they don't know I'm a hero."

Erica felt a knot in her stomach. She leaned over and kissed Ted on the cheek. "I don't think that'd be a good idea."

Ted forced a smile and kissed Erica back. "I know." He took a deep breath and let it out. "I won't. It just all seems too unbearable sometimes."

Erica turned Ted's head toward her. "You can handle all of this, Ted. There'll be moments when it's too much, but if you can deal with it 90 percent of the time, you'll be better than any living soul there ever was."

Erica felt Ted's fingers brush against hers. She was divided right down the middle between wanting him to go and wanting him to curl up next to her in his bed.

Ted looked up as if he heard something through the silence. "Duty calls."

Erica narrowed her eyes as the loudspeaker interrupted her thoughts. "Ted Finley to the principal's office. Ted Finley to the principal's office."

Erica wondered how often Ted was using his new mind reading abilities on her. "They're here?"

Ted nodded. He offered his hand to her, and she took it. They walked down the hallway for what could be the last time in a long while. A few students, assuming Ted was in trouble, let out a few accusatory howls. Erica figured this wasn't the part of school he'd miss the most. Everything they had to convey to each other was done through the pressure of their joined hands. By the time they reached the office, Erica was squeezing Ted as hard as she could.

Agents Vott and Harding were sitting in the office when they arrived. Harding turned his head to the side, as if he didn't expect Erica to be there. She gave him an evil eye in response.

"Enough, you two." Vott took out a folder and passed it to Ted. "There's been another attack. This time in North Carolina. We're moving things—"

"I know." Ted squeezed Erica's hand back. "It's time to go."

"We'll give you two a minute." Vott nodded to Harding. "No flipped tables this time, okay?"

Erica wasn't sure if her eye could get much more evil. After the agents left, Erica wrapped her arms around Ted and pressed herself into him. He did the same and they stayed like that for over a minute.

She pulled back to look him in the eyes. "Call me when you get there."

He took a deep breath and smiled. "Yes, ma'am. I wish you could come."

"Don't worry." She kissed his neck. "You'll be back soon."

Erica wished she knew that statement was a certainty. Ted walked through the office doors, and before long he was gone.

The rest of the day was a blur. Erica didn't retain any information that was sent her way by teachers explaining the next eight months. She barely recalled a single word of the high-pitched yammering of Winny and Beth after school. Erica put off a group meeting with Dhiraj and the gang until the following day. She needed time for some mental recovery. Later that evening, Ted's call to let her know he'd arrived was brief. She recognized the description of the Lychos immediately and gave what pointers she could for their apprehension.

She lay awake in bed well past midnight. The cushy mattress pad beneath her might as well have been concrete. There was only one person in her bed that would soften things, and he was several hundred miles away. As she considered going downstairs for a snack, she heard a noise in her bathroom. The instinctual fear and readiness that came with the chance for battle made her smile.

Home invader, you picked the wrong chick to cross.

She rolled out of bed slowly and crouched down low. The door to her bathroom began to creek open. When the dim figure crept into view, she waited until just the right moment to strike. With a swift kick through the legs, the man toppled to the ground. Erica tried to jump on top of him, but the intruder rolled away at the last second and kicked up to his feet. She popped up off the ground and rapidly punched at him. He blocked two blows before a third one knocked him on the jaw. When he tried to swing back, Erica ducked his arm and leapt onto his back. As she began to squeeze, the man turned on the bathroom light.

Erica could see in the mirror that she was choking the life out of Yoshi. She growled, hopped off and pushed him into the sink. "Damn it, Yoshi."

Yoshi wore a sheepish grin as he rubbed at his throat. "Sorry, Kikuchiyo. I didn't mean to startle you."

Erica ran her hands through her hair and walked into other room. Yoshi followed. They sat on the edge of her bed.

"It's Erica." She shook her head. "What are you even doing here?"

Yoshi brought his hands together and sat up straight. "I think you need to see this." He removed a photograph from his pocket.

Erica snatched it out of his hand. "You could've called." She looked at the picture in the light.

She'd seen the image shared all over social media. It was Senator Kable and Sophie Kent.

"Yoshi. In the modern world, when you want to share a picture with someone, you post it on their page. You don't break into their house in the middle of the night."

Yoshi grinned. "Facebook isn't allowed in the Academy, but evidence is."

Erica looked at the picture more closely. "Why is this evidence?"

Yoshi took the photo back and tucked it away. "There were over 100 pictures taken of the senator in the hospital. The picture with the girl was the only one without multiple patients."

Erica felt her heartbeat start to decrease after her fight or flight response dissipated. "You think the senator had something to do with her disappearance? It's not a lot to go on."

Yoshi nodded. "I'm going to Florida to investigate. Leave school. Come with me."

Erica's instinct was to tell Yoshi he was crazy. If she kicked him out now, there was still a chance she could get an hour or two of shuteye. Once that feeling passed, she let herself ponder the thought. With Ted off working for the government, potentially for the rest of senior year, did she even need her high school cover any longer? Besides, the government knew who she really was anyway and there was no telling how they'd treat her going forward if the war were to escalate.

"I don't know, Yoshi. I've got a life here."

Yoshi probed her with his eyes. "One that wasn't even yours to begin with."

He has a point.

Yoshi stood up and shook out the leg she'd kicked. "I want to leave as soon as possible. Let me know your decision." He walked to the window and turned back. "You can't protect him right now, so please, protect me."

With that, Yoshi opened the window and leapt out.

Erica lay back down on the bed. Now her chances of getting a few winks before school were even less likely. Yoshi's offer to investigate the Florida incident was tempting. She knew that if she did so, there was no way she'd put her former inhabitant's parents through the same hell again. Erica couldn't run away. If she planned to go she'd have to tell them the truth.

CHAPTER
20

On the second day of school, Natalie felt a major energy dip in the Treasure High hallways. She could've attributed it to the other students realizing that they weren't just back to see friends but to do work. In reality, she knew it was because resident superhero Ted Finley had left with no definite return date in sight. Aside from their brief encounter in the hall, she hadn't seen much of her ex-boyfriend since he returned to town. Natalie didn't know how to feel when Ted so willingly accepted Travis as her boyfriend. Did she want to see jealousy in his eyes? Maybe. She guessed that since she didn't have many lingering romantic feelings for him, it was fair of him not to throw a hissy fit.

During fifth period study hall, she received a note that had made its way around the room. It didn't survive without a little doodling graffiti of an eagle wearing Viking horns and a separate picture of what may have been a bare butt. Natalie opened the note. It was typed, so she couldn't tell who it was from, though she imagined Travis wouldn't have gone to the trouble. With Ted out of the picture, there was only one likely candidate, and that person wanted to meet her in the audio/video room after last period.

"Great. Just what I wanted after my last period lecture. Another lecture."

Natalie considered blowing off the requested meeting, but sure enough, she found herself outside the audio/video room a few minutes after the final bell. Jennifer leaned on the wall beside the door. She was completely oblivious until Natalie tapped her on the shoulder. Jennifer's eyes sprung open as if she'd been in a deep trance.

"Oh, hey."

Natalie leaned beside her. "You alright?"

Jennifer sighed. Natalie had heard all about the field hockey scuffle from her former teammates. To say it was out of the ordinary for Jennifer to beat up an opponent would be an understatement.

"Yeah." She looked at the A/V room door. "Dhiraj doesn't know about the fight. Or the suspension. Please, don't tell him."

"I'm not in the habit of lying to my friends."

Jennifer nibbled at one of her fingernails. "I'm not either, okay? The suspension lasts another couple of days. I promise I'll tell him soon."

Natalie let out a deep breath. "Your secret's safe with me." She opened the door to the room. "Let's just get whatever this is over with."

Jennifer nodded and led Natalie inside. She spied a museum's worth of old equipment as she walked in. She heard a noise on the other side of the room. Natalie's surprise level hit zero when she saw Dhiraj in the corner fiddling with a digital video projector. Jennifer sat down beside him.

Dhiraj clicked the final plug into place. "There we go. Hey, Nat."

Natalie threw her backpack onto an empty chair on the far side of the room. "Hi. Should I expect to be here a while?"

Dhiraj grinned. "As long as it takes."

Jennifer gave Dhiraj a disapproving look and pointed at her watch.

Dhiraj pointed at her. "Right. I meant 20 minutes until Student TV comes in here."

Natalie slumped into the chair beside her bag. "Good. Wasting 20 minutes doesn't sound so bad. Can we get this over with?"

Dhiraj pulled his lower lip over his top one. "Don't hate, Natalie. Don't hate." He pushed a couple of buttons as the lights dimmed and a video began playing.

Natalie recognized the music and black and white text almost immediately. With election season on the horizon, the attack ads had already begun. Only, this one had nothing to do with politics. A black and white picture of Travis appeared on the right side of the screen.

"Travis Conner willingly joined the Go Home Alien movement even though he knew the truth about Ted Finley."

The voice was obviously Dhiraj trying to do the deep "attack ad" voice. Natalie couldn't help but laugh at his high-voiced effort to find his lower register.

A particularly unattractive photo of Travis fighting for position in a football game popped up on the screen.

"When Travis Conner had the choice between honors classes and busting heads on the football field, he picked helmet-to-helmet combat."

A third image came up, this one of a bloody wrist bandage.

"Travis Conner has gotten in six reported fight incidents in the last three years, not including his attempt to corner Dhiraj Patel in the bathroom, with two other friends as backup."

Natalie sighed and watched the last image pop up on the screen. It looked like it was snapped at some party, given the drunk face Travis was making.

"Is this the guy you want by your side this senior year? Vote against Travis for boyfriend."

The voice sped up as a sentence appeared at the bottom of the screen. "Paid for by the Natalie's Friends Against Travis Conner Fund."

When the video came to a close, Natalie grabbed her bag and reached for the door handle. Dhiraj sped across the room and put his shoulder into the door before she could open it.

"Hey! You're not even gonna comment on the production value?"

Natalie retracted her hand and stared into Dhiraj's eyes. She went about her usual practice of hoping she could set fire to his face using her look alone.

"You shouldn't have spent the money."

As she reached for the handle again, Dhiraj wedged himself between her and the door. She threw up her hands and sat down on an empty chair.

Dhiraj followed her to her seat. "I don't understand how a guy who was in an anti-Ted cult and who tried to punch me in the face is suitable dating material."

Natalie knew this was what would face her if she revealed the relationship. She'd pretty much ignored Travis after the incident at the GHA headquarters for the rest of junior year. When the two of them found themselves at the same college for concurrent basketball and football camps, they literally ran into each other in the cafeteria. Travis' tray smacked into Natalie's so hard that her plate of spaghetti and meatballs ended up all over her shirt. While Natalie just wanted the incident to be over, Travis' coach demanded that the linebacker immediately wash the stain out before it set. She pulled on a practice pinny from her bag and headed through a large, swinging door. When the two of them went into the kitchen together, it was the first time they'd been alone since he shot her in the back in the GHA lobby.

"Sorry about the shirt." Travis didn't look up at her as he rinsed out the red stain under the warm water.

He had a swollen bump on the side of his cheek. She assumed it was the result of a tackle gone wrong. Natalie wanted to stop looking at it, but she felt drawn to his face.

"It's fine." Natalie looked around the room to make sure they were really alone. "I never got to thank you."

Travis finally looked at her. The look of confusion on his face was so apparent, Natalie almost had to laugh.

"Natalie Dormer wants to thank me? I feel like that's less likely than winning a state championship."

She smirked. "Okay. Okay. You were obviously an idiot. And you shot me in the frickin' back."

Travis turned off the water and gritted his teeth. "That's true. But it was just with a rubber bullet."

"Anyway...." Natalie attempted to push out the memory of the sharp pain that bullet had caused her. "You got yourself kicked out of the cult to save us. It was a selfless act."

Travis poured some more soap on the stain and attempted to scrub away at it. "Not completely selfless. Even though you pretended to have feelings for me, I wasn't pretending. I cared about you."

Natalie grumbled and spoke under her breath. "I wasn't pretending."

Travis leaned in. "What was that?"

Natalie looked toward the exit and then back at him. "I liked you. For real. I don't know why, because you're a terrible person."

Travis smiled at that.

She continued. "Lord help me, I actually missed you afterwards. It must've been a bout of insanity. One that I'm thankfully cured of."

Travis sprayed water all over Natalie. She suppressed a shriek and blinked to get the liquid out of her vision. Before she could retaliate, she was completely drenched. Natalie pounded on Travis' chest with her fist.

"You jerk!" She slammed the other fist into him as well. "I'm gonna destroy you."

Travis scowled. "Not if I destroy you first."

They locked lips and started making out right there in the college cafeteria kitchen. Natalie's fists became flat and felt for his chest and his back. Travis tossed away the shirt and lifted Natalie up onto the edge of the sink. She felt the passion coursing through her body and wanted nothing more than to have Travis close to her. That feeling didn't go away all summer long.

Natalie rubbed her hands together as Dhiraj waited for an answer.

Jennifer stayed a few feet behind her boyfriend, as if trying to keep herself safe from the confrontation. "I hate to say it, Nat, but Dhiraj has a point."

Natalie snorted out of her nostrils. "First of all, I want to point out that Travis and I have been dating all summer long and you two didn't notice because you were so lovey-dovey."

Dhiraj and Jennifer shared a happy glance.

Natalie stretched out two fingers from one hand and tapped them on the other.

"Number two, people can change. Jen, you used to have to worry about Erica drinking too much or doing something stupid 24/7. And Dhiraj, Ted couldn't even open a jar of peanut butter and now he's off saving the world." Natalie leaned her back against the wall. "Can't a massive douchebag turn over a new leaf?"

Dhiraj opened his mouth, but nothing came out. He looked back at Jennifer and she shrugged her shoulders.

He tried a second time. "Look, Natalie—"

"Go on a double date with us."

It took Natalie a second to realize that she'd been the one who made the ridiculous suggestion. Maybe her friends' approval mattered more to her than she realized.

Dhiraj raised his eyebrows. "A double date?"

She groaned. "Yeah. Who knows? Maybe we'll even have fun."

Dhiraj seemed like he was about to launch into another rant, but Jennifer gripped his shoulder before he could start.

"Let's do it."

Dhiraj looked uncomfortable. "Fine. We'll do it. But we're probably not gonna like him."

Natalie felt a sense of pride over beating back the intervention. "Good. And I probably still won't care."

CHAPTER
21

Sandra felt warm around the hundreds of people crammed into the college auditorium. She couldn't imagine how hot her husband must been have behind the podium with the lights shining off his face. She kept her face as neutral as possible as President Blake delivered a response during the first Presidential debate. Her husband's demeanor on the other side of the stage was calm with a slight smile. He looked as if he were in on a joke that he wanted to clue millions of people into. Sandra smiled and glanced down at her attire.

Her light blue dress was more expensive than her entire wardrobe combined had been when she was a waitress. The diamond from her massive engagement ring glistened in the light. She recalled the days she'd spent toiling in the back of Page's Diner, her wrists aching from the heavy trays she lifted from the kitchen. The only pain she'd felt since then was the five-story fall to her death and the beating she'd taken from Erica LaPlante. If her husband's plan went off without a hitch, she might never need to feel any kind of pain ever again.

Sandra was only a few feet from the moderator's table. YNN blowhard Rudy Bolger had somehow secured the spot that was usually intended for serious, neutral journalists. Sandra knew the order of the questions Bolger would ask. With foreign policy out of the way, it was time for the one that would make or break her husband's campaign.

"Thank you, Mr. President." Bolger's intonation made him sound every bit the ratings hog he was. "We'll start with you for the next question. In the last two weeks, we've seen devastating otherworldly attacks in Treasure, Pennsylvania, and Chapel Hill, North Carolina, which seem to have shown that we are truly not alone. How would you handle encounters like this in the future as we deal with creatures from another realm?"

Sandra watched President Blake shift ever so slightly behind the podium. She caught her husband's eye, which rewarded her with a twinkle.

He's got him. He knows he has no chance.

President Blake stood straight up to hide his fear. "Thank you, Rudy. The White House strongly condemns these otherworldly attacks as cowardly acts of terrorism. We also offer our condolences for the lives lost during these senseless and ruthless incidents."

Blake seemed to collect his thoughts for a moment and looked straight ahead into the camera. "We have mobilized Ted Finley and a team of trained agents from the Department of Homeland Security to deal with the problem. Finley and the agents are tracking down the creatures as we speak. In the next four years, with Ted by my side, the White House will work to end these attacks by reaching out to these other worlds, thereby becoming the first Presidency to engage in diplomatic relations with another dimension."

Bolger nodded with a wide expression for the camera. It wasn't focused on him, though. It was focused on Blake, who appeared visibly shaken by his effort to answer a complex question. Bolger pointed toward Sandra's husband with his fingers in the shape of a gun.

"Senator Kable, same question."

Sandra smiled in sync with her husband. It was time for the shark to eat.

"My staff and I likewise offer our heartfelt condolences to the families who've been affected by this tragedy. As President, I won't rely entirely on a superhero for help. You know who should be a hero? The President of the United States of America."

Despite the instructions that the audience should remain silent during the answers, several students expressed their fervor with a hearty whoop. Sandra kept her laugh to herself.

"As President, I'll create a new governmental body to better understand the other worlds, and unlike my opponent, I'll share all the information with the public. We are the United States. We don't like getting pushed around."

After all the questions had concluded, a production assistant led Sandra to the stage. As she shook hands and took pictures with the Blake family, Sandra felt self-conscious about her appearance. While she was in her early 20s, she'd been made up to look much closer to 40. She was told it was a voter thing. It was one of many things she'd been told to do of late. Sandra thought about the hidden tattoos on her hand and shoulder when she walked arm-in-arm with her husband to a private area.

"How'd I do?"

She smirked. "You know how you did."

He returned the same look. "But I want to hear it from you."

Her husband was powerful enough that he didn't truly need her. She had no clue why her opinion even mattered to him. While it could've been a kind gesture to a loved one, Sandra had a sneaking suspicion that not everything was as it seemed.

She waited until they had reached a room with her husband's campaign staff to honor his request.

"I think you beat the pants off him." She kissed him on the cheek. "Which gives me an idea for later."

Her husband's face turned pink. When the members of his staff noticed his entry, they began cheering. None of them was louder than Terry, the slimy individual who ran the campaign. He snuck in between the two of them and placed his arm on both their shoulders. Sandra did her best to smile, even though all she could think about was getting his arm off her.

"You killed it, Mr. Senator. The networks are saying he won it on the economy, but nobody cares about that right now. Everyone is scared about the attacks, and as far as they're concerned, you're the one who should be protecting the United States."

Sandra beamed while her husband took on an almost bashful appearance.

He made a fake sigh of relief. "Thanks, Terry. And thank you everyone for all your hard work. I couldn't have done this without your tireless research and preparation."

When Terry took her arm of Sandra's shoulder to join in the applause, she took a step away from him and put her hands together as well.

"Obviously, it's terrible that all this is happening. If I could take back those lives lost—"

Her husband's voice broke. For all the acting lessons she'd taken during and after high school, his ability to fake believable emotions was miles ahead of hers.

Terry offered a reassuring pat. "I know, sir. But if you become the leader of the free world as a result, maybe they'll all have been worth it."

Sandra watched as the other people in the room gave a slow nod. She wondered if Terry and the others would stay with them even if they knew of the senator's atrocities. Her husband put his arm back around Terry's.

"Thank you, my friend." He looked back toward the rest of the room. "You all deserve a celebration. I would join you, but I've heard my wife has her own celebration in mind."

The staffers laughed, and after a few handshakes here and there, the Kables were off. Despite the staff's best efforts to keep which hotel they were staying in a secret, Sandra and her husband were mobbed as soon as they exited their vehicle. One photographer who seemed to want an extra-close photo really got on Sandra's nerves. She briefly ruminated on how easy it would be to snap his neck. Senator Kable seemed to sense her bloodlust, and he guided her away from the eager photographer.

She'd been a nobody as a waitress; she wasn't sure if being a celebrity was better or worse. By the time they'd gotten through the mob, Sandra felt exhausted and collapsed on the hotel bed. She wiped at her makeup and facial prosthetics that made her look like the ideal first lady. It didn't take long for her to take herself back to her real face. She didn't care that she'd need an hour in the makeup chair the next morning before she left the room. Her shoulders relaxed and she breathed a sigh of relief.

Sandra walked into the bathroom and watched her husband perform the same ritual. He removed the toupee from his scalp, revealing scars on the left side of his head under a graying patch of thin hair. He frowned back at Sandra with a look like he knew the image before them still wasn't right. Kable reached behind his left ear and unpinned the fake skin from his face. As he peeled it off, the man looking back at them was much more genuine. He laid the half-mask down on the hotel bathroom counter.

Some would call her husband's true face unfinished, but she knew this was the only version of him that looked complete. She'd known it the second he saved her from the school gymnasium; it'd been reaffirmed when the two of them blew up the police van the following day.

Sandra put her hands around his waist. She kissed the back of his neck and leaned her head on his shoulder.

"I love seeing you." She ran her hands over the scars on the left side of his face. "I wish I could see you like this all the time."

He smiled. The broken side of his mouth was unable to curl nearly as much as the side that still looked human.

"Do you think the world would accept how I truly look?"

She thought of her own disguise as she placed her face beside his. "After all this pretending is over, we can just kill all the people who don't."

Kable put his hand around Sandra's back. He dipped her deep, sending all the blood rushing to her head like she'd had too much champagne. Sandra squealed with joy as he pulled her back upright.

"You know just what to say to make a man happy."

She grinned and gestured toward the bedroom. "I think it's time for that celebration now."

He nodded and flipped off the light in the bathroom. The nightlight reflected off his mask. On the counter lay the face of the next potential President. As he carried her into bed, Sandra couldn't help but think that the title "First Lady" had a good ring to it.

PART THREE

CHAPTER
22

Erica sat down on her bed next to Jennifer. As she looked around the room, she relived memories of everything that had happened there: secrets she'd told, conversations she'd had, and kisses she'd shared. As with all her other lives, however, most of her memories weren't really hers. Erica knew she was living in a borrowed life, and while she prided herself on her secrets, this was a time for the truth.

"Are you okay?" Jennifer placed her hand on Erica's back.

The small, circular path Jennifer's hand took matched one that the previous Erica had felt on hundreds of occasions. For the new Erica, it may have been the first time she'd experienced it.

Erica knew her previous inhabitant had never appreciated Jennifer. The loyal friend had done everything in her power to keep the old Erica from self-destruction. While it didn't work, Jennifer could have been voted the least responsible for Erica's murder.

Erica sighed. "In most missions, nobody knows who I am, and I treat my 'family' as part of the mission." She ran the tops of her fingers against the soft bedspread. "It's not like that this time."

Before Erica could tuck her chin and look at the carpet, Jennifer blocked the move with her free hand and offered a reassuring grasp.

She knows me. At least, she knows parts of me.

Jennifer peered into Erica's eyes. "You could always sneak away like I did. Maybe it'll only last a couple of days."

Erica shook her head. "I don't know that for sure. Besides, losing me again would kill Mom and... Erica's parents."

Most of Erica's missions had been shorter than this one. From previous experience, she knew that the more time she stayed, the more attached she'd become.

Her throat started to close up. "I can't put them through that again."

Jennifer shifted her position to face Erica with her entire body, crossing her legs over one another. "And telling them their daughter is dead is going to be better?"

Erica looked away, spying the patched-over hole in the wall she'd caused when Redican had wiped her brain. She wondered what would have happened if her first use of unknown strength would have involved shoving her parents or some other act of violence.

"I'm putting them in danger by being here." Erica sniffled. "Better to just rip the Band-Aid off and tell them the truth."

Jennifer nodded and squeezed Erica's shoulders with a hug. "I'm here for you."

The affection made Erica want to let out all her emotions. Her boyfriend/mission was hundreds of miles away. She was about to devastate her parents. A cocktail of sadness, fear and anticipation wreaked havoc with her hormones. But she knew she had to be strong, and she did her best to release the emotion as she'd learned to do in a previous life at the Academy in Japan.

"Thanks, Jen." Erica returned the hug. She took a deep breath and pulled back. "I've been meaning to ask you about something else."

Jennifer blinked. "So you heard?"

"I'm just not sure why you're keeping it a secret."

Jennifer stood up and walked to one of the windows. She wiped some dust off the blinds. "I don't know. Embarrassment. Not really understanding why I fought that girl."

Erica felt ashamed. Here Jennifer was standing by her side. Who was supporting her?

"You need to tell Dhiraj."

"I know. I'm just waiting for the right time."

"No such thing." Erica grabbed a pillow for her lap. "I think I'm about to prove that."

They went downstairs shortly after they were sure Mr. and Mrs. LaPlante were home. Erica's father was sifting through some papers on the couch with a sports news recap show on in the background. Her mother unwrapped the plastic from a gourmet make-at-home pizza. Erica had nearly forgotten it was the cheat day on her mother's carb-free diet.

"Hey guys." Erica's voice shook. "Can I talk to you in the family room about something?"

Mrs. LaPlante gave Erica an odd look. Even after almost a year of the more polite version of her daughter, such etiquette caught her off guard. She glanced between Erica and Jennifer.

"Really, honey, if you were going to be a lesbian, couldn't you have picked someone a little more flashy?"

Erica's eyes grew wider, but not have as wide as Jennifer's. They took a step apart.

Erica shook her head. "Mom. It's not about my sexuality." She glanced back at her friend. "And Jennifer is plenty flashy. Can you guys just come in here?"

Mrs. LaPlante sat down next to her husband, who, after some prodding, finally switched off the TV and gave Erica his full attention.

Erica had already practiced what she was going to say in her head, but sitting before the two people who had clothed her, fed her and put a roof of her head made the words seem wrong.

"The last year has been amazing. You two are great parents." A nervous pain grew in her stomach. "You just aren't my parents."

Mr. and Mrs. LaPlante's reactions were as different as steel and cotton. Her father's face grew stern and cold, while her mother's countenance surprised Erica. She almost looked relieved.

Mr. LaPlante leaned forward and spoke quickly. "Erica. I can assure you that your mother and I... we have the birth certificates and everything."

Mrs. LaPlante put her hand on her husband's chest. "I don't think that's what she means, dear."

Erica looked into her mother's eyes.

She knows. How does she know?

Mrs. LaPlante sighed and her voice started to waver. "You're not my daughter, because somebody killed her, right?"

The color went out of Mr. LaPlante's face. Erica wasn't sure how to respond. Jennifer tapped her friend on the shoulder, reminding her what she was there to do.

"Yeah." Erica felt the pain grow within. "How did you know?"

"You told me." Mrs. LaPlante touched her husband's leg. "Earlier this year. You said that you died."

It all made sense now to Erica. In addition to busting a hole through the wall, the brainwashed version of new-Erica must have had visions about her body's death. Seeing something that grotesque in her mind must have been worth sharing.

"I'm sorry. I didn't mean for you to find out—"

Mrs. LaPlante waved away Erica's words. "No, no. I should've known my own daughter. You acted so differently when you came back. We just wanted to believe."

Mr. LaPlante remained silent, and Erica wished he would say something. She supposed that one positive reaction out of two wasn't so bad.

He finally broke his silence. "If you're not her, why even come back here? Why give us that false hope?"

Mr. LaPlante's words broke Erica's heart. She wanted to move across the room and hold him. But that likely wasn't going to be an option anymore.

"The people who gave Ted his powers put my spirit into your daughter's body. I still have all of Erica's memories. I know she didn't express it, but she loved you deeply."

Erica's father gave a single laugh. "Maybe you got the wrong memories."

Erica looked back at Jennifer, because she couldn't look her father in the eye any longer. It hurt too much.

Jennifer took the hint and spoke. "Erica did love you guys. This new one does, too. You should've seen how hard it was for her to tell you this."

Mrs. LaPlante grabbed a tissue from the side table and dabbed her eyes. "What happened to my daughter?"

Jennifer brushed her hand against her forehead. "A guy she was dating killed her. But, I made sure he went to prison."

Jennifer and Erica took turns answering the rest of the questions surrounding the murder. Erica felt some relief over the top of the anxiety. The secrets were out, and her mission would have to adapt. After exhausting all their questions, Mrs. LaPlante cried softly while her husband remained stoic.

He refused a tissue from his wife. "Erica, if that's even what I should call you, what do you want from us?"

Later that evening, Erica got what she needed. Mr. and Mrs. LaPlante agreed to emancipate her and give her a roof over her head as needed for the rest of the school year. While her father had asked what she wanted, Erica couldn't bare to request the truth. She wanted things to remain as they were, with her parents treating her like a daughter. That aspect of their relationship remained up in the air.

Later that night, Erica felt drained as she lay down beneath the sheets of her bed. She could've slept right then and there, if she didn't have to make one more revelation of the truth. Erica pulled out her tablet and dialed up Ted for a video call.

"Hey!" Ted seemed to have all the energy Erica lacked.

"Hey. How's North Carolina?"

Ted didn't appear to notice Erica's lack of verve. "Warm. And we haven't found the bad guys yet. How are things in—"

"I told my parents who I really was."

Ted's grin left him. His voice dropped an octave. "What?"

Erica sighed. "Yoshi and I are going to investigate the attacks. And if I can't be out there with you, I can't be in Treasure."

Ted leaned forward and rubbed at the back of his head. "Erica. We don't know how long this'll last. Maybe we'll stop 'em by the end of October and there'll still be—"

"Ted, I had to tell them at some point."

Ted glared into Erica's eyes through the screen. As if she hadn't been made to feel bad enough already that day.

He looked up at something off-screen before looking back at the screen. "I'm sure that was hard to do."

Erica's nervousness diminished slightly. "It was."

He leaned his temple down on his hand. Erica found his attempt to smile through his dissatisfaction incredibly cute. She mimicked his position and pretended for a moment that she was right beside him.

Ted sighed. "It's been one hell of a week."

Erica matched his breath. "It has."

He sat up and moved the tablet accordingly. The shift in perspective made Ted's chin look way bigger than it actually was. "You've gotta do what you've gotta do, and I won't stand in the way of the mission. Please be careful out there."

Erica pursed her lips together. "Of course."

Ted looked over his shoulder at something before turning back. "Look, I have to go on a night patrol. We've been doing it all week. I wish I could—"

"Ted?"

"Yeah?"

"Lychos. They're like big dogs. Keep that in mind if you find one."

Ted frowned. "Ok. Goodni—"

"Ted?"

"Yeah?"

"I miss you." Erica concentrated on the little video camera on her tablet. She sent all the love she could muster into the tiny circle.

Ted closed his eyes for a moment to soak in her words. He opened them with a sigh. "I miss you, too. I hope you're doing the right thing."

Right then, she vowed to herself that before the month was up, she'd hold Ted Finley and kiss him like he'd never been kissed before.

"I hope I am, too."

CHAPTER
23

Two nights later, Ted used his powers to move a fallen tree to his left. He was starting to get familiar with these woods after a few days of patrolling, but he was tired of flying or jumping over the same barrier. At least it gave him something to do, because at this point, there'd been no clues whatsoever.

Ted had Erica on his mind as he and Allison held their flashlights on the dirt and leaves in front of them. The trees were much taller than the ones behind his house, but they reminded him of the pond and the smell of Erica's perfume as she lay beside him. He wished Erica had consulted him before she made such a major decision. Even his parents didn't know Erica's full story, but she said it wouldn't take long before the word spread. He figured he wouldn't have been able to convince Erica to continue living a lie, but maybe he could've delayed it just one more month. The threads of normalcy in his life were being snipped, one by one.

Ted was supposed to be in school getting his college applications together. He was supposed to be enjoying everything that came with being a senior. Instead, he was trudging through the woods with the federal government monitoring his every move. If there was one positive, it was his new handler, Allison. Her blond hair was lighter than Erica's and hung straight down to the base of her neck. She was smaller than any of the other agents Ted had met in the last few months, but she was far stronger, faster and more capable than she looked. While he'd made efforts to keep things close to the chest, spending so much time with an attractive female made him spill the beans pretty quickly.

"So, she's not going to be a high school student anymore?"

Allison's voice played softly against the backdrop of crickets and the wind.

"I guess not. Who knows how long she'll be gone. I just wish she were here. I think you'd like her."

Allison laughed. It was more like one sharp note than a rolling giggle. "I tend to get along with girls who don't take crap."

Ted smiled. If he had to be away from Erica, he might as well spend his time with someone who was almost as cute with the same take-charge attitude. They reached a clearing in the forest and saw a railroad track cutting through. Allison sat down on the track and Ted took a seat next to her.

"Here's my question." Allison shook out her hair and ran her hands through it, then tied it into a ponytail. "Can you trust her?"

If Allison had asked the question six months earlier, he couldn't be sure how he would've answered. Erica hid the sword and the books from him. She neglected to tell him that there were other powers at his disposal. She kept all sorts of information from him and used her "protector" status as justification for holding back. Since that time, however, she'd been much more forthcoming.

"I definitely trust her. I wish the government felt the same way."

Allison put up both her hands. "Hey, don't look at me. I'm all for more help in the situation. The guys up top are just scared of something they don't understand."

Ted definitely trusted Erica more than he did the federal government. After all, he couldn't forget that before he made his summer deal, someone with power had helped to forge the malicious Go Home Alien movement. He turned his flashlight toward Allison's face.

"And what about you?" He moved the beam of light to point up at his chin. "Are you scared?"

"Why should I be scared?" She hopped up and looked down at him. "I've got a lovesick but capable superhero to protect me." Allison offered him a hand. "Just a few more hours to go."

A rustling noise caught Ted's attention. Allison must've heard it too, because she moved her flashlight in that direction. She raised her eyebrows toward Ted.

"You ready?"

Ted nodded and took her hand before moving back into the forest. Allison pulled out a tranquilizer gun. She had told him that each dart had a dose of the knockout drug that could bring down three grizzly bears. Ted hoped that was enough.

They continued to move forward, and the rustling sound grew. It was accompanied by a soft chewing noise. As Ted and Allison approached, the chomping became clearer. It reminded Ted of a room full of people eating barbecue chicken with their mouths open. He had a feeling that wasn't what awaited them.

Allison motioned for Ted to join her behind a tree. She motioned around the trunk and Ted squinted to adjust to the dim light.

Illuminated by a half moon, one of the Lychos beasts leaned back on its hindquarters, enjoying a meal of raw deer.

Allison motioned for Ted to join her back on the other end of the tree. "Remind me not to watch Bambi after this."

Ted nodded in agreement. "What's the plan?"

"I'll hit him with the darts. If they don't knock him out, you'll have to."

"Fun times. I'm ready."

She smiled. "Good. On my mark."

Allison used her fingers to count down from three. When she reached zero, she and Ted leapt out from their hiding place. Three darts came zipping out of the tranquilizer gun and flew through the crisp air. One hit the Lychos directly in the neck, while another got it in the chest. A third one was about to zip wide, until Ted used his powers to snatch it out of the air and plant it in the creature's leg. The beast screamed in pain, its voice filling the forest with a guttural groan. It kicked the deer carcass, sending blood and guts everywhere.

Ted put up his hands and blocked the decaying shower from hitting the two of them.

"Thanks." Allison loaded several more darts into the gun.

"Don't mention it." Ted looked at the beast. "Do you think that was enough?"

Since kicking the deer and screaming, the Lychos hadn't done much of anything except for stumble once or twice.

"I think s—"

The Lychos reached behind itself and pulled a 20-foot tree out of the ground with a powerful rip. It took only a moment for the creature to turn the tree sideways and throw it directly at them. The huge projectile made a whooshing sound as it barreled ahead. Allison dove away and rolled down a small hill. Ted put both hands up once again and stopped the massive tree just two inches in front of his face.

Ted moved his hands like he might if he were gripping a baseball bat and the tree moved in the same position. "There's nothing like a good piece of hickory."

The Lychos roared and Ted swung his arms forward. The tree's trunk whipped into the creature's body. The swing sent it at least 10 feet into the air before the beast came crashing down in the distance. Ted relaxed his hands and flew through the air toward the creature. The Lychos had fallen on a small, thick tree, and a sharp branch stuck out of its leg. It was completely motionless. Ted looked inside the creature's mind and found no activity whatsoever.

"If you'd been nicer, we could've signed a treaty. Get it, a tree-ty?"

The dead creature didn't respond. Ted's laugh didn't last long, as he heard a scream back in the direction he'd come from.

"Allison."

Ted flew toward the noise and saw his partner. She was backing away from the other two Lychos, and she was running out of room. Ted eyed the creatures between him and Allison and started flying at top speed. All of a sudden, one of the beasts turned around to face him and raised its arms. As it did, Ted felt himself lose complete control over his body. He tensed up the muscles he usually used for flying. They did nothing. He continued moving incredibly fast with a complete lack of control. Fear washed over his body.

"Holy crap!"

Ted covered his face as he whipped through several branches. The wood scratched his arms and cheeks, leaving sharp prickles of pain on his skin. As he was about to make impact with the ground, he uncovered his face to learn of his final destination. He slammed into a bush, the impact rattling Ted's brain and causing some of the branches to punch through his clothing and into his skin. The adrenaline kept him alert when he got to his feet. A gash on his arm throbbed and he held his hand to it. When he took his palm away, it was covered with blood.

"Oh, man."

Ted could feel the wooziness from the blood loss battling his adrenaline. For now, the latter was winning, particularly when he heard another scream from Allison. He ripped off his shirt and tied it tightly around the gushing wound.

They blocked my powers. They're not just hairy and ugly. They're dark souls, too.

Ted tried to access his powers again to lift off the ground. It was no use. He ran toward the noise.

"Looks like I'm gonna have to do this the old-fashioned way."

CHAPTER
24

Natalie looked up at her bedroom wall to see the display of her final eight candidates for college. The first visit was coming up in just a couple of days, and she could feel the tension building in her back and neck. Then again, that could be tension for her upcoming double date with Dhiraj and Jennifer. It took her about 20 minutes to decide on a green tank top and blue jeans, even though she knew her outfit would have little to no impact on the upcoming event. With about a half hour left until she had to meet Travis, she opted to check something off her to-do list by calling Christina Finley.

Natalie pulled up the video call app on her phone and swiped until she got to the contact labeled Ted's Cool Sister. Christina had been the one who'd added the entry last year. Ted's sister took the call and met Natalie with a giant smile and a toss of her golden hair.

"Well, if it isn't the girl who used to date my gross brother."

Natalie rolled her eyes. "I think there are 20 things I'd rather be defined by."

Christina's face crinkled as she grinned. From her hair to her thin face, there was little on the surface that connected her to the Finley family. Even her boisterous laugh seemed like it belonged to another gene pool.

"Too bad. Until I'm proactive enough to change your entry on my phone, that's what you're gonna come up as. What's going on?"

Christina had been a big supporter of Natalie's relationship with Ted. While she didn't often have high praise for her sibling, Ted told Natalie of how often Christina would say how lucky he was or how he was going to be a WNBA player's wife someday. Christina was an athlete in her own right, as one of the starting pitchers for the Southern Ohio softball team. She threw a shutout in the College World Series during her freshman year. The two of them were often mentioned in the same breath when it came to Treasure sport prospects.

Natalie returned the grin. "Just getting pumped about next week."

"Me, too!" Christina leaned back in her chair. "You do drugs, drink whiskey and engage in illegal acts of violence, right?"

Natalie shook her head. "Can you let me get into college before you ruin my life and reputation?"

"Boo!" Christina gave Natalie a lewd gesture before reverting to her smile. "Suit yourself. You excited about your double date?"

Natalie's spirits dropped. "Uh. I guess."

Christina continued as if it were the most natural thing. "See, Dhiraj told Ted, and Ted told me. When I was at Treasure, Travis Conner was some sweet freshman meat. Nicely done."

Natalie felt the butterflies dive-bombing her stomach and every other vulnerable part of her anatomy. She didn't expect to be talking about her love live with her ex-boyfriend's family members.

"Yeah." Natalie chewed her lip. "Christina, have you ever dated a bad person?"

Ted's sister pondered the question for a moment. She laughed to herself multiple times before responding. "Um, try twice this semester. I dated a guy who broke up a marriage in his hometown. After I found out, I continued to date him for three more months until he cheated on me."

Christina laughed at herself again. Natalie wasn't sure why it was so funny, but she found herself joining in. "That's terrible. Why'd you go out with him?"

Christina turned her head to the side and focused her eyes on the camera. "Ms. Natalie, there are boys who would be great to settle down with, and there are boys who are all fun and trouble. There's nothing wrong with spending an extensive amount of time in column number two."

Natalie pulled into Travis' driveway. His house was located next to the old Torello home. Jason and Phil's parents had moved out after the collapse of the GHA. Natalie considered coming inside, but when Travis walked out the front door, she was happy to be spared the awkward parent conversation.

Travis was more dressed up than Natalie. He wore a tight, grey button-down that exposed his thick arms and round chest. She imagined herself ripping the shirt from his body as buttons scattered across the car floor.

Fun and trouble.

Travis got in the passenger side and buckled his seatbelt. He didn't reach over to kiss her like normal. Then again, today was different. It was their first public date.

"You alright?" Natalie pulled out of the Conner driveway. "You're not your usual annoying self."

Travis cracked a smile. "I feel like I'm headed to a firing squad."

Natalie made the turn out of Travis' neighborhood. "Dead man walkin'."

"Just so you know, I plan on completely embarrassing you."

She slapped his leg before returning her hand to the steering wheel. "I want Dhiraj off my back. If you're not on your best behavior, I'll delete your number from my phone."

He rolled his eyes. "You wouldn't."

"You wanna try me, football?"

Travis grunted. "Fine. What do you want me to talk about?"

"Anything other than the GHA or how you tried to punch Dhiraj in the face."

"Hey, Travis, remember when your cult gave Ted's mom second degree burns and you and your friends cornered me in the bathroom?"

Natalie peered out from behind her menu and gave Dhiraj the evil eye. She'd been to O'Malley's multiple times with her family, but on this visit the lighting seemed dimmer, the laughter from the conversations around her more ominous.

Dhiraj ignored her glances and stared straight ahead at Travis, despite Jennifer's efforts to get his attention.

"I hear the chicken is good." Jennifer pulled on Dhiraj's shoulder. "Are you gonna get the chicken?"

Dhiraj gave one last stare to Travis before he nodded to his girlfriend.

Natalie heard Travis' breathing pick up its pace. She put her hand on his leg and held it steady, hoping its presence would calm him.

"They aren't my friends anymore." Travis looked back at his menu. "I think I'll get the chicken, too."

Dhiraj grumbled. "Fine, I'll get the fish."

"Seriously?" Natalie put down her menu and crossed her arms. "Are you really not going to get the chicken because he got the chicken?"

This series of evil eyes she gave seemed to make a little progress on wearing down Dhiraj's angry veneer.

His eyes darted away from her. "It did look good."

Natalie shook her head. "Can we talk about something else?"

Jennifer presented the date's first smile. "Great idea. Are you excited for Southern Ohio?"

"Of course," Natalie said. "Christina says there'll be some debauchery."

The comment piqued Travis' curiosity. "Really?"

Dhiraj sneered at Travis, but the other three ignored him. Particularly Natalie.

"So she claims." She tapped her menu on the tabletop. "I'm probably just going to watch." Natalie gripped Travis' thigh. "Probably."

After a several second lull, Jennifer piped back up.

"And Travis, what're your college plans?"

Travis looked at Natalie as if he was unsure he was allowed to participate. She glared at him until he started speaking.

"A lot of it comes down to football. If I don't get a scholarship, I might not go."

Natalie narrowed her eyes. "This is the first I'm hearing of this."

Travis chuckled. "That's because we don't usually talk that much."

"Ugh." Dhiraj made a face like he'd just eaten rotten eggs. "This is not dinner table conversation."

Natalie was getting the hang of ignoring Dhiraj. "So you might not go to school?"

Travis scratched the side of his head. "My parents don't really have any money saved up. I kind of need a full scholarship if it's gonna happen. It's not like I haven't been planning for this for years."

A waiter came by and took their orders. All four of them got the chicken. Natalie leaned down on her hand and rubbed at her temple. She couldn't believe she'd been dating someone for several months without knowing something so important.

After giving the final order, Dhiraj creased his forehead.

"What do you mean, you've been planning this for years?"

Travis cleared his throat. "You know. When I dropped all those honors classes freshman year. I wasn't in the top 10 percent of smart kids like you and Ted. I had a better chance of getting money for college if I focused on football. So that's how I've spent all of high school."

Natalie had essentially known she'd be getting a full ride for the last few years. But, if something had ever happened, she knew her parents would be able to pay for her education. She couldn't imagine what it would feel like to be financially dependent on her hoops skills. And anything she could come up with felt scary.

Judging by the silence, Jennifer and Dhiraj didn't know how to respond, either. Travis took the opportunity to continue.

"It sucks, though. I had good friends in those classes, but not anymore. And half the football team was in the GHA. Ever since I gave Ted that tape and got Cobblestone locked up... I'm not exactly their favorite person. Now I've got nobody."

Travis shifted away from Natalie and stood up. "Maybe it was a bad idea to do this. I'll walk home."

Natalie reached for Travis, but she wasn't the first to get to him. Dhiraj stood up and used his arm to block Travis from leaving.

"Wait, man." Dhiraj let out a deep breath. "I'm sorry. I didn't know about all of that."

"It's ok. I'm sorry for trying to beat you up and everything the GHA did."

Dhiraj nodded. "Why don't you stick around?"

"You want me to stay?"

"Want is a strong word."

Jennifer socked Dhiraj in the side.

"Ow!" Dhiraj rubbed at the forming bruise. "What I'm trying to say...." He looked at Natalie. "Maybe if we talk it out, I can figure a way for you to go to college with a partial scholarship."

Travis gave Dhiraj a dubious look. "You'd do that for me?"

Dhiraj looked back in her direction. "If Natalie's willing to give you the benefit of the doubt... then so am I."

Natalie realized she was holding her breath and let it out all at once. Travis smiled at her and extended his hand to Dhiraj.

"Thanks."

Dhiraj hesitated but eventually accepted the gesture. "You're welcome."

Everybody sat back down, and the next three hours were much lighter in comparison. As Natalie watched Dhiraj and Travis laugh together, she let all the tension melt out of her.

This is how it's supposed to be.

She looked across the table at Jennifer, who raised her eyebrows and smiled. Natalie grinned back.

One more year. And it's gonna be a good one.

CHAPTER
25

Yoshi watched as Erica stared back at her parents' house. She looked every bit the teenage girl whose body she inhabited. He could hardly believe she'd bested him during their bedroom tussle. Yoshi wondered if Erica had felt the same attachment to the people around her when she died in Kikuchiyo's body so many years ago. After all this time, a part of her was still the best friend he ever had.

Yoshi pulled the car out onto the highway. "You've gotten soft."

Erica chuckled. "Can I blame it on being a teenage girl?"

Yoshi had gone years without hearing a single joke, but the last couple of weeks was starting to warm him back up to humor. He almost smiled. "No."

Erica looked at her phone before tucking it away. "I was part of a family, Yosh. If it hadn't been for the attacks, I might've kept up this lie for good."

Yoshi had been beside Kikuchiyo's body when the protector crossed over into his friend's life. There was no need for keeping secrets among the members of the Academy. They knew all there was to know about the Realm of Souls and the ongoing war. Yoshi's mind went back to the battle that pulled them apart. He thought of flames, blades of ice and the charred flesh of his dearest friend.

"Do you remember Japan well?"

Erica leaned her head back into the chair. Yoshi still hadn't gotten over the fact that this skinny teenager held the memories of over a dozen lives.

Yoshi felt Erica's eyes upon him.

"The memories of my other lives come in and out of this one." She took a deep breath. "Ever since you came here, I'm remembering a lot more from Japan. You fought well that day."

Yoshi felt the regret bubbling up to the surface. "Not well enough to save you."

Erica leaned her elbow against the passenger side window. "I was there to protect all of you. By sacrificing my life to save others, I achieved my mission. It's part of the job description."

Yoshi stared out at the cars ahead of him. "I knew you'd return in another form. I thought the only way I'd ever see my friend again was if I was chosen as the living soul." His blood simmered. "But Ted received the power. Not me."

Yoshi glanced over at Erica. He could tell she weighed her words carefully before responding.

"The light souls chose well with Ted. They would've chosen well with you, too."

Yoshi looked back at the road. "Who would you have chosen?"

Erica smiled. "Thankfully, I'm not involved in such high-level decisions."

Yoshi let out a small laugh. It felt good to do so.

Erica cleared her throat. "So, what'd the school think of you leaving?"

Yoshi thought about his dozens of requests to leave the Academy and the equal number of refusals. He remembered the crimson that covered his blade after he'd slit the throats of two Academy guards. He'd wiped the sword on fresh snow before he took a path along the side of a slick mountain to get away undetected.

"They begged me to go. They knew my skills could help your mission."

Erica nodded. "We're glad to have you on board." She turned on the radio and blared music for the rest of the afternoon.

Later that night in the room of a four-star hotel – Erica's parents wouldn't have permitted anything less – Yoshi watched as his friend emerged from the bathroom. He wondered what he would have thought if Kikuchiyo had come before him wearing all pink with a suggestive phrase printed on the backside.

Erica took the toothbrush out of her mouth. "What?"

Yoshi realized he was staring. "It's nothing."

She finished brushing and spat into the sink. "I know. I'm a girl." Erica began speaking in Japanese. "But remember, I'm also an old friend. I'm glad we can take this journey together."

Yoshi grinned. "Me, too."

After Erica fell asleep, Yoshi took a long walk out on the balcony. The warm air reminded him of the Academy's heat training room, where they would fight with sweat dripping from head to toe. Yoshi wiped some perspiration from his brow just as his phone buzzed against his thigh. Yoshi noted the familiar number and walked far out of earshot of their hotel room.

"Yes?" He paced in the parking lot. "Everything's going as scheduled." Yoshi nodded as if the person on the other side could see it. "I won't let you down, Senator Kable. Goodnight."

Yoshi hung up and looked into the sky. "It won't be long now. I'll have Kikuchiyo. I'll have the power." He looked back at the door to his hotel room. "And there's only one person who can stop me."

CHAPTER
26

Ted brushed the dirt off his clothing and felt the sting of sweat pouring into another unwashed cut. His bleeding arm pulsated, but he did his best to ignore the pain and dizziness. He tried to levitate himself off the ground to see if his powers were still blocked. Ted strained his muscles and visualized himself soaring through the air. Despite his best efforts, his feet stayed firmly planted.

Back to average.

One of the Lychos let out a large growl and swiped in Allison's direction. Ted couldn't see her clearly in the darkness, but he heard the pop of her tranquilizer gun. A yelp of pain shot through the forest as a dart made a direct hit. But as with the first creature, the substance inside the dart seemed to make little difference.

"Ted!" Allison ran further away from the beasts, darts shooting over her shoulder as she went.

Ted dashed off in her direction.

Think. What would Erica tell me to do?

Ted passed by a three-foot long tree branch.

She'd say to use my surroundings.

Ted whistled as loud as possible. One Lychos turned around, and then the other. As the moon reflected off the hairy beasts, Ted could see three darts sticking out of one and five out of the other.

She is one hell of a shot.

Ted waved the stick in the air. "Hey, puppies. Good puppies."

Ted watched as the creatures' eyes followed the stick. "Just like big dogs. Let's see if they like to fetch!"

Ted tossed the branch in the opposite direction. The two creatures watched the piece of wood as it made an impact with the ground. Then they looked right back at Ted.

"It was worth a try."

Ted started to run, and the Lychos immediately gave chase. He placed each footstep as carefully as he could, knowing that one trip could result in death by giant dog. Ted's heart pounded and he could feel his lungs being pushed to the limit. The crisp, green smell of the trees was quickly being replaced by sweaty fur and dog breath. The growling and barking sounds behind him grew louder as he dashed through a patch of trees that were closer together. Ted sidestepped through them and looked behind him. The Lychos slowed down, unable to squeeze between the trees as Ted had.

Ted grinned as his chest heaved. "Looks like we need to put you guys on the diet dog food."

As the Lychos unveiled their claws, a sound like a perfect sword coming out of its sheath rang through the woods. They sliced several trees at once, clearing a path for themselves in just a few moments.

"Next vet visit, we're clipping those nails." Ted went back to running and spied the clearing in the forest from earlier. As the Lychos gave chase, he knew he couldn't keep this up forever. His heart was beating even faster than it had during his multi-state flight.

Ted reached the railroad tracks and heard a train whistle in the distance. He spied a faint white light that was getting brighter with every passing second. The Lychos exited the forest with a snarl and looked around for Ted. Seeing them outside of the tree cover made the creatures look even more intimidating. Their legs and teeth were twice the size of anything he'd ever seen on TV. It was something straight out of a nightmare.

Ted heard the train whistle again and stepped off the track. "This is where I make my last stand."

He pounded his hands together and screamed as loud as he could. The Lychos both jumped at the noise before realizing it was just the diminutive hero headed in their direction. One creature swiped at him, but Ted kicked his paw away. He rolled forward and kicked again with all his might. His shoes made impact with the beast's knee, causing the Lychos to fall forward. Ted jerked his body to the side to avoid being crushed.

The other beast immediately leapt on top of Ted. He gripped the creature's wrists to avoid being sliced. As it snarled in Ted's face, he wondered if he'd ever smelled something so putrid. It was like a landfill mixed with a gas station toilet.

"You must be a hit with the lady Lychos."

When the creature lunged for his face, Ted released the grip in one hand and punched the creature right in the neck. When it clutched at its throat, Ted rolled away and pushed himself up to standing. The train grew louder as it approached.

As Ted tried to bring the fight closer to the tracks, one of the creatures snatched him up by the back of his neck and lifted him off the ground. He felt the claws cut at his skin. Ted jerked back and forth until he slipped through the creature's grasp, sending him back to the ground. He got up right away. When the Lychos reached for Ted again, he jumped over the paw and grabbed hold of the creature's shoulder. Ted pulled himself up onto its back and started boxing it beside the ears.

"This is for going on the carpet."

The Lychos howled in pain and lurched forward, flipping Ted into the air. He landed on his feet before viewing the white light of the train fast approaching. The ground shook beneath his feet.

"I'm gonna have to time this right."

Both Lychos seemed to have already recovered from his assault. He watched the saliva drip from their sharp fangs. The creatures extended their claws until they looked like pale, white knives.

"We got off to a rough start, guys, but with enough training, I think we can get back on track."

The beasts charged after him and Ted slipped underneath their claws, running at full speed for the train tracks. He wondered if Natalie would be proud of his fifty-yard dash time as he pushed his legs to bring him up the slight incline. The sound of the train surrounded him and drowned out the noise of the approaching creatures. Ted's eardrums rattled and the ground shook beneath his feet as he reached the edge of the track. The train's whistle blared as the operator saw the boy on the tracks. Ted continued to run at full speed with the beasts right behind him.

I'm not gonna make it.

The train bore down on him and sparks flew as the operator tried to use the breaks. Ted put every last ounce of strength into his legs. He leapt past the other side of the tracks, his left foot barely clearing the engine as he tumbled to the ground.

He barely heard the loud "whap" sound over the skidding of the breaks, but when Ted turned back, he saw that the train had smashed into the creatures at full speed. The locomotive sent both of the Lychos flying, with one ending up on each side of the tracks. Sparks from the train's still-engaged brake system illuminated the broken creature nearest Ted. His powers restored, Ted felt himself lift off the ground and move toward the beast. The massive creature was broken and bloody. He sat down beside it. On one of its arms, he spied the black tattoos that indicated it was a dark soul.

"As if you needed an advantage." Ted watched as the train finally came to a complete stop. With the noise diminished, he heard something else.

"Ted!"

Between two cars, Ted saw Allison come into view. One arm hung limp at her side, but at least she was alive. Ted flew through the gap and landed in front of her.

"Hey, are you okay?"

Allison wrapped her good arm around Ted. She was shivering from the ordeal.

Ted hugged her back. "Don't worry. They're dead."

He looked to his left to verify. The Lychos on that side of the tracks appeared to have been struck even worse than its counterpart had. Ted looked back at Allison. The sweet smell of her hair filled his nostrils.

She breathed deeply into his chest. "I have not been trained for this."

Ted smirked. "What? They don't simulate an invasion by giant dogs from another dimension?"

Allison pulled away from Ted. "Nope. I'll tell them to update the manual."

As Ted felt the adrenaline leave his body, the train and the forest around him began to spin. He reached for his head and bent one knee onto the ground.

Allison crouched down and put her arm over his shoulders. "Ted?"

Her voice seemed to echo as everything started to go dark. He looked at his makeshift tourniquet. The blood had seeped all the way through and it was damp to the touch.

"Hospital."

Ted watched Allison pull out her phone as he grew more and more weak. Ted swore he heard Allison calling his name when the world around him slipped away.

CHAPTER
27

Jennifer was trapped. Sandra, the former waitress and now devilish dark soul, stood to her left. Yarrick, the Russian brute from Nigel's gang, was to her right. If she tried to run and jump off the stage, it was likely the Torello twins would kill her. There was only one complication. Mr. Faraday, a teacher whose praises she'd sung throughout the school, was in Yarrick's clutches. She fought back tears and looked at her options.

I need to help him. They'll kill him for sure.

Sandra cackled. "Come on, Jen. Aren't you going to save your teacher?"

Yarrick tightened his grip around Faraday's neck. Her teacher struggled to get air past the Russian's massive forearm.

"Jennifer." Faraday's voice was all rasp. "Please!"

Jennifer's heart felt primed to explode from her chest. She took a few steps toward the Russian.

"So timid." Yarrick grinned. "It is like she wants teacher to die."

Jennifer felt Sandra closing in on her from behind. She took one more step toward Yarrick before she cut toward the backstage door.

"Jennifer!" Faraday's scream was loud and clear despite the blocked airways. "No!"

Jennifer's very being wanted to turn around, but she resisted the effort. She gripped the handle to the backstage door and slammed it behind her.

She expected to be in the hallway that led to two adjacent dressing rooms. Instead, she saw the high ceilings of Mr. Patel's office building. Her hand was no longer on the door to the school auditorium. It was gripping the handle to the large glass door that had locked behind her.

"What're you doing?!"

She caught Dhiraj's eyes. He appeared to be filled with terror. She turned away and saw the brainwashed mob approaching on the other side of the glass.

"Come on!" Dhiraj ran back toward her and pulled at her arm.

Jennifer was petrified and couldn't move a single muscle. "I can't!"

Dhiraj grunted as he tried to lift her. "We need to go!"

The members of the mob began pounding on the glass. While it had previously seemed impenetrable, cracks began to show.

"I'm too scared." Jennifer could hear the defeat in every syllable she spoke. "Let me die."

"No!" Dhiraj lifted her off the ground.

He'd only taken a single step when the glass shattered behind them. As broken shards landed on the ground, a series of hands reached through the door and pulled at Dhiraj's back. Jennifer fell to the ground, landing on the broken glass. When she looked behind her, Dhiraj had been completely pulled through the door.

"Jennifer!"

The mob began tearing at her boyfriend's clothes. She once again felt helpless. Jennifer reached toward him.

"I'm sorry, Dhiraj." She turned away and ran. "I'm sorry."

Dhiraj's pained screams echoed through the lobby as Jennifer hit the elevator button. She stepped inside and the doors closed behind her with a ding.

When they opened up, Jennifer was no longer indoors. She walked out into the forest clearing just outside the Treasure city limits. Jennifer saw two people in the distance and walked toward them. She could feel her body shivering, though she couldn't tell if it was from the cold or the sights she'd seen. As Jennifer got closer, she made out the figures before her.

Erica LaPlante, clad in her cheerleader attire, had just put her arms around Deputy Daly.

Jennifer felt the life seep out of her. "No."

She watched as Daly pulled a knife out of his jeans. Jennifer stared straight ahead. It was as if she were a tree planted in the ground, unable to do anything but witness the impending murder. Daly thrust his knife into Erica's side. As her friend crumpled to the ground in pain, Erica looked straight into Jennifer's eyes.

"Save me!" The blood streamed out of Erica's side. "Jennifer!"

As Erica mentioned her name, Daly looked straight up at her. He took another knife out of his jeans, this one much longer and sharper. Jennifer's body shook.

She took one last glance at her dying friend. "I can't." Jennifer fled at top speed into the mouth of the cave.

Before long, she ran into a dead end. She felt around on the stone for a way to escape. Jennifer turned around when she heard the sound of footsteps. While she assumed it would be Daly, she saw something completely different. Ted, Erica, Dhiraj, Natalie and her father stood in front of her. They all shared the same look: pity.

Erica approached her, brandishing the sword. She shook her head. "You could've helped us, Jen. You should've helped."

Before Jennifer could reply, Erica slashed the sword directly through her face. A sharp cut of pain spread through her cheek as the alarm brought her out of slumber.

Jennifer sat up in her bed with tears in her eyes. It took her a minute to recognize the ringing sound of the alarm. After she shut it off, she sat there in silence as long as she could, head in hands.

"All your friends are fine. It's all gonna be okay."

Her attempt to comfort herself wasn't completely true. Ted was in a hospital in North Carolina. She had no idea where Erica and Yoshi were, but she missed her friend something fierce. The field hockey suspension gave her nothing but time to think, and most of those thoughts brought her great pain. While Jeannie Moss now worshipped the ground she walked on, that wasn't enough to stop the emotions that accompanied these recurring nightmares.

Jennifer smiled and nodded through Dhiraj's entirely one-sided conversation on the way to school. Part of her wanted to tell him about everything. About the suspension. About the fear that exploded within her whenever she closed her eyes. She felt like she'd done enough to him in her dreams – there was no need to give him anything to worry about in real life.

Besides, she figured Dhiraj was dealing with Ted's hospitalization in his trademark way: by avoiding the subject. If he was allowed to gloss over the fact that his best friend needed several bags of blood transfused into his body, then wasn't she permitted to lie about field hockey and her general disposition?

By the time lunch rolled around, Jennifer could barely keep her eyes open. Dhiraj sat by her side as Natalie and Travis ate across from them. Natalie's boyfriend had taken Erica's old seat, and the whole lunchroom conspired to keep the fifth seat open. That's where Ted used to sit.

"Cents?" Dhiraj tapped Jennifer on the shoulder. Wherever she'd been, it certainly wasn't in range of the conversation.

She forced a smile. "Sorry, what?"

He grinned back. "I was just talking about the gatekeeper. What do you think she's up to?"

Jennifer had enough demons she was dealing with in her head. It was overwhelming to consider fighting off something that could actually fight back.

"I don't know." She opened her eyes wide to keep herself awake. "You were the ones who saw her. Not me."

Dhiraj put his arm around her. "I know. You're just such a good sleuth. You're like a hot version of Sherlock Holmes."

Jennifer couldn't resist the eye roll. "Elementary, my dear boyfriend... I've got nothing." She gestured across the table. "What about you guys?"

Travis scratched his head. Jennifer didn't mind his presence at the table, though Dhiraj had put up resistance about letting him into the inner circle. Natalie said it was either let him in or watch her leave.

Travis put down his sandwich. "Does it make any kind of shape when you connect the dots?"

Jennifer flipped over her napkin and pulled a pencil out of her backpack. For all her lack of rest, she was able to draw a fairly accurate map of the U.S. The other three stared in awe at her capabilities.

"A mapmaker, too?" Dhiraj kissed her cheek. "Maybe your Halloween costume should be a sexy cartographer."

Natalie tossed a fry that landed right between Dhiraj's eyes. "Shut it, puppy love."

Jennifer stifled a laugh and connected the dots between Treasure, Florida and North Carolina. "It just looks like a line so far."

Natalie snatched the napkin from Jennifer. She stared at the three points on the makeshift map. "What do the attacks have in common?"

Jennifer strained to form a coherent thought. Each of the attacks had been so different. The Florida hurricane incident involved the kidnapping of a young girl. The attack in Treasure was more like a robbery. The last one was more public than the other two had been and eight people remained missing. Judging by the pictures of the Lychos, she wouldn't be surprised if they'd been digested.

Dhiraj interrupted her thoughts with the bite of a carrot stick. "I don't know. Maybe Erica and Yoshi'll find something."

Jennifer pictured Erica going up against a gang of Lychos and Draconfolk. She saw the protector fending off one or two before ultimately succumbing to the swarm.

She pouted. "I don't know. I worry about her."

Natalie flared her nostrils. "Come on. I know she's your friend, but she's got a freakin' samurai by her side. Besides, she isn't exactly dainty."

Jennifer thought back to her dreams and the blood dripping from Erica's side. She chewed on her lip. "I know. I just wish she were here."

Dhiraj glanced over at the empty chair and sighed. "I wish they were both here."

Travis slapped the table and they all perked up. "Quit whining, you guys." He put his arm around Natalie. "Soak this up. Who knows where we'll all be next year."

Jennifer took in a deep breath. She didn't mind the subject change one bit.

Natalie removed Travis' hand from her body. "Um, I'll be on national TV kicking butt for some school that's lucky to have me."

Dhiraj grinned. "I'll be running Ted Finley LLC while rocking a 4.0 at Harvard."

Dhiraj's eyes fixed on Jennifer's. She wanted to answer it in just the way he wanted, but they hadn't talked much about their future. At least, she hadn't.

"I don't know what I'm gonna do." She worked her tongue around her mouth. "Maybe I'll keep an eye on Erica."

Dhiraj put his hand on her lower back. "Didn't you do that for most of high school?"

Jennifer felt the exhaustion come over her once again. "It's different now." She came off whinier than she wanted to. "She's trying to save the world. So is Ted. It's hard to think about college when giant lizards and dogs are going around killing people. And we're just sitting here, helpless."

Silence filled the table, allowing the other noises of the lunchroom to trickle in. When Dhiraj leaned toward her, Jennifer turned away. They remained speechless.

Travis cleared his throat. "See? None of us really know what's gonna happen. Personally, I see me and my entourage going to my girl's away games."

Natalie raised her eyebrows. "You think we're gonna last till the end of the month? Let alone next year? I'm dating a crazy person."

Travis made a kiss face and Natalie stuffed a handful of fries into his mouth.

When lunch ended, Jennifer dumped out her trash and left the cafeteria as quickly as she could. The smell of fried foods gave way to the familiar scent of floor polish. Dhiraj caught up with her and matched her stride.

"You really don't have any plans for next year yet?"

Jennifer shook her head. "No. I really don't."

Dhiraj bit his bottom lip. "Well, I was going to save this for a better time, but…."

Jennifer stopped as Dhiraj fished something out of his backpack. He took out a folder filled with several sheets of paper. Jennifer took the documents and leafed through them.

She squinted. "College applications?"

He smiled. "Read the school names."

Jennifer looked them over. "Boston University. Boston College. Northeastern–"

"They're all in Boston." Dhiraj put his arm around Jennifer's waist. "I know I'm going to Harvard. I want you to be right around the corner."

Jennifer wasn't sure how to react. She didn't even know what schools she would apply to. If any.

"Dhiraj, I said I didn't know–"

"I need you." He had a pained look on his face. "I know it's 10 months away, but I want us to be together for the long haul."

Jennifer felt warmth course through her. It was her first positive sensation in over a week.

Maybe that's a sign.

"Okay."

Dhiraj did a double take. "Okay? Just like that?"

The warm feeling doubled. She smiled. "Just like that."

Dhiraj wrapped his arms around her and pulled her in tight. "You don't know how happy that makes me."

Jennifer hugged him back. "I'm glad."

For the first time in recent memory, Jennifer felt like she was needed. Like she could actually help someone. She'd do anything to stop the self-loathing and the nightmares. Maybe even move to Boston.

CHAPTER
28

Erica and Yoshi walked around the south end of the collapsed hospital building early in the morning. The air smelled like smoke, even though nothing nearby appeared to be burning. Sheriff Norris had worked his connections to give them free reign to examine any potential evidence. Dropping Ted Finley's name didn't hurt, either. The rest of the city was still in deep recovery after the hurricane, but Erica felt a sense of pride that Ted was able to save so many lives. Since most excavation equipment was being used on other parts of the city, the collapsed hospital building had remained largely untouched. Erica walked on top of the rubble and thought back to Adam, the living soul she'd had to kill by bringing down a building on top of him.

"What're we gonna find here, Yoshi?" Erica kicked a piece of cement in his direction.

The samurai caught it with ease and placed it back in the pile. "Proof." He looked left and then right. "Proof of something."

Erica scanned the top of the pile several more times. If something had brought the entire building down, it was likely buried far beneath the top of the pile. Even using her enhanced strength, there wasn't a safe way to reach the base of the foundation. Erica wondered if anyone would've even been able to hear any kind of detonation over the winds of the hurricane.

After another 10 minutes of searching, Erica and Yoshi left the site for a makeshift temporary hospital a few blocks away. As they entered, the head nurse came right up to them. She had a vibe that could best be described as stern and sweet.

"If it isn't Super Ted's girlfriend. I recognize you from the tabloids."

Yoshi smirked at Erica, but she ignored it to focus on the nurse.

"Are you Nancy?"

"I am. Your man floated me through a hurricane and saved me and my patients. I don't know what we could do to ever pay him back."

Erica smiled. "He told me you were brave. Let me ask you a few questions about that night and we can call it even."

The building looked like it was set to be retail space before the hospital took it over. The owners had protected the property well and were happy to donate the space for the next couple of months.

"They say it's about trying to help their fellow man." Nancy gestured to a few plastic-folding chairs. "I think it's so they can get their pictures in the paper, but we'll take it either way. What do you two need to know?"

Erica took out a notepad and a pencil. Dhiraj had offered her a space-age tablet for note taking, but there were some things Erica still preferred to do the old school way.

"We have a theory about what brought the hospital down. Was there anything strange in the days leading up to the hurricane?"

The nurse laughed. "What wasn't strange? Senator Kable's people were in and out all week for his visit. Volunteers were coming in to try to waterproof the building. If you told me it wasn't an episode of one of those hospital TV shows, I woulda had a hard time believing you. Pure drama."

Erica looked at Yoshi.

He cleared his throat. "Was anyone keeping track of all the people who came in and out?"

The nurse laughed. "You talk?"

Yoshi's face revealed a sly smile. "Only when necessary."

She cackled, her laughter reverberating throughout the small space. "There's only one man who even had a chance of controlling that mess. Charlie Potts. He runs the hospital with an iron fist. Well, ran."

Erica wrote down the man's name. "What do you mean ran?"

The nurse sighed. "Day before the Hurricane, Charlie cashed in all his sick days from the last 20 years."

Erica tapped her fingers against the chair. "Maybe he thought it'd be easier if he came back after the storm."

"Charlie Potts doesn't do easy. Not sure what came over him. I swore I saw him the day of the storm, walking around like the life had been taken clean out of him."

Yoshi nodded. "Can you tell us where to find him?"

The nurse's face grew stern. "Usually, no." She brightened back up. "But for Team Ted, I'm willing to bend the rules."

Charlie Potts lived alone in a part of town that hadn't been as impacted by the storm. They didn't have any trouble getting over by car. The house didn't look very big, but Nancy had said the man hardly spent any time away from the hospital. No need for home improvement if you're living at work.

Erica knocked on the door. She heard something metallic fall to the ground. After that, there was nothing but silence. Erica tried knocking again. "Mr. Potts? We're friends of Ted Finley's."

Yoshi smiled. "You think he'll recognize you from the tabloids, too?"

Erica was about to smirk back when they heard a glass fall to the ground and break. She put her shoulder to the door and easily broke the deadbolt. The first thing she saw was a series of broken objects scattered along the hardwood foyer and hallway. It looked more like a break-in than the house of someone taking a staycation. Someone zipped in front of her too quickly to be identified.

"Looters?" Erica saw that Yoshi had already crouched down into a fighting stance.

Yoshi's knuckles cracked as his hands became fists. "One way to find out."

They followed the last direction the figure went, taking care to avoid stepping on broken glass. She heard heavy breathing from the corner of the room and pulled the cord for a nearby lamp. The light shined on the face of

Charlie Potts. He shivered against the wall like a trapped animal. His clothes and hair were disheveled. The man's eyes darted in every direction.

He seemed to look directly through Erica and Yoshi. "I'm not me. I couldn't be me."

When Yoshi took a step forward, Potts ran through the kitchen and into another room down the hall. A trail of blood followed behind him. Erica assumed it was from stepping on the broken glass with bare feet. Yoshi kicked some of the shards out of his path. "The nurse said he was put-together."

Erica walked into the hallway. "Emphasis on the was."

She knocked on the door to the room Potts had entered. "Mr. Potts? We just came from the hospital. Nancy was asking about you."

Potts came running right toward her. There was nothing on his face that suggested sanity. Instinct caused her to punch the man directly in the head, and he fell right down onto his back. His chest moved up and down, but otherwise the man was motionless.

Yoshi peered over her shoulder. "Questioning people is harder when they're unconscious."

Erica grunted at her partner. "There'll be two people unconscious if you don't shut up. Let's get him onto the bed.

Potts woke up a few minutes later. Erica and Yoshi had tied his hands and legs to keep him from running. The man's body shook as if there was an unlimited supply of energy just bursting to get out. His eyes continued to look around frantically.

"I'm not me. I'd never do what he said."

Erica sat down on the bed beside him. "What who said, Charlie?"

The man shouted in response. "Don't you know what it's like to not be you?"

She put her hand on his arm. "I actually know that feeling pretty well."

The human contact and the tone of Erica's voice seemed to calm the man down, but several other attempts at questions resulted in similarly cryptic remarks.

"We're getting nowhere." Yoshi tapped at the side of his head. "You know what you have to do."

Erica sighed. She avoided going inside the minds of crazy people whenever possible. She wouldn't describe it as a pleasant experience.

"Fine. But you're treating me to a cheeseburger afterwards. Damn teenage body is hungry every 20 minutes."

Yoshi agreed.

Erica shot a blue bolt of energy between her hands and moved toward Potts' head. "Don't worry, Mr. Potts. It'll all be over soon."

Potts screamed and Erica entered his mind.

All of a sudden, Erica was inside the hospital before the storm. Everything was white and pristine. She saw Charlie Potts walk around the corner at a breathtaking pace. Erica met his stride.

"Mr. Potts."

"Miss, you'll have to report to reception. I've got a meeting I'm only five minutes early for."

Erica laughed to herself. "I'll just tag along if that's alright."

"It's not."

Erica slowed her gait to stay a step or two behind the man. He entered a conference room, but before he could shut the door behind him, Erica wedged it open with her foot. The brightness of the hospital gave way to complete darkness. Erica could still see Potts' back, and he was speaking with someone, but it was unclear who it was.

Potts shouted at the individual. "You need to get out of this hospital!"

Before Erica could hear what the other person had to say, Potts collapsed to the ground and the scene before her changed.

Now they were deep in the hospital basement. Potts was muttering to himself, but nowhere near as much as he had been in his own house. He carried a large backpack.

"Destroy the hospital. I would never do that. Who am I?"

This time, Potts didn't complain that she walked by his side. "Who is making you destroy the hospital, Mr. Potts?"

"Kable's men think I'm a terrorist. I would never do this."

Senator Kable.

When Potts reached the corner of the room, he took out a long knife and started hacking at the walls. He tore a small hole and placed a metallic device with a digital display inside.

"Why did Kable's men put you up to this?" Erica felt the memory start to close in on itself. "Mr. Potts?"

"I'm not me. And you're not supposed to be here."

Potts stabbed at Erica with the knife, which she barely avoided before they both woke up.

Erica's head stung. Yoshi was holding her by the waist.

She rubbed her forehead. "Did I fall down?"

"Almost." He steadied her. "What did you see?"

"Potts bombed the foundation. Seems like someone with Kable programmed him to do it." Erica looked back at Potts, who was now practically catatonic. "We're never gonna find that bomb or any security footage."

Yoshi nodded. "What should we do?"

Erica looked at Potts. Kable ruined the man's life and tried to kill Ted in the process.

"I'm gonna call Ted."

Erica looked at her phone. She'd had trouble getting reception ever since they'd gotten to the hurricane-affected area. She gave Yoshi a nod and walked outside. Erica finally got reception in the middle of Potts' lawn, at which time she received half a dozen voicemails.

"What the heck?"

Erica bypassed the messages and called Ted.

After three rings, a woman's voice answered. "Erica. We've been trying to reach you."

Before she could reply, Erica heard a scream from inside the house. She couldn't make out the words, but it sounded like, "I know you! It's you!"

It was Potts. He repeated the words multiple times over before she heard the sounds of a scuffle. Erica hung up the phone and ran to the front door. When she burst in, Yoshi was standing next to Potts. The man she'd just questioned was dead in a pool of blood. The crimson substance slipped between the cracks in the hardwood floor.

Yoshi breathed heavily. "I tried to stop him."

Erica looked down at the knife in Potts' hand and the blood pouring out of his neck.

"What did he say? I heard him screaming something."

"He thought he recognized me. Then he grabbed a knife and slit his own throat."

Something didn't add up for Erica. She leaned against a wall as she looked back at their fallen witness. "We need to call the police."

Yoshi shook his head. "No. We need to get to Senator Kable."

"We talked to the hospital. They'll know we were here. We can't just leave."

Yoshi took Erica by the shoulder. "They won't understand."

Erica wasn't sure if she understood. She took a deep breath. "We're going to call 9-1-1. We'll say we broke in because we heard him screaming. I'm not running away like I'm guilty."

Erica looked deep into Yoshi's eyes. She tried to find any trace of a lie. There was none.

He nodded. "Okay."

Erica silenced a call back from Ted before calling in the emergency.

CHAPTER
29

Ted's memory was shaky for the next day or two. He'd see a flash of emergency technicians loading him into an ambulance and then darkness. He'd recall bright fluorescent lights of the hospital and a crowd of doctors around him. Then he'd slip back to black. When he was conscious, Ted felt a dull ache throughout his body. In one of few clear moments he retained, he figured he was under a heavy sedative that kept him from feeling much of anything. When he went unconscious, Ted was plagued by memories of the challenges he faced. He thought of the Lychos and the train bearing down on him. Ted pictured the shimmering blue portal and the silhouetted gatekeeper stepping out. More than anything, he thought of Erica lying there next to him. At one point, he may have even called out to her as a nurse gripped his hand.

When he woke up much less groggy, he was surprised to see his parents standing over him. They were flanked on either side by more than a dozen vases filled with flowers. The reds and purples and yellows gave some character to the white room. Both of his parents had tears in their eyes and his mother squeezed his hand harder than he ever thought possible.

"Hey." Ted's throat was dry.

His mother's cheeks turned red as she smiled. "Hey, honey."

"Why... why are you guys down here?"

Ted's father cleared his throat. "Just because you're a big shot government operative now doesn't mean we stop being your parents."

Ted's stiff neck preventing him from nodding as much as he wanted to. "What happened?"

Mrs. Finley explained that in the process of beating the Lychos, he lost a considerable amount of blood. Fortunately, the hospital was able to patch him up and replace everything he'd lost.

"You should've seen everyone." Mr. Finley beamed. "They were running around here like the Pope had been shot."

Ted laughed. It hurt to do so, but he wasn't going to let pain get in the way of a good chuckle. "How long have I been—"

"Two days." His mother brushed his arm with her hand. "And we've got someone here who wants to see you."

Ted's mouth opened at the hope that Erica was there. When Allison walked through the door with her arm in a sling, he tried to hide his disappointment. She had a few bumps and bruises on her face, but he seemed to have taken the worst of the damage.

He moved his hand up in a sort-of wave. "You made it."

Allison walked up to the bed and gave him a hug with her good arm. She smelled of fresh soap and shampoo, which made Ted realize just how unfresh he must've smelled.

"All because of you." She pulled away from the bed. "You've got great parents. They showed me all your baby pictures."

Ted wasn't sure if his new blood had yet learned how to rush to his face. If it had, he was certain his cheeks were flushed. "You brought my baby book?"

Mrs. Finley looked appalled. "Of course not. What kind of embarrassing parents do you think we are?" She smiled. "I scanned the baby book so that all the pictures are on my phone."

Ted groaned. "Mobile humiliation. Ain't technology grand?"

Allison laughed. "You were a cute baby. Even though you could never keep your diaper on." Ted's brain told him to run away and hide, but the machines connected to his body wouldn't let him. "I—"

Allison held up her hand. "Just kidding, she filtered out all the naked ones." She checked her watch. "I've gotta get to DC for a debriefing. When you're good to travel, you'll be joining us."

Ted might've chosen a few extra days of pain and blood loss over any more meetings. He nodded and Allison bid them adieu.

After a bit of catching up, Ted asked about Erica. They said she was prepared to jump in on a video feed as soon as he was ready. He considered using his powers to shove them out of the room, but he didn't want to seem entitled. They left of their own free will when Ted connected with his girlfriend.

"I leave you alone for five minutes and you end up in the hospital."

Erica's face was so beautiful that he didn't mind the sarcasm.

"You should see the other guy... other wolf, I mean." He grinned, but the only thing that would really make him happy was having her there beside him.

"I'm glad you're okay."

He smirked. "I'm glad you have a pretty flexible version of okay."

"You're alive. You're not missing a limb. Those are the cut-off points."

He stuck out his tongue. "So, did you guys find anything?"

Erica looked behind her. There didn't seem to be anyone around, but there was a concerned look on Erica's face. As if someone could be listening in.

"We think Senator Kable might be involved with the gatekeeper somehow."

Ted's eyes grew wide. The man had been in a vehicle with him and seemed like your everyday politician, albeit one targeting the highest position in the land. Maybe Ted hadn't quite gotten a handle of his mind-reading abilities.

"Do you have proof?"

Erica's concerned look returned. "We had a possible witness who may have helped the senator take down that hospital you were in."

Ted's instinct told him to put his hands up to his face, but the tubes sticking out of him wouldn't permit it. "What the hell?! I need to talk to this guy."

Erica's eyes went dim. "He's dead."

Ted could tell there was more to the story, but Erica seemed like she was in no mood to tell it.

"Where are you now?"

"We're going to go scope out the senator's place up in Pennsylvania. Maybe we can find something more concrete."

Ted didn't like the "we" in Erica's response. He'd feel much better if she was going alone.

"I still don't trust him."

She nodded. "He's devoted to the cause, Ted. But I'll be careful."

Ted detected a hint of doubt in her demeanor. He wanted to push it, but he started to grow tired from the conversation.

He shook his head to try to get the cobwebs loose. "I want to come with you."

Erica's face creased from laughter. "Two things. One, you're currently under the employ of the federal government. Two, you look like you're too weak to move."

Ted defiantly sat up hard. "I'll be fi–" His head started to throb as dizziness came over him. Ted closed his eyes to keep the room from spinning.

Erica noticed and pursed her lips. "I rest my case."

Ted took in a deep breath and the sensation dissipated. "Just be careful, okay?"

She nodded. "Always. You, too."

"I miss you."

Erica bit her lip. "I miss you a lot. We'll see each other soon."

"I hope so."

After the call, Ted thought long and hard about the senator's place in this game. He could've been a dark soul like Nigel, but most of them tended to fight and kill, not run for office. There was a chance he was a disgruntled being from another world, like Redican, but there was no way to tell that from a hospital bed. And what of the candidate's request that Ted endorse him? Ted wanted to focus his energy on recovery, but he couldn't stop the thought that played on multiple fears: what would they do if the next President were a ruthless murderer?

CHAPTER

30

On the first day of school, Dhiraj had felt like the big man on campus. He thought that he finally had control over everything that would bring him the best year ever. Natalie's tryst with Travis, Erica's reveal of the truth to her parents, and Ted's mission and subsequent injury were sending things into a tailspin.

Dhiraj spent a few hours crafting the next TedFinley.com email blast. Despite Ted's protestations to say anything, Dhiraj convinced him that the hundreds of thousands of subscribers needed to know that he was okay. The emails were usually a cinch. He'd make a few funny quips about being a hero, plug one of the many Ted tie-in products that kept the business afloat, and thank the fans for being a part of the whole shebang. On that day, every time Dhiraj wrote a sentence it felt wrong. He couldn't figure out how to write a tasteful joke given the attacks and the missing people.

Dhiraj paced the length of his room, flipping a pencil around between his fingers.

"People are dead or dying. Ted almost died." He sighed. "What happened to the tabloid stories of sex scandals or alien love children? Those were way easier to deal with."

Dhiraj finally opted to go with a short and sweet approach. He typed out the message.

"Dear Ted Heads,

I'm overwhelmed by your support these last few days. Due to the tireless work of the staff at UNC Hospitals, I'm on the road to recovery. We're still investigating what caused these attacks, but as soon as I know something concrete, you'll be the first to know. Please visit this page where crowdfunding campaigns have been set up for the families impacted by the attacks.

I never would've recovered if it weren't for all your love. Thanks for taking this heroic journey with me. Until my next up, up and away message!

Heroically,

Ted"

He scheduled the message for the following morning and barreled through his homework. Usually, he and Jennifer would do their work together, but a field hockey exhibition match at another school took that option off the table. His relationship was about the only thing that was going as planned. He itched to call her, but he knew it was important to let her have time to herself as well. Dhiraj zipped through his homework as fast as he could before driving over to Natalie's.

When the front door to her house was unlocked, Dhiraj let himself in. He made himself at home, pouring a large glass of orange juice and heading up to Natalie's room.

"Hey, you guys should lock—"

As he came into view of the doorway to Natalie's bedroom, he saw something that almost made him drop his juice. There was Travis, completely shirtless, kissing Natalie deeply on top of her bed. The two of them didn't notice him at first, and he couldn't stop himself from staring at the two muscular, attractive people making out in front of him. His self-consciousness got the better of him and he cleared his throat. Travis leapt off Natalie, hitting the edge of the mattress and landing on the floor. Natalie sat up and turned apple-red. When she saw who it was, she etched a scowl into her face.

"Dhiraj." She growled through clenched teeth. "How nice to see you. You really should have called ahead."

Warmth spread through Dhiraj's cheeks. "I'd apologize, but I feel like I just got a free show. Maybe the appropriate response should be thank you."

Travis stood up, rubbing the hip he'd just slammed into the ground. "You're welcome." He smirked. "I always said we should set up a cam—"

"Both of you, out of my room!"

Travis grabbed his shirt of Natalie's desk chair. "I gotta go anyway, babe. New plays to study."

When Travis tried to kiss Natalie on the forehead, she swung at his midsection. He deftly avoided it and walked toward the doorway.

"Moneybags."

Dhiraj nodded. "Conner."

With that, Travis was gone.

Natalie grumbled and gave Dhiraj a death stare. "What don't you understand about the words 'both of you'?"

Dhiraj ignored the bunched-up bedspread and sat on the corner. "Oh, I thought you meant him and his ego. They're practically two separate people."

Natalie pulled a sheet over her head and groaned, letting herself slump back against the headboard. "What do you want, Dhiraj?"

He pulled the sheet away. "I wanted to interrupt your passionate love life."

Natalie kicked at Dhiraj from under the covers. "You know, I bet they wouldn't even give me life in prison for killing you. Just a slap on the wrist. They'll call it the 'dangerously annoying' defense."

Dhiraj laughed. "I know a good lawyer. Though he might not represent you if you murder his son."

Natalie sighed and let out a chuckle. "What do you really want?"

Dhiraj placed his glass of juice down on Natalie's computer desk. "We're supposed to be having the time of our lives, Nat. Senior year has laid a big, fat egg so far."

Natalie shifted to a cross-legged position. "We're best friends with a superhero who's fighting evil villains from another world. Having fun isn't exactly something we can count on anymore."

"I kind of miss the way things were before."

Natalie raised her eyebrows. "Things were easier but they weren't better. We were idiots. We didn't know about the dark souls or the other worlds or anything."

Dhiraj looked out the window into the night sky. "Ignorance is bliss."

"Ignorance is pointless. Aren't you the one who says it's always better to have more data than less?"

Dhiraj had given Natalie that line when it came to detailed statistics about the Treasure High basketball team. He wasn't sure if it applied to changing his entire worldview overnight. When Dhiraj didn't answer, Natalie threw up her hands in the air.

"Ugh! Shouldn't you be talking about this with your girlfriend? That's what she's for."

Dhiraj's eyes narrowed. "She's at a field hockey game. As a former captain, I figured you'd know that."

Natalie's face twitched. "Of course I knew that. I'm just annoyed with you."

Dhiraj knew of Natalie's prowess on the court, but her poker face left much to be desired. "Is there something going on with Jen I should know about?"

Natalie rubbed at her eyes. "Leave me out of this, Dhiraj. I swore I wouldn't tell. It's not worth worrying about."

A panic came over Dhiraj. What was Jennifer holding back from him? Why would she want Natalie to keep it a secret?

Dhiraj put on his much better neutral face. "Fine. I won't. Thanks for the chat."

He hopped off the bed and walked away.

"Dhiraj, wait. You're not going to tell her I said anything, right?"

Dhiraj faked a calm grin. "Of course not. Sorry again for interrupting Kissfest Live."

Before Natalie could reply, Dhiraj had bolted out of the room. He sat behind the steering wheel of his car for a moment and practiced his deep breathing techniques. They didn't seem to work as his hands began to sweat.

Is Jennifer going to break up with me?

Once the thought crossed his mind, he couldn't take it back. Now all the deep breaths in the world couldn't calm him down. Dhiraj's hands and feet did the work his mind couldn't, directing his car to Jennifer's house. He pulled up to the opposite side of the street and looked toward the house. Sure enough, he could see Jennifer through her window.

Why would she lie to me?

Dhiraj pulled out his phone and pushed the Jennifer icon on his speed dial. He tried to think of what he'd say if she picked up. Would he pretend that Natalie hadn't said a word? Could he possibly bring himself to confront her right off the bat?

Dhiraj didn't have the chance to try either. He watched through Jennifer's window as his girlfriend pushed the button to send his call to voicemail. He stammered as he tried to start his message.

"Hey, J—Jen. It's your m—man with a plan. I just wanted to see how your game went. Call me later."

Dhiraj hung up and tossed the phone onto the passenger seat. He didn't feel like a senior anymore. He just felt heartbroken.

CHAPTER
31

Erica and Yoshi parked their car a few blocks away from Senator Kable's estate. In researching the man behind the eight-foot-high decorative walls, Erica found a politician with a past that was so pristine, it could barely be believed. When the attack ads hit full force during the election, Erica wasn't sure what President Blake's TV spots would focus on. In her experience, whenever a person didn't have any skeletons in their closet, there were several dozen of them buried in the basement.

Erica followed closely behind Yoshi. The samurai had been quiet when police questioned them about the death of Charlie Potts. It turned out that the cops had been called to the Potts residence multiple times in the last week. His late night screams and erratic behavior had gotten the attention of several neighbors. They weren't surprised the man might take a knife to his own throat.

Erica wasn't as convinced as the officers had been.

After a few laps around the compound, Erica and Yoshi both agreed about a relative blind spot between two cameras. They'd have to leap over the wall at just the right moment. Yoshi went first, using a parkour-style move to lift himself to the top of the wall. Once there, he leapt over with ease and disappeared from view. With a running start, Erica used her enhanced strength to fly through the air and grab hold of the wall. She could feel the cement scrape against her fingertips as she lifted herself above and over and then rolled as she landed to absorb the impact. The grass beneath her was cool and damp, as if it'd been recently watered. The building ahead of them was even more impressive than it'd been when obscured by the walls. It was dark red and covered with intricate sculptures from top to bottom. Erica figured she could fit her parents' house at least six times over in the building before her. Unfortunately for Kable, that also made it harder to guard.

Erica wiped at the dew on her pants. "Where to?"

Without hesitation, Yoshi pointed to a half-open window that seemed to lead to the basement. Erica's pulse quickened.

This is too easy.

They moved one at a time to avoid the cameras until they were just outside it. The samurai opened the window all the way and ushered Erica inside. She searched his face. There was nothing out of the ordinary. Erica gestured to the window.

"I insist."

Yoshi nodded and lowered himself into the room. Erica waited a moment for him to call back to her before she did the same.

Erica turned on a pocket flashlight and moved it from left to right. While there didn't appear to be a camera, there were several computers set up in a sort of corner office. Erica set her flashlight on the ground to free her hands and turned on one of the computers. She took out a flash drive Dhiraj had given her for just these sorts of occasions.

"What does it do?" Yoshi looked completely at ease.

Erica smirked. "Computers have been around for about ten percent of my lifetime. I'm lucky I know the difference between a Mac and a PC."

After being jacked in, the flash drive opened up a program that allowed them to bypass the password screen without a problem. They spent the next several minutes searching through computer files. There was no mention of portals, the hospital bombing or the gatekeeper.

Yoshi peered over Erica's shoulder. "Look up Sophie Kent."

The search yielded one result: a backed-up email on the computer from Senator Kable to his campaign manager.

"'I really like Sophie Kent's story. Can we make sure I get a picture alone with her?'"

Erica's eyes narrowed. "It's not incriminating, but it's certainly suspicious." She took a picture of the email using her phone. "I want to take a look around."

Yoshi nodded. "Okay. I can keep searching."

Erica shook her head and spoke in Japanese. "Two heads are better than one."

He smiled and reached over her to shut down the computer.

They wiped down their fingerprints, exited the room and crept up the stairs to the main part of the house. The basement led up into a massive library. The smell of old, hand-bound books reminded her of lifetimes past. Erica wondered how many of the books were decorative and how many he'd actually read. Before she had a chance to wager a guess, the light in the room turned on. She prepared to run back through the basement, but a familiar-looking woman appeared in the room's entryway. Erica had seen Senator Kable's wife on TV multiple times, but there was something different about her in person.

"Erica LaPlante." Kable's wife sounded completely awake despite the late hour. "I recognize you from the tabloids."

Erica looked back to Yoshi. Her partner was gone. It was as if he'd vanished into thin air. She focused her attention back on the senator's wife.

"Mrs. Kable. I'm sorry to wake you. Your guards let us—"

"I've heard enough lies on the campaign trail." Mrs. Kable took off her robe to reveal the black tattoos of the dark souls on her arm, as well as a rainbow-colored butterfly tattoo on her hand. "We may as well tell the truth, protector."

The recognition was immediate.

Sandra.

Every part of Erica screamed within her, telling her that escape was the only legitimate plan. "I liked you better with shorter hair."

Sandra tossed her hair and tied it back into a ponytail with one quick motion. "Appearance means everything to voters." She started to circle around the room toward Erica. "You'd think it'd be the issues. Or the voting record of the candidates. Nope. The people don't want a butch first lady."

Erica held her ground. She was close enough to the basement exit that a quick knockdown of her attacker could allow her to escape.

"But they'd be okay with an evil one?"

Sandra laughed. "I wouldn't be the first."

Before her quip had a chance to settle, Sandra charged straight ahead. Erica blocked the first punch, but the next three landed. The two body blows knocked the air out of her while the fist to the jaw took her to the ground. Erica tried to kick up, but Sandra swept her legs before she could do so. Sandra locked her thighs around Erica's arm and twisted it against the joint. Pain shot through Erica's body. She reached back, locked her hand around the heaviest book she could grasp and heaved it in Sandra's direction. Erica's attacker ducked the weighty tome, but the movement allowed Erica to kick Sandra away from her arm. As the dark soul came running back toward her, Erica spun her leg into Sandra's neck. Sandra shouted with pain and went down to one knee. Erica took the opportunity to kick Sandra in the side of the face. The dark soul's head bounced against the carpet and her body went motionless.

Erica rubbed at her arm and was about to run back down the stairs when she felt a sharp pain in her back. She reached for the source and pulled out a long, thin dart. Erica turned around toward the direction the dart had come from and saw a man she'd only previously met through the television screen.

"My wife wanted to handle you alone, but husbands have to support their spouses from time to time."

Kit Kable shot another dart out of the gun, which hit her directly in the stomach. Erica could feel the drug start to work its way through her bloodstream. Her eyelids started to feel like anvils.

"But she's—"

"A dark soul, yes." Kable moved in closer, still pointing the weapon. "And you're a protector. At least, you were."

Before Kable could get any closer, Erica ran past him at full speed. She could barely see where she was going, but she used her instinct to jump through a window. Erica couldn't feel the sharpness of the glass or the thud of the ground. All she knew was that she couldn't let herself get captured. Erica cued her muscles to push her toward the wall, but she started to lose feeling from head to toe. She pulled out her phone and tried to reach the text message screen. Like everything around her, it was becoming blurry. Erica felt the phone slip from her hand as her body went limp and landed on the grass beneath her.

PART FOUR

CHAPTER
32

Ted woke up to the text in the middle of the night. Half of the tubes that had previously tethered him down had been removed, giving him the freedom he needed to reach the device.

"Going to the Academy in Japan. Will explain when I land."

He immediately texted back to get more info, but none came. The phone's display told him it was three in the morning, and his fight or flight response told him he wouldn't sleep again that night. He called Dhiraj, but his friend didn't pick up. He considered waking his parents, but he had no idea what they could do about it. After several calls went through to Erica's voicemail, his sleepless brain attempted to sort through the facts.

Why would Erica go to Japan without telling him? As far as he could figure, either it was some kind of light soul "need-to-know basis" thing or Erica wasn't the one sending the text. When they'd last spoke, she didn't seem at all convincing when it came to Yoshi's trustworthiness. There was also the matter of the gatekeeper still on the loose and the potential involvement of Senator Kable. Erica could've been tossed through one of those portals for all he knew. And Yoshi could've been the one who did the tossing. He clenched his fists when he thought of the samurai.

Ted let himself drift off to sleep around six in the morning, but half an hour later he woke up to the sounds screaming from the hallway. His anxiety had come alive when he slept, as all the items in his room began thrashing against the walls. The empty bed beside him had completely flipped on its top. To keep the nearby nurses at ease, he resolved to stay awake and controlled for the rest of the morning.

Ted's eyes felt the strain of sleeplessness when Agent Vott entered his hospital room. Vott stepped over a toppled chair like nothing at all was amiss.

"Good news. The doctors have cleared you to go." Vott looked back at the chair. "Bad dreams?"

Ted ignored a headache that shot through his skull. "Something's wrong with Erica. I need to go home."

Vott shook his head. "You need to go to Washington, DC."

Ted's voice grew low. "And you're going to stop me from flying out of here?"

Vott looked away and sighed. "Tell me what's wrong."

Ted explained the situation to the DHS agent. Even though he knew Vott wasn't exactly Erica's biggest fan, at least he seemed sympathetic to his plight. The agent sat beside Ted on the hospital bed.

"Look, Ted. We don't want you to go flying away in your condition, but we'll help you locate your... girlfriend." Vott put his hand on Ted's shoulder. "You need to meet us halfway, though. Come to DC. At least it'll get you closer to home."

Ted knew that Vott had a point. He had no interest in taking back to the skies at less than full strength. Sitting up straight still gave him trouble; he couldn't imagine what flying through the air at top speed would do.

"One more condition."

Vott mumbled something to himself. "What's that?"

"I want a meeting with Senator Kable."

Ted bid his parents adieu and changed into something a little more protective than a paper gown. During the flight to DC, Ted learned that Kable had just flown to DC from Pennsylvania. That put him in his house around the same time Erica and Yoshi would've been there. Ted seethed as he thought about the samurai and what the senator might have done with Erica.

Vott came through on his promise and set up a meeting with Kable in a DHS conference room only a few hours after Ted's arrival. The room was sterile and pale, as if Ted hadn't even left the hospital room. He set there alone for several minutes until Kable poked his head in.

"Mr. Finley. So good to see you again."

Kable's confident smile made Ted clench his teeth. Perhaps sensing Ted's hostility, Kable avoided a handshake and left an empty chair between himself and the hero. The senator placed a manila envelope on the table and looked into Ted's eyes.

"I've got a busy schedule, but I was happy to squeeze you in." His grin made Ted want to rip the man's teeth out. "How may I help you?"

Ted cleared his throat. "If I decided to endorse you, when were you going to tell me about your connection with the gatekeeper and the disappearance of Sophie Kent?"

The senator put on his best shocked face. "Those are strong allegations, Ted. Are you sure you aren't still feeling the effects of those heavy painkillers?"

Ted's heartbeat quickened. "I know you were involved. I know you were home last night when Erica LaPlante paid you a visit."

The senator smiled. "I was."

Ted hadn't expected to hear the truth. He leaned in. "And...?"

"Erica and her samurai friend did visit, but they were turned away because it was the middle of the night."

Ted used his power to search through the senator's thoughts. There had to be a lie mixed in with the truth. As he attempted to read the man's mind, Ted felt the dizziness come over him again. He steadied himself with his hand placed firmly on the table.

"I don't believe you."

Senator Kable dumped out the contents of the manila envelope in front of Ted. His look turned from polite to stern. "Ted, believe it or not, I came here to protect you."

He pushed one paper in particular over toward Ted.

"What's this?" Ted picked it up and looked the document over.

It was an inter-office memo between the President's chief of staff and a name Ted didn't recognize. There was a lot of jargon that didn't make sense, but the mention of the Go Home Alien movement caught his eye.

"To make a long story short. President Blake was the one who funded the GHA."

Ted's jaw hit the ground. The organization that had put his mother in the hospital. The people who imprisoned Natalie and tried to frame her as a terrorist. If this document meant what Kable said it did, President Blake was behind it the whole time.

Ted looked back at the door that led to the hallway. "How do I know this isn't a trick?"

Kable stood up. "The only trick, Mr. Finley, is how the government tricked you into working for them. A trick that worked quite well, I'm afraid."

Ted stood up to meet Kable's eyes. When he did, the anger that coursed through his veins caused all the chairs in the room to slide into the wall.

"What else do you know?"

Kable offered his hand to Ted. "Everything I know is in a pile right there. Like I said before, I'm terribly busy today, but it was great talking—"

Ted walked between Kable and the door. "We're not finished. You know something about Erica and the attacks."

Kable walked right up to Ted's face. The hot breath from the senator's mouth warmed Ted's cheeks.

"There are a dozen men outside who would be willing to die for me. The only ones on your side put your mother in the hospital. I don't know anything about your girlfriend, so I think it's best to play the odds, Super Ted."

Ted suppressed his ire and stepped to the side.

Kable grinned. "Good talk. Let's do this again sometime, shall we?"

Before Ted could devise a retort, the senator had left him alone in the room. He sat back down at the table and pored over the documents. While he didn't understand most of them, enough was made clear. If the documents were genuine, President Blake and the GHA were as one. After a few minutes went by, Agent Vott walked in.

"Did you get everything you needed?"

Ted spun around in his chair. "Did President Blake fund the GHA?"

Vott's eyes gave it away even before his brain did. Ted had been through Vott's head a hundred times over, but the sheer mention of Blake tied to the GHA told him everything he needed. Vott took a deep breath and closed the door behind him.

"We never meant for your mother to get hurt. We thought Cobblestone could be controlled."

Ted's rage bubbled over. The three chairs nearest Vott cornered the agent by the door. "My mother could've died. Natalie could've gone to jail." Ted felt his power grasp around Vott's throat. "You lied to me."

Vott tried to pull the grip away from his neck, but there weren't any hands to remove. If Ted wanted, he could've used all his strength to end the man's life. He released his hold and Vott slumped into one of the chairs.

"I'm done. I'm going home. Tell Harding I left the signed football in his office."

Ted opened the door.

"Ted, wait!"

He looked back at Vott. A man who'd seemed so honorable and intimidating before now reminded Ted of a rat.

"I'm sorry."

Ted blinked without a reply and slammed the door behind him.

When he got to the parking lot, he heard a pair of heels clacking after him. Ted turned back to see Allison running toward him as fast as her footwear and arm injury would allow. He slowed down to let her catch up.

"I heard about what happened." Allison shook her head. "I don't know what to say."

Ted looked through her mind. It didn't take long to find that she knew nothing of President Blake's plan or the GHA. Nevertheless, she was still part of the organization that'd done him wrong.

"Say goodbye. I'm going home."

Before Ted could walk away, Allison blocked his path with her good arm. "I know. Let me take you there."

Ted considered his options. He could use the government credit card to book a last-minute flight, but who knew how long that would take. If Allison drove him, he could be there in just under three hours.

Ted nodded. "Okay."

"Okay."

The two of them remained silent for most of the trip. He appreciated the space Allison was giving him. His thoughts failed to show him the same kindness. In addition to Erica's unknown whereabouts, now he knew that the most powerful man in the country was the one pulling the strings on that hateful organization.

No more trust. Just Erica and me. That's it.

Ted's train of thought was interrupted by a familiar sound. It was louder than the last time he heard it and lasted much longer. He looked out the windshield of Allison's car and realized they were on a bridge. Ten feet above the road, a fleck of blue caught Ted's eye in the center lane. The portal expanded rapidly until the shimmering gateway became large enough for a bus to fit through.

"Holy crap."

Allison couldn't have put it any better. Before he could put his own thoughts into words, a giant creature came tumbling out of the gateway. It landed with a crashing thud on the cars below. Ted's heart skipped a beat as the bridge shifted beneath them.

CHAPTER
33

Natalie and Travis stood outside the security gate at Philadelphia International Airport. Travelers bustled past them, carrying what looked like all their worldly possessions for a three-day trip. Natalie knew she could make her rolling duffle last two weeks if she needed to. She'd engaged in some small talk with Travis for the last five minutes or so over the cacophony of chatter, but it was getting to be that time. Natalie had been surprised when Travis said he'd drive her there; after all, her parents were more than willing. Then he proceeded to act weird the entire car ride, much jumpier than normal. As he continued to yammer in the airport, Natalie stopped him mid-sentence with a hand around his jaw.

"Hey!" She squeezed, pressing his cheeks toward his mouth. "What the hell is wrong with you?"

Natalie released his face and Travis scrunched up his nose. "Ow. What do you mean?"

She grumbled. "You're being a freak and I have to go. So, if there's something on your mind, just say it."

Travis' shoulders slumped. "Alright." He gestured to the security line. "This is my dry run."

Natalie looked at the security line and back at him. "Explain."

Travis looked uncomfortable, as if he didn't know what to do with his hands. "Next year, when you fly on outta here to be the next superstar, that'll be it. No more us. My life'll go back to normal."

Natalie looked at the clock above the security line. She knew that if she didn't head in that direction soon, she'd be taking the bus. She put on her best compassionate face. "I don't know why you're playing this good guy act so hard."

He threw his hands in the air. "That's just it. It's not an act. You've got me, Dormer. You really do."

Natalie looked into Travis' eyes. She loved kissing him, and when the two of them were physical. Heck, he was only a rung or two below the kind of guys you might see shirtless in an underwear ad. Natalie didn't mind them taking things to the next level of public dating. It was less work than sneaking around, but was Travis Conner actually her serious boyfriend? She wasn't at all sure.

She took his hands and ignored the passers-by who'd started watching them. "You gotta get yourself together here. I like you too, okay? I'm literally gonna be back in three days." She kissed him on the lips. "Try not to freak out."

They locked lips again for one last kiss before Natalie picked up her bags.

Travis looked a little relieved, though his posture was still droopier than normal. "Text me... text me when you land."

She tried out a girlfriend smile, but it didn't ring true. As she walked away and joined the herd of travelers, she felt something pull at her stomach.

Crap. Travis Conner is falling in love with me.

Christina Finley was waiting for her at her destination with a ridiculous sign that spelled out Natalie's name in pink glitter. When Natalie was within reach, Ted's sister put her into a tight headlock. Two-plus years of college had brought out Christina's "wild child" tendencies, but Natalie had always noticed them in Treasure. Her loud laughs became louder, her fast speech picked up its pace and her curves became curvier. The gap between her and her brother became a chasm after her time away. But it's not like anyone could tell they were brother and sister, anyway.

Christina smiled the entire car ride to town. "So, how's my dork brother doing in the hospital?"

Natalie let out a sigh. Everything she'd heard about her ex was second-hand. "I've talked to him about two seconds since summer. Hopefully he's recovering. I guess being a superhero isn't all its cracked up to be."

Christina laughed. "Oh, he'll be fine. You know, dropping his name has gotten me more than a few gentleman callers. If he doesn't want the attention, I'm happy to take it."

Natalie laughed. "You'll get yourself on TMZ if you don't watch out."

Christina made a sexy face as if she was posing for a picture. "Is hero's sister too sexy for her own good? Nine pictures that prove she's a goddess."

Natalie's first walk through a college dorm was eye opening. Christina lived in a co-ed building, and it didn't take long for Natalie to see one guy in his underwear and another in a towel. The latter was somehow even more muscular than Travis. It wasn't entirely eye candy though, as she took in the scent from at least three rooms in thorough need of a deep clean. As they walked across the outdoor balcony, she also unintentionally spotted two half-naked bodies shifting on a bed through a wide-open window. Natalie turned away as quickly as she could.

Well, this'll take some getting used to.

Christina's place was in the same four-room suite as the uncensored nudity. Ted's sister said nothing of it and led Natalie inside. The dorm room was smaller than she expected, with two beds raised on wooden slats, allowing for a little extra maneuvering underneath. Softball team posters and artwork covered the dreary, off-white walls. There was a musty odor that seemed like it'd been recently masked underneath a layer of antibacterial spray.

Christina gestured to one of the lofted beds. "Tara practically lives in her boyfriend's room, so she agreed to let you use her bed."

Natalie nodded and dropped her stuff beside a dresser. "So, this is college?"

Christina smirked. "No. This is a dorm room. Let me show you college."

Christina pointed out countless buildings and athletic fields in just over half an hour of walking all around campus. Natalie couldn't believe how big everything was. And there were so many people walking around everywhere. Natalie knew she was one of the top prospects in the country, but even she felt tiny in the vast plot of land and the sea of students. She wasn't sure if she could handle it.

Natalie shook her head. "How do you not get lost here?"

Christina laughed. "Oh, come on. It's not that crazy. Besides, you're gonna be going to like four different places, tops."

When they walked toward the basketball stadium, they came upon what seemed like the only unpopulated patch on a campus otherwise teeming with co-eds. As soon as Christina pointed toward the dome, Natalie saw a familiar face emerge from behind one of the trees. A woman with jet black hair who looked like she'd just left a comic convention held a metal staff in her hands.

"Someone's doing Halloween early this year. Hey, witch! Hey!"

Natalie clamped her hand over Christina's mouth before the gatekeeper could turn toward them.

"Shut up! You're gonna get us killed!" She pulled Christina behind a bush.

Christina nibbled at Natalie's fingers. Natalie pulled them away. "Alright, I'll be quiet. Who is that chick?"

The woman twirled her staff in the air and slammed it into the ground. A portal opened up and three creatures emerged. They looked like two giant wolves and one of the lizards Natalie had ridden with Erica. The sun glistened off the wolves' massive fangs.

"What're those?"

Natalie slapped her hand back on Christina's mouth and pulled them tight against the tree. She heard one of the beasts begin to approach. Even its slobbery breath sounded angry as it moved toward them. Natalie knew that if one of the creatures spotted them, the whole bunch would have no issue sharing the two of them as a mid-afternoon snack. She felt Christina's pulse quicken against her chest.

"Get over here, you filthy creature." Sela Fortbright sounded impatient, as if she'd been herding these three all morning.

The wolf gave one last sniff before joining its pack. The beasts ran off behind the stadium, and the gatekeeper went back into her portal.

For once, Christina was speechless. She got free of Natalie's grasp and stared at the gateway. Natalie walked toward the portal, but it had closed up before she could get anywhere close.

She pulled out her phone and dialed Ted's number. "Come on, Ted. We need some heroism right about now."

The call rang several times before going to voicemail. Christina continued to stare at the place the gateway had been. She was shaking.

"What the hell was that?"

Natalie flared her nostrils. "Something bad. And we might have to be the ones to stop it."

CHAPTER
34

When Jennifer got the mass text from Erica, she started examining it right away. An immediate text back received no response, and about a dozen texts over the next day resulted in the same lack of contact. She felt the same pangs of nervousness she experienced when the old Erica disappeared. Jennifer knew that things were much different now, but she promised the new Erica that she'd watch her back, too. Jennifer didn't waste any time hacking into her father's computer late at night to take advantage of Sheriff Department resources. Sure enough, there were records of Erica and Yoshi buying and getting on a flight to Japan.

"Why would they go to Japan if all the attacks have been here?" Jennifer squinted at the screen, as if zeroing in closer would somehow reveal the truth. "If there was a good enough reason for her to go, Erica would've told Ted. She would've told all of us."

The nervousness of the past week faded away. Now Jennifer had a mission.

She knew that Erica was a part of multiple lives before this one. It was possible that they'd never experienced the real her, and that the protector would be willing to fly across the world at the drop of a hat, but Jennifer had to believe the part of Erica that was their friend would care enough about them to provide more than a mass text.

The next morning, Jennifer made some calls to Florida, which is where the purported Japan flight originated. With each clue she obtained, something inside her felt more alive. She got in touch with the makeshift hospital the pair had visited. A nurse named Nancy confirmed that Erica and Yoshi had been there and that they'd visited the house of former hospital administrator Charlie Potts. Jennifer asked if she could get Potts' number, but after several tears and sniffles, Nancy told her about the man's purported suicide. The death seemed more than suspicious.

Jennifer dashed down the stairs to the kitchen as her father prepared to dig into a massive sandwich piled high with meat and cheese.

She relaxed her face and gave her best puppy dog daughter eyes. "Dad? Can I go to Florida to investigate the disappearance of Erica?"

Her father gave the sandwich a disappointed look and placed it back down on its plate. He raised his eyebrows at his daughter. "Honey, that sounds expensive. And we don't even know that Erica is missing."

Jennifer intensified her pleading eyes. "But, Dad, it's official police business."

The sheriff groaned and pushed his sandwich away. He pulled out a chair for his daughter. "No, it's not. Can we talk this out?"

Jennifer stomped over to the chair and collapsed into it. She crossed her arms. "Every moment we wait, Erica has less of a chance of surviving."

Her father did his best to look compassionate through his hunger. "What's in Florida?"

"A suspicious suicide. A phantom plane. Erica might be down there, too!"

"Jennifer. You're not responsible for what happens to Erica."

Her eyes narrowed. "Yes, I am."

The sheriff leaned back in his chair. "Well, you don't have to be. She's here to protect Ted and the world. Have you seen her fight? She doesn't need protection."

Jennifer grumbled. She'd seen Erica fight off Nigel's gang in the caves. Secondhand, she'd heard about her laying the smack down on the mind-wiped students. In both instances, she'd nearly died.

"Just because you can fight doesn't mean you're safe."

Sheriff Norris put a hand on her shoulder. "I'm not sending you to Florida. Even if you can cobble together the money, I don't think you should go. You've got school and college applications—"

She pushed her father's hand away. The anger bubbled throughout her body. "None of that stuff is gonna matter if the world ends. We need Erica. If only there was a way to track...."

Jennifer paused for a moment. She looked at her father and remembered the day of the school attack. He'd driven his truck through the front doors and nailed one of Nigel's thugs, but he'd done it by instinct alone.

"Dad? How'd you find Erica the day of the school attack?"

He sighed. "It felt like I could sense she was in danger. I couldn't even control my own facilities. It was pretty frightening, actually. I'm glad she took it out of my head."

Jennifer stood up. "I'm gonna call Dhiraj. We need to track her that way again."

Her father took a conciliatory tone. "I told you, honey, I can't do it anymore. She took it out."

Jennifer stared straight into his eyes. "I'm not talking about you."

The orderly led Jennifer, Dhiraj and Sheriff Norris into the clean, white room. They sat in three chairs on one side of the table. When her father folded his arms, she and Dhiraj did the same. Jennifer had thought this was a good idea when she came up with it, but the anticipation was making her reconsider. There was a major chance the plan would go terribly wrong, but she wasn't sure she had any other choice.

The door to the room opened once again; this time a man with long, gray hair entered, led by two orderlies. He looked significantly different from the last time Jennifer had seen him, but his face and eyes remained the same. The two attendees sat the man down in the chair across from them. He moved slowly, as if weighed down by something heavy on the inside. When he met their stares, it took him a moment or two before he recognized the people across the table.

"If it isn't Sheriff Norris... his lovely daughter... and Dhiraj Patel." Albert

Redican's intelligent smile shined through a worn-down exterior. "How nice it is to see you."

CHAPTER
35

Ted stared in awe for a few moments as he took in the sheer size of the creature. It vaguely resembled the Lychos, but it was more than five times larger. When it let out a roar, the shockwave of sound smashed half the car windows in a quarter-mile radius, including theirs. Before Ted could say anything, Allison was on the phone with the DHS. When she'd explained the situation, she waited for a short response. Allison turned her attention to Ted.

"We need to get it off the bridge."

Ted nodded and opened the car door. He could feel his arm throb as he pushed the handle outward.

Good thing I'm in perfect health.

Ted went flying off in the creature's direction. The people in the cars the giant had landed upon were alive, but barely. The nearby vehicles had done their best to clear a path for the beast, but given the traffic jam, there wasn't much they could do. Ted flew as low as he could, recalling his crash landing during the last battle. He aimed straight for the creature's hairy belly.

"If you take me down, I'm taking you down with me."

Ted pictured a rocket blasting off as he aimed for the beast's midsection. The creature locked eyes with him just before Ted made impact. The blow knocked the giant Lychos off its feet and up into the air. Passengers in the creature's path abandoned their vehicles. The creature bounced off the center support beam for the bridge, leaving a dent in its wake, before it slammed down on the now-empty cars. The bridge lurched beneath Ted's feet after the

Lychos landed. As the creature sat there, dazed, Ted got a better look at it. Like its smaller family members, this beast had the black tattoos of the dark souls on its arm. Ted tried to fly up into the air once again, but his powers failed him, instead leaving him with a hint of the dizziness he'd felt after the blood loss.

"Looks like Papa Wolf is onto me."

It was. The creature slowly got to its feet and growled at Ted. It kicked a nearby car that still contained passengers. The vehicle smashed through the guardrail and hung over the edge of the bridge. The screams from the car made Ted's pulse quicken, tamping down the dizziness. The creature lumbered toward him, pushing several cars out of its path. As the beast reached out its arms to grab Ted, he rolled, jumped up on the hood of a car and leapt to grab a hold of its furry back.

The creature screamed and twisted its torso to try to shake Ted free. Ted held on and tried to use his powers on the teetering car. To his surprise, the vehicle lifted back onto the bridge with ease.

It needs to see me to block my powers. As long as I can hang on—

The beast shook its back so violently that Ted lost his grip completely. He was about to come crashing down on an SUV when his powers kicked in, stopping him a few inches before his face hit metal. He dropped the last few inches when the creature turned toward him. Ted's face pressed against the roof.

"Not a fan of a fair fight, I see."

The Lychos ran toward Ted and the SUV. The creature looked ready to snap him in two as its fangs chomped up and down. He looked around at his options as the beast closed in. He made a split-second decision to leap on the car beside him, right as the creature swiped at the SUV. The beast's claws ripped the roof clean off of the car as Ted landed shoulder-first on the other vehicle. The pain from his recently-healed arm wound was blinding. The dizzy sensation returned, but Ted gripped the car to steady himself.

"Come on, Ted. Keep it together."

When the beast realized it hadn't killed Ted with its previous swipe, it grabbed for his new location. Ted popped up, ran and leapt to another car, and then another. With each jump came another swipe from the beast. Every leap made him even dizzier. The creature roared with anger as Ted continued to evade it. As he made one more leap, Ted lost his balance completely, collapsing onto the roof of a blue minivan.

He felt his hope slip away as he watched the creature run toward him. His last effort to use his powers failed and the beast's claws made the familiar sword sound as they approached his head. Ted closed his eyes and heard several gunshots ring out. When he opened them, the beast's back was to him. Between the creature's arm and the bridge, Ted could see Allison holding her gun in her free hand and firing another round of bullets into the chest of the Lychos.

"You want dinner?!" Allison's voice carried surprisingly well amidst the chaos. "I'm your main frickin' course!"

The creature roared and moved away from Ted. He pushed away the pain and sought vengeance. He reached out with his hand and found himself in the mind of the beast. Ted wasn't sure how, but he'd gained complete control over its body.

"I think I've got an itch you can scratch."

With its razor-sharp nails still extended, Ted forced the creature to bury the claws in its own chest.

Ted assumed he'd been shot or stabbed, because there was no other way to explain the unreal pain that went through his body. He looked down to see no blood or knives, just his hands in the same position as the Lychos claws. He watched the beast collapse forward, as he wrenched his consciousness out of the now-deceased mind. Ted's body convulsed on top of the minivan. The memory of the pain remained as he clutched at his burning chest. Allison had been by his side for at least a minute before he realized it.

"Ted?!" Allison touched his face. "Ted?"

His heart was beating so fast, he thought he might pass out again.

Allison stroked his cheek. "You're okay. You stopped it."

Ted looked up into her calm eyes. He started to breathe more slowly. The memory of the claws driving into his chest began to fade, as did the pain from his arm.

Allison smiled. "There we go."

Ted looked past Allison to see the Lychos on the ground, its claws sticking into its blood-covered chest. The creature was motionless.

"Didn't his mom tell him not to play with knives?"

Allison looked at the creature and then back at Ted. Her eyes widened. "You were in its head. You made it stab itself and you screamed because you felt it too. Did you know you could do that?"

"The control part, yes. The killing it and feeling its pain thing, no." He touched at his chest, which continued to feel wounded. "I wouldn't recommend it." He put his arm around Allison's shoulder. "Can you take me home?"

She nodded and helped him down from the roof. He stumbled by her side as they got to the creature's corpse.

"What're we gonna do if this keeps happening?" Allison asked.

"If what keeps happening?"

She swallowed. "If they keep getting bigger."

CHAPTER
36

Erica's head felt as heavy the previous few days as it did today. At least, she thought it'd been a few days. It just as well could've been an hour or six weeks. The drugs they were pumping her with made her thought patterns cloudy. She was in a small room with no windows that made it nearly impossible to tell what time of day it was. That seemed like it was by design. Senator Kable's design.

From what she'd seen in the last week, Erica felt like she had more than enough evidence to bring a case against the senator. That is, if she and Yoshi were ever able to escape.

Yoshi.

Erica hadn't seen the samurai since she'd left the basement. Perhaps if she hadn't been so interested in snooping around, the two of them would've escaped with what they needed.

No. He wouldn't have let us. He knew we were there.

Erica had tried to get out of the bed on multiple occasions. On what she thought was the second day, she actually succeeded, but that only resulted in a face plant on the cold, wooden floor below. When a nurse rolled her back over, Erica tried to attack the attendee. Her strength was so sapped by whatever they were pumping her with that the nurse didn't even realize Erica's malicious intent.

"It's okay. We'll get you right back into bed, Ms. Kable."

Erica figured the senator told them she was a wayward cousin whose bad behavior could ruin his chance at election. Whatever the story was, they didn't know who she really was. Her efforts to speak were typically met by confused looks, and even if she could put a whole sentence together, she wasn't sure it would do her much good.

On the third day — at least she hoped it was the third day — Sandra entered the room. After ruling out the possibility she was an apparition, Erica strained to get up. She made only a tiny bit of progress on her pillow before Sandra pushed Erica's arms down on the bed.

"It's so rewarding to see you like this. It kind of puts the entire war into context."

Sandra looked different than when Erica had last seen her. There was makeup caked on her face that made her look more mature. Erica supposed that Sandra's natural, punk appearance wouldn't fly as a newlywed to a Presidential candidate. She looked at least a decade older than she really was.

Sandra must've noticed the path of Erica's eyes and touched her own face. "Yes, it's hideous, isn't it? I'm in the makeup chair for an hour every day. I wish there were an easier way, but infiltrating the White House makes it all worthwhile."

Erica wanted to scream. She wanted to stab Sandra in the throat with a nearby needle and run. The emotion coursing through her body came out as little more than a simple cough. She could feel the saliva trickling down the side of her neck.

"Aw, you're like a baby, Erica." Sandra dabbed at the drool from the corner of Erica's mouth with a tissue. "And we'll keep you this way as long as we want."

Sandra gave Erica a playful pat on the face and headed toward the exit. Erica strained with all her might to get the words out.

"Kill me."

The sentence was so scratchy that Sandra had a difficult time making it out at first. Once she did, the former waitress smiled with glee.

"Wouldn't that be something?" She ran back over to the bed and leapt onto Erica. Erica was so drugged up, she could barely feel the weight of the dark soul on top of her.

Sandra grabbed one of the pillows from beneath Erica's head. "Wouldn't it be great if I just choked the life out of you? You would die in agony and we could drop your lifeless corpse on your boyfriend's doorstop."

Sandra pressed the pillow against Erica's face. She braced herself for the lack of oxygen, but before she could even be deprived of one breath, the dark soul took the pillow off.

"But then, you'd go back to the Realm of Souls and tell them all about me and Kit and the plan." Sandra placed the pillow back underneath Erica's head and planted a kiss right on her lips. "So we're not going to kill you. You and your friend still have some value to us."

Erica's rage dropped by half.

My friend. Yoshi's still here.

Sandra got off the bed and walked back to the door. "By the way, it's been really fun getting everybody's worried text messages. Too bad they'll all be dead before they find you."

With that, Sandra left.

Another day passed. During the middle of the night, Erica had seriously considered biting into her own tongue. If she bled enough, she could die and cross back over. Losing this body and life would be one of the worst things she'd ever had to endure. They'd likely keep her on the Realm of Souls to help coordinate the mission. Meanwhile, Ted would remain on Earth. There was a chance she'd never see him again, but she'd have the intel the light souls would need to fight against Senator Kable and Sandra.

Kable. Who is he?

Erica assumed he was a dark soul like Sandra, but there was no guarantee of that. Perhaps he was like Redican, another person who'd been harmed by the war between the dark and light souls. Someone who wanted Ted to fix all the problems in the world. If only things were that simple.

Erica let the night go by without trying to injure herself. She felt less hazy the following morning, and her arms and legs seemed to move a bit more freely. Erica hoped her body was starting to develop a tolerance to the drugs. Short of someone finding and rescuing her, building up an internal resistance was her best hope of getting out. When a bright light filled the room, Erica squinted her eyes to adjust. There was a figure in the doorway carrying a tray.

At first, she assumed the silhouetted man was Senator Kable, finally paying her a visit after he'd taken her out. But it wasn't Kable. It wasn't Sandra, either. Her lips curled into a smile when she realized it was Yoshi. As he approached her, the smell of eggs and bacon wafted over. The joy that built inside her began to recede.

He's bringing me food. He's working with them.

Erica felt her fingernails dig into the mattress. Yoshi's face was completely neutral as he took the chair beside the bed. Erica's mind filled with curses and questions. Between the rage and the medication, Erica conveyed everything with one simple word.

"Why?"

Yoshi scooped up a forkful of scrambled eggs and moved them toward her mouth. She chewed and swallowed. There was no reason to refuse the food. Besides, maybe it would give her body what it needed to resist the drugs.

"The years since you died weren't easy." Yoshi's words were dry and practiced. "Nobody could replace Kikuchiyo, and I knew the only way I'd see him again was to be the best."

The food caused Erica to cough, and Yoshi raised a glass of orange juice to her mouth. The eggs went down hard, burning her throat as they passed.

"I became the best." He gripped the fork tighter as if it was a weapon. "And yet, I was still passed over."

Erica was torn. She'd been tricked and betrayed by someone who felt like a brother to her. Then again, she knew the unusual ways of the light souls could be downright frustrating.

"When the senator contacted me with an opportunity, I knew it wasn't about reuniting with my friend anymore." Yoshi stared deeply into her eyes.

His look was dark and twisted. The boy Erica had known in Japan was long gone.

"I knew it was about power." His smile sent a shudder down Erica's spine. "And power can be earned... or taken."

CHAPTER
37

Natalie and Christina's first stop was campus security. A balding man who resembled a turtle ambled over to the two of them. When Natalie blurted out the details, the man took notes for the first few seconds before raising his eyebrows.

"So you're saying there are lizard-people on campus?"

Natalie grumbled at the man's tone. "Yes, like the ones on the news a couple of weeks ago."

He nodded and pasted on a smile that Natalie immediately wanted to smack off.

"I hadn't heard about that." The man put his notepad back underneath the counter. "Was that before or after the mutant spiders took over New York?"

Natalie was about to hop over the counter when Christina held her back.

Christina looked into Natalie's eyes and took a deep breath. Unintentionally, Natalie did the same. She felt some of her rage dissipate.

"Don't worry." Christina patted her on the shoulder. "I got this."

Natalie crossed her arms and looked back at the turtle man.

Christina cleared her throat. "Sir, important question before we leave. Who gets blamed when the students die?"

That wiped the grin right off the rotund man's face.

He stammered. "Ex—excuse me?"

Christina grinned as if she were in a beauty pageant. "See, one of these monsters put a half dozen police officers in the hospital in Pennsylvania. Since the students don't have proper combat training, I imagine these 'lizard-people' will kill some students." She paused for a moment to flutter her eyelashes at Natalie. "I just wanted to know who gets the blame here after they get killed."

The turtle man didn't respond. He simply picked up the phone and made a call to someone with real power. His tone of voice went from joking to meek in a hurry. By the time he hung up the phone, he looked more like an albino turtle.

"Thanks, ladies. Please go back to your dorms. We're instituting an immediate curfew."

Natalie nodded. "Good to know someone smarter is doing the thinking for you."

Christina waved goodbye and they made the trek back to her dorm room. The mass exodus of thousands of students to their rooms or off-campus apartments was amazing to behold. When the dorm came into view, Natalie looked up at eight stories of insanity. At least three sets of speakers blared hip hop as dancing and screaming filled every balcony. She watched as one girl ran down the hallway at full speed in her flip-flops. She didn't make it to the end before slipping and landing straight on her back. The students around her cheered.

Natalie looked behind her as more teens packed themselves together. The hundreds of conversations muddled to the point she could barely hear herself talk.

"I wonder if we stand a better chance with the lizards."

Christina raised her eyebrows twice. "Oh, come on. I know you're not used to fun in Treasure, but we're gonna have some tonight."

Several players from the basketball, softball and field hockey teams started up a party in one of the study rooms. Natalie tried to focus on meeting people who could be her future teammates. Instead, all she could think about were those creatures out there. Someone handed her a plastic cup filled with a sweet-smelling liquid. Natalie smiled politely at the person before placing it down on the windowsill. She'd watched enough TV and movies to know that mystery drinks could spell trouble.

Natalie looked around at dozens of athletes and other students acting like they were having the best time of their lives. She felt her chest tighten. Plenty of people had chatted with her and told her why their school was the place for her to be. At that moment, she just wanted out of that room.

She shifted between the bodies and walked until she found a quiet outdoor stairwell and sat. A breeze mixed with the chill of the concrete beneath her thighs made her shiver, but at least she could form a cohesive thought. She considered texting Travis or Dhiraj. Maybe even Ted.

Natalie wondered if she was cut out for the social aspects of college life. After all, before Dhiraj and Ted chatted her up, she wasn't much for using words. She played and trained and played some more. When she left her friends, would she be able to find new ones, or would she always be the person in the corner?

The door at the top of the stairs opened, which made the music louder until it shut. Natalie looked back to see a boy who couldn't have been much older than a freshman walking down toward her. He held one of the plastic cups she'd turned down and sat beside Natalie.

Natalie considered using her death stare to get the guy to leave, but she didn't want to be labeled as an ice queen.

The boy's eyes were barely open he spoke. "I know who you are. You're the one they're all recruiting."

Natalie did her best to put on a normal smile. "Hi, I'm Natalie."

She extended her hand, which he grasped and shook way too high and too low. "Sam. I'm thinking you should go here."

Sam took another sip from his cup and nodded as if she'd asked him a question.

"Oh yeah?" Natalie put a little distance between them on the step. "Why's that, Sam?"

Sam left his cup on the step and ran down the stairs. The boy almost tripped on the second to last step, but he regained his balance before reaching the ground-level pavement. He seemed almost proud of himself for standing.

"I'm gonna show you." He motioned her over. "Come with me."

Natalie sighed. "Sorry, Sam. I'm really comfortable right here."

Sam looked harmless, but Natalie knew better than to sneak away with some guy she'd just met. Plus, it was starting to get dark.

"Oh come on. I'm gonna show you a part of campus that gets really pretty at ni–"

One of the creatures Natalie had seen earlier ran so fast toward Sam that she might've blinked and missed it. Natalie only needed to catch a hint of green to identify the Draconfolk before it threw the boy over its shoulder and dashed into the nearby trees. Natalie yelped and knocked over the syrupy liquid from the cup beside her. She felt her heart pounding.

"What happened?"

Natale looked back to see Christina at the top of the stairs. "One of the lizards just took Sam into the forest!"

Christina reached her side. "Really? Harmless Sam?"

Natalie wondered briefly what a nickname like that could do to a kid. "He's gonna be Bloodless Sam if we don't save him. Come on."

Natalie didn't think twice about running off into the trees, and Christina followed right behind her. It wasn't until she remembered just how much trouble one of these things had caused her and Erica that she doubted her decision. Natalie felt the endorphins build in her system. Leaves crunched beneath her feet as she tried to get a view of Sam, but it was far too dark to trust her eyes. Before she could get her bearings, she heard the beast approach from the side.

When it tried to get a grip around her waist, Natalie gave it a sharp elbow in the jaw and ran. Her eyes darted in either direction to find a potential advantage. The creature was so close behind her that she could hear its gurgled breath. She ran for a large tree, leapt, kicked off it with her left foot and swung the right foot toward the lizard's head. It didn't expect the attack and took Natalie's shot right to its face. The beast brought one hand to its cheek and let out a gurgled yell. Natalie stomped hard on the lizard's foot, and when it bent over she socked it in the neck. The creature reached for its throat with one hand and for Natalie with the other. Its claws tore through her shirt as she tried to wrench free. The lizard tightened its grip and she could feel the sharp nails digging into her arm. The creature yanked Natalie closer.

Her face was about three inches from its face when the beast opened its mouth and screamed. The stench of the breath mixed with her fear made her stomach turn inside out, but she refused to back down. As she screamed back in the lizard's face, Natalie heard something zip through the air and nail the lizard in the face. The beast yelped in pain and released its grip. Natalie hadn't seen the first projectile coming, but the second one whizzed beside her head and struck the lizard in the chest. She backed away and looked toward the thrower. Christina Finley windmill-pitched another softball-sized stone in the lizard's direction. This one hit the beast square in the head with a crack and sent it straight to the ground.

Natalie gave it a light kick in the side to see if the beast was still conscious. When it didn't move, she smiled at Ted's sister.

"That was awesome." Natalie rubbed at her arm. The creature hadn't drawn that much blood, but the pain lingered.

"Nowhere near as cool as that kick off the tree. Did you see Sam?"

Natalie shook her head. As she did, she spied another hulking shape coming her way. And then another. "We better get back to the dorm."

Natalie and Christina were about to exit the woods when a blue portal opened up right in front of them. It whirred with electricity as the bright ring grew wider. Natalie half-expected another Draconfolk to come popping out. Instead, it was the stout, pale woman she'd come to know as the gatekeeper. Natalie's stomach flipped once again.

"Natalie Dormer and the sister of the living soul." The gatekeeper tossed her hair. "I see you've met my friends."

CHAPTER
38

Jennifer tried to keep her gaze away from Redican's eyes, as if looking deeper into them would make her lose her mind. She glanced at her father and Dhiraj. They wore similar expressions. From the corner of her eyes, she could see how much the man across from them had aged since he had become a substitute teacher at Treasure High the previous school year. Erica had told her that the powers of the book were too much for a non-living soul to handle. The only reason he survived at all was because the book was created from a part of Redican's realm. Jennifer half-wished he'd met his maker, particularly after he'd forced Ted to choke Erica half to death. The other half remained neutral; given the chance, he could be of some use to them.

After a minute of silence, Redican rolled his eyes. "You can look at me. The orderlies have me nice and drugged up." He relaxed his face and eyes. "Besides, so much of my power came from the book, I'm as harmless as a fly now."

A look from the orderly in the room betrayed Redican's lie. The front desk had already informed Jennifer and her guests about several incidents. The one that caught her attention was the time Redican made everyone see him as a little girl who'd accidentally been locked in overnight. The head doctor was on the phone with the police when he saw a glimmer of who the girl truly was.

"Flies carry disease." Dhiraj looked tense. Then again, he'd been oddly tense the entire ride over there.

"Indeed they do." Redican smiled. "How's school? Have they gotten another long-term sub to replace me? You know, the pay teachers get these days is alarming. They should—"

"Enough." Sheriff Norris looked as though he wanted to burn a hole in the side of Redican's face. "You almost killed students at that school, my daughter included. This isn't an opportunity for small talk."

Redican nodded and sat up straight in his chair. "I didn't think this was a social call." As he looked at the three of them, his body shook with strain.

Jennifer felt a presence in her mind. She put her hands to her head, realizing that Redican was rifling through her thoughts. Judging by the way Dhiraj and her father were reacting, he was doing the same with them. Jennifer felt the tension in her head ease.

Redican's body relaxed. "Erica's missing, huh?"

Jennifer felt dirty and wondered what else he could learn in there. Could he see things even she didn't know were inside?

The sheriff grunted. "I have a feeling you knew that before we came in."

Redican shifted in his chair. "I don't know what you're talking about."

Jennifer leaned forward. "They told us you tried to escape about a week ago."

Dhiraj scoffed. "From what we heard, it was pretty pathetic."

Redican grumbled. "These drugs. I don't even know what I'm doing half the time."

Her father's eyes narrowed. "Erica put her spell on you. I know what it does. She did it to me."

Redican frowned. Jennifer imagined a person who could control minds didn't love it when he got a taste of his own medicine.

"Fine." Redican put up his hands. "You got me. I tried to run away. I was compelled to, but I didn't get very far."

Redican stretched his legs apart, the rattle of his shackles echoing throughout the small room. "It was quite embarrassing, actually. They drugged me and wrestled me to the ground in front of all my new friends."

Dhiraj smiled. "Sounds like exactly what you deserved."

Redican scowled. "Rubbing it in won't get you what you want."

Jennifer felt like their moment was slipping away. She took a lighter tone. "We don't know where Erica is. We think that you tried to escape because you knew where to look."

Redican smiled as if he had the upper hand for the first time in months. "I have a feeling you're right. It's obvious that whatever this connection is with Erica, it's strong. I think I'd be able to help..." Redican put his feet, shackles and all, on top of the desk. "I just don't think I want to."

The sheriff looked like he was about to dive across the table and reach for Redican's throat. Jennifer stayed her father. "What if we made a deal with you?"

Dhiraj and Sheriff Norris spoke in unison. "What?!"

Jennifer waved them away.

Redican tucked his armed behind his head and leaned back. "I like deals. I'd be interested to hear the terms you're offering."

After the sheriff signed the bottom line of the document, the four of them walked outside. Redican's hair looked even more silvery as it billowed in the wind.

"You miss the little things when you're holed up in a cage." Redican held his hand up and let the wind waft through his fingers. "What's next?"

The sheriff opened the back door for him. "We were hoping you'd tell us."

The former sub was about to get in the backseat when he seemed to hear something. He looked out into the sky.

"I will." Redican reached out as if to touch the clouds. "Once we get going, I'll be able to lead you right to her."

CHAPTER
39

Sandra held her husband's hand as they watched the news from the couch. Their DC residence wasn't nearly as spacious as the Pennsylvania home, but that didn't bother her. It reminded her of the final apartment of her former inhabitant's life. She looked over at her husband, whose eyes were fixed on the television. Sandra considered kissing his neck when a special report interrupted her would-be foreplay before it had begun.

Rudy Bolger came on the air, looking as if he'd been rushed from makeup to his desk. His Cheshire grin told Sandra that something ratings-worthy was on the horizon.

"Good evening. President Blake has announced that he's made a major shift in his campaign, including an about-face on the face of his domestic policy." Bolger leaned into the camera and cupped one hand over his mouth. "I wrote that one." He went back to his original position. "Blake has changed his tune about superhero Ted Finley."

Senator Kable squeezed Sandra's hand so hard that she thought it would begin seeping blood. She wrenched it away from his grasp. She wanted to scold her husband, but the look on his face spoke the words "proceed with caution."

"President Blake has gone so far as to declare war on the other world. A literal World War. Let's see part of his speech in Iowa."

The screen cut to President Blake standing behind a podium. Local government leaders filled the space behind him while a few rows of spectators could be seen before him. The nervous leader who'd stumbled on questions during the debate was no longer. It appeared the man had his swagger back.

"I don't agree with Senator Kable on a lot of issues, but he was right about one thing: I need to take action. I've liquidated the Ted Finley task force. Instead, I'm issuing an executive order declaring war against this new world."

Kable stood up with a jolt. He grabbed the remote control off the coffee table and promptly slammed it into the wall. The device smashed into a dozen pieces, which tumbled to the carpet.

"With God as my witness, the United States of America will end these attacks and protect the world from terrorism. It's our world and we'll protect it with everything we've got."

A chorus of cheers echoed throughout the venue before the camera cut back to Bolger. The twinkle in the man's eye made Sandra's stomach sink.

"The policy change came at a welcome time for the President. Poll numbers were shifting toward his opponent, giving Senator Kable a two-point lead."

A graphic appeared on the screen showing the latest polls. Sandra's husband squatted down and placed his hands on the coffee table. With a skyward jerk, Kable flipped the table completely over as it landed with a thud. He walked into the kitchen and pulled out his phone as Sandra looked more closely at the numbers.

"With a single policy shift, President Blake is now polling as the victor with a two-point margin over his challenger. An impressive four-point swing."

Sandra moved cautiously ahead so she could look at the scene unfolding in the kitchen. She deduced that her husband was speaking with Terry, the campaign manager.

"You told me it looked like things were in the clear!"

A wine glass shot from one end of the kitchen to the other, crashing against the wall with a ping and shattering on the countertop. Her husband's tone was getting louder and angrier with each word.

"We should've gotten out ahead of this, Terry! You're telling me we don't even have a statement ready?!"

Another glass zipped across the kitchen as Senator Kable paced back and forth. Sandra cringed as the sound of glass breaking once again reached her ears. She walked up to the TV and hit the power button. There was no need to watch the group of pundits talk about what she already knew. Senator Kable's plan had been working, until it wasn't.

She tiptoed to the opening between the kitchen and the living room.

"Don't speak to me like a child!" Kable voice grew low. "I could end your career in a heartbeat."

Another glass went whizzing by, but this time Sandra had to duck to avoid the contact. She turned back to see the glass break quietly on the carpet. When she looked back at her husband, he'd hung up the phone and was staring straight into her eyes.

"Honey, I–"

Sandra felt the air slam into her gut as she flew backward across the living room. She crashed into the wall, feeling a crack in her shoulder before her hip landed on the ground. Crumbled drywall fell on the top of her head. Sandra's shoulder burned as her husband loomed over her. Senator Kable didn't even seem to notice his fallen wife.

"We need to go further."

Sandra shifted to her left to see if she could get her shoulder back into place. It only stung worse when she moved. "But how?"

Kable paced as Sandra got to her feet and shook the white powder from her hair. She knew they'd have to get someone in here to patch up the hole before they had any company.

Kable's movement stopped. He looked up with a smile. "We need a hero."

Sandra sighed. "Ted knows about you, dear. He'll never turn."

Kable shook his head. Sandra looked into his eyes, and now felt like she was face to face with the devil himself.

"We don't need Ted. I'll be the hero." Kable's grin grew wide. "And you'll be the villain."

CHAPTER
40

Ted shivered for most of the car ride back to Treasure. He'd been through a lot of challenges in the last year, many of which made him worry about death. After killing the giant Lychos while he was inside its mind, now he knew what dying felt like. It was dark and black. The feeling was endless. As far away as he felt from Erica at the moment, Ted wondered if he now had a connection with her on a deeper level.

Allison broke the heavy silence. "Look at the bright side. At least you're still alive."

Ted made the slightest of acknowledgements. "All of the pain, none of the release."

He could feel Allison's glare on the side of his face.

"You're saying that you want to die? That's hardly constructive."

Ted stared off out of the passenger side window. "No. It just would've taken some of the weight off my shoulders."

Allison scoffed. "You know, you've still got people out there who care about you, Ted. You don't have to carry that burden alone."

Ted finally looked over at Allison. She looked older somehow. Like she was a parent giving him advice.

"Nobody else is a superhero."

"Plenty of people are superheroes. They just don't have powers. You think you're the only one who has troubles or responsibility?"

Ted's face grew warm. "If I fail, all those other heroes die. All their burdens are mine. And I don't know what I'm doing."

There were a few moments of silence before Allison took a deep breath. "You'll figure it out."

Ted instinctively searched through Allison's mind. As far as he could tell, she really meant what she said.

"How do you know?" he asked.

"I don't. But you'll do it, because you have to."

Allison pulled into the Finley driveway and put the car in park. After she turned off the engine, they sat there for several minutes. Ted leaned his head back against the seat and attempted to have his muscles release the tension of the events of the last few days. He let the pain, suffering and death seep out of him and into the seat. He knew Allison was right. Necessity would give him what he needed to pass his next set of tests. At least, he hoped it would.

"I'm sorry." Ted took Allison's hand. It was colder and longer than Erica's. "I really appreciate you trying to cheer me up."

Allison ran her thumb along Ted's palm. "You're going to stop the bad guys. You're going to find Erica. I know there's a lot of pain and suffering out there. Just remember the good stuff, too."

Ted nodded and undid his seatbelt. He leaned over and hugged Allison. "I will. Be safe."

She squeezed him back. "You too. Now, go save the world."

Ted unloaded his luggage from the car and waved goodbye to his short and storied career as a government operative. As he walked up to the front porch, he saw a shadow shift before him. When he got closer, the samurai stepped out from the black. Ted froze. The man was the last person to see Erica alive, but Ted had no way of knowing if Yoshi was involved in her disappearance. He proceeded with caution.

"I thought you were in Japan." Ted left his bags in the middle of the front walkway.

Yoshi met Ted halfway. "Senator Kable and his men sent that text after they took us captive." His voice wavered. "I barely escaped with my life."

Yoshi's distress sounded genuine. Ted's efforts to get the truth from the samurai's brain remained unsuccessful. Ted tried to hide his frustration.

"Where is she?"

Yoshi cracked his knuckles. "I can show you. But you'd better be ready for a fight."

Ted looked deep into the samurai's eyes, but they didn't give anything away. He had yet to trust Erica's former friend from the moment he met him. But if the man truly knew where Erica was, then Ted had no choice but to follow him.

"What's one more fight? I'm ready."

As Yoshi navigated him away from Treasure and onto the highway, Ted realized that he'd never been alone with the samurai. While he remained unsure of Yoshi's loyalty, at least he could find out more information during their time together.

"How long has the Academy been around?"

"Over 300 years." Yoshi seemed pained to discuss his former residence.

Ted pressed on regardless. "And they know about me? And the war?"

Yoshi flared his nostrils. "When you became the living soul, we were some of the first humans on Earth to know about it."

"How?"

"One of our elders had a vision. He saw you, your name and where you lived." Yoshi glanced over at Ted. "What's it like?"

"Being the living soul?" Ted let his guard down, allowing the thoughts of the fellow drivers into his head. To his surprise, fewer thoughts than normal trickled in. "It's the gift that keeps on giving."

When Yoshi leaned in, unsure of what Ted meant, he elaborated.

"It's like having all and none of the options at once. You have to be strong enough to balance the world on your shoulders."

Yoshi nodded. "Sounds like an impressive duty. Turn onto this exit here."

Ted followed the next few directions and pulled into a stripmall parking lot. The shops had been long abandoned, judging by the grass growing through the sidewalk cracks. Ted's hope grew.

This would definitely be a good place to hide someone.

Yoshi led him around the back of the building to a locked white door surrounded by brick. The samurai gestured to Ted, and he got the hint. For some reason, the lock was difficult for him to disengage with his powers. He felt tired, as if he'd jogged up the stairs too quickly. As Yoshi opened the door, Ted searched for Erica's mind. He couldn't detect her, but with his powers glitching, there was a chance he simply wasn't strong enough.

Ted followed Yoshi inside. The room was larger than it looked from the outside, and it seemed as though it could easily house a small grocery store if it'd ever been finished. Everything was bathed in a concrete grey hue. When Ted closed the door behind them, only a sliver of light came into the room through a broken vent near the ceiling.

"Where is she, Yoshi?"

Yoshi slipped into the shadows, and the sound of his footsteps seemed to disappear, despite the echo-prone interior. Ted kept his back up against the door, recalling his mistakes in the fight last year against Sandra in the school gymnasium.

"Your princess is in another castle." Yoshi's laugh bounced off the walls.

Ted wasn't sure what he was surprised at more: Yoshi's laughter or his knowledge of 1980s Nintendo games.

Yoshi continued. "You'll have to get through me if you want to find her."

Ted crouched down in a fighting position. "You told me to be ready for a fight. I've been ready ever since you got to town."

Ted saw Yoshi's face creep out of the shadows. The samurai's calm demeanor had morphed. His emotionless exterior now bore a massive smile.

"It'll be an honor killing you, Ted Finley."

CHAPTER
41

Natalie stared with awe as the gatekeeper slammed her staff to the ground and another five portals opened behind her. Each portal yielded several Draconfolk each, and the creatures all lined up in a controlled formation. By the time the portals closed, Natalie could count 16 in all. She glanced back to see the two beasts who'd been chasing them join the ranks.

"How coincidental it is to see you again." The gatekeeper looked beautiful and confident. "Too bad it's not under the greatest of circumstances for you."

Natalie held up one hand. "Hey, there's no need to go around killing people. I mean, we get the point, you can summon up wolves and lizards and stuff. It's very impressive."

The gatekeeper's smile glinted in the moonlight. "Why, thank you. I've never seen such politeness on Earth. If any of you could survive, I'd pick you."

The gatekeeper gestured back to her army of giant lizards. They began to move forward.

"Wait!"

Even the lizards halted in their tracks from the shrill sound of Christina Finley's voice. "We surrender. On behalf of the university, we surrender. Can we discuss the terms of our peaceful ceasefire?"

One of the Draconfolk gave what seemed like a confused gurgle and turned toward the gatekeeper.

Natalie stepped forward. "Erica told me the gatekeepers were fierce, brave and honorable warriors. Let's be diplomatic."

The gatekeeper didn't even pause to consider the offer before bursting into laughter. "Oh, my poor girls. That was a completely different person."

Natalie's stomach squeezed. "I know that your old memories are in there. A part of you wants to keep us all alive."

The gatekeeper gave her squadron a smirk. "It's easier for someone with my strength to suppress those pacifist thoughts." She waved the Draconfolk ahead. "Remember, it's not personal. Just politics."

As the gatekeeper and the Draconfolk moved toward them, Natalie and Christina backed up until they found themselves against a tree. The bark that made Natalie's back itch was the least of her troubles. They shared a glance.

"You know, Dormer. I always held out hope you'd be my sister someday."

Natalie let out a nervous laugh. "Thanks. Me, too."

The gatekeeper crunched through the leaves and got within striking distance of Natalie and Christina. She held up a fist to stop their progress. The gatekeeper drew back her staff and prepared to strike.

"Goodbye, ladies. I'll send Ted your rega–"

A bullet zipped through the air and clipped the gatekeeper on the shoulder. Blood spattered across the leaves below. Natalie looked behind her and saw what looked like the entire school riflery team brandishing their weapons.

The student leading the pack wore a confident smile. "Ma'am, step away from our recruit and we won't fire again."

The gatekeeper lifted her staff into the air, but before she could slam it into the ground, another bullet cut through the air and hit her arm. She screamed and gestured for the Draconfolk to move ahead. Natalie's eardrums hummed with the sounds of gunfire. She watched as several of the lizards took bullets to the chest and arms. As a few of the creatures got close, another wave of students came through, this one comprised of martial artists and wrestlers. Two heavyweights tackled one of the lizards to the ground and started punching it, while five kickboxers surrounded another and assaulted it until the creature collapsed. Natalie was amazed to see so many incredible athletes surrounding her, and the gatekeeper and her small battalion were quickly overmatched.

Christina pulled at Natalie's shirt. "We'd better get outta here."

Natalie nodded, but as they charted a safe path, she heard an exchange between one of the Draconfolk and the gatekeeper.

"No. We're holding them back until the rally."

That was all Natalie could make out as Ted's sister pulled her out of the forest. As she made one last turn back, Natalie watched as the gatekeeper and the one uninjured Draconfolk jumped into another blue portal. When one of the wrestlers slammed the final standing creature to the ground, the group of athletes cheered and exchanged high fives.

When Natalie and Christina exited the woods, they gave each other a big hug. Natalie pulled away first. "What was that, some kind of 'athletes in trouble' phone chain or something?"

Christina laughed. "Something like that. You alright?"

As far as Natalie could tell, her arm had stopped bleeding. Aside from being shaken up and prepared to die, she was as put-together as ever. As Natalie nodded, she saw Sam limping out of the forest. He had a large gash on his leg, but it didn't appear to be life-threatening.

"Harmless Sam!" Christina ran toward him. "Are you okay?"

The adrenaline seemed to have cut down on Sam's level of intoxication. "Yeah, stupid scaly bastard."

Christina's look of concern was something new for Natalie. "We should take you back to my room. Patch that up until the paramedics come."

He agreed and the three of them tried to recover in Christina's dorm. Natalie's temporary bunkmate fashioned a tourniquet from an old Treasure High long-sleeve tee and wrapped it around Sam's leg. They sipped water and waited for an ambulance to arrive.

Natalie ran the words of the gatekeeper over in her head. Christina, now in full caretaker mode, felt Natalie's forehead.

"You're quiet. Are you gonna pass out?"

Natalie brushed Christina's hand away. "No, I'm just thinking. Why would she say killing us was just politics?"

Christina checked Sam's wound. "I don't know. Maybe she was just trying to be quippy."

Natalie shook her head. "No. I heard her talking about a rally with one of the lizards. Do you think she meant a political rally?"

Sam cleared his throat. "There's a rally coming up in Pennsylvania. It's a home pride thing for the senator."

The two girls looked at Sam. He shrugged. "What? I'm a poli-sci major."

That's when it all started to make sense. Natalie's mind felt like a puzzle that had just been put together. She talked it out before the pieces could no longer make sense. "The attacks have been in Ohio, Pennsylvania, North Carolina and Florida." Natalie looked into Sam's eyes. She smiled. "You know what all of those have in common?"

Sam gave her a cockeyed glance. "Farming?"

She rolled her eyes. "Maybe you should change your major. They're all battleground states in the election. Toss-ups. Kable needs to win them if he's going to beat Blake."

Christina squinted at Natalie. "You're saying Senator Kable is working with the gatekeeper and staging attacks to try to win an election?"

Natalie smirked. "It's probably not the most underhanded thing anyone's ever done to get into office." She started to pace around the room. "I need to get back home, stat."

Christina pouted. "What about your visit? You haven't even met most of the team yet."

Natalie began packing her bags. Her shoulders and neck felt tense, but she knew this was the only possible solution. "If we let Kable get away with this, who knows if there'll even be a school next year."

CHAPTER
42

Jennifer gripped the inside of the car door as tightly as she could. While she was the one who'd convinced her father to drive away from the facility with Redican in tow, she hoped the man wouldn't find his way into her mind again.

"There was a text message that said Erica was in Japan." Sheriff Norris glanced up into the rear-view mirror. "Is that where she really is?"

Jennifer looked in the mirror as well. Dhiraj was pressed against the left window, as far as he could possibly be from Redican. The former substitute teacher seemed to enjoy the uncomfortable personal space.

Redican laughed. "I'm not a GP–" He went completely silent.

Jennifer turned back slowly to study him. He looked like a robot that'd been put into sleep mode.

Dhiraj waved his hand in front of Redican's face. "Looks like we got a dud. Should we take it back?"

Jennifer was about to tap Redican on the shoulder when he burst back to life. Dhiraj let out a tiny yelp.

Redican ignored Dhiraj's girlish squeal. "No. I'm not sure how I know that, but no. She's much closer than that."

Jennifer felt relieved and more anxious at the same time. Using Redican to find Erica had been a good idea so far, but there was no way to know what the consequences might be.

"Where?" Jennifer's voice came out like more of a squeak than she'd intended.

Redican shook his head as if trying to get something loose. "An hour and a half away. Two, tops."

Redican gave the sheriff driving directions a few moments before each turn. They found themselves back on the highway before long, and Jennifer watched as the former teacher became less mechanical.

"Looks like my brain is mine again." He snorted. "For the time being, at least. Perhaps we can play a car game in the meantime?"

Dhiraj gave a hesitant laugh. "You don't seem like the license plate bingo type."

Redican smiled into the mirror. "I've got a different game in mind. It's called Secrets."

Before Jennifer could reply, she felt Redican invading her mind once again. It was much stronger than the sensation had been inside the facility. She knew he was getting stronger. It was like dozens of thoughts were being called up at once without her permission. She saw a childhood carnival with Erica and Ted, the moment she fired the bullet that clipped Deputy Daly's ear, the angry mob trying to break through the front door of the office building, and multiple other memories at once. Her head felt heavy and hot with more thought processes going on at once then she ever thought possible.

Sheriff Norris noticed his daughter's discomfort. His voice filled the car. "Leave her alone!"

"Stop it!" Dhiraj shoved Redican into the other side of the car.

Jennifer felt the tension leave her head as she slumped back against the chair. There was a sharp sting at the base of her skull.

"Owww." Jennifer tried to massage the soreness away with her fingers. "What'd you do in there?"

"I was just gathering some information for our game." Redican looked more vibrant than before, as if he'd sapped some of Jennifer's energy. "Who'd like to go first?"

"This isn't funny!" Dhiraj fumed. "Stay out of our heads."

Redican took on his best teacher voice. "Dhiraj, can you honestly say you don't want to learn your girlfriend's secrets? There are some good ones to choose from."

Jennifer wanted to turn around and put her hands around Redican's throat, but she felt so lethargic from having him in her head, he probably would've dodged any kind of attack.

Sheriff Norris' voice shook with anger. "You're here for one reason, Redican. If you don't stop, I'll put you in solitary for the rest of your life."

Redican rested his arms behind the back seat, stretching out as wide as he could, as if he owned the place. "You can't do that, Sheriff. You need me. Just like your daughter needed to be suspended from field hockey."

Jennifer felt her stomach drop.

Dhiraj looked confused. "Is that why you were home the other day?"

She turned toward the back. "What other day? Were you spying on me?"

"I must've been," Dhiraj said. "How else would I have seen you hang up on me?"

Jennifer shook her head and looked to her father for support.

He wore as dour an expression as Dhiraj. "What'd you do to get suspended?"

She smacked the dashboard. "I got a little overzealous protecting a teammate."

Redican chuckled. "Overzealous? You gave the girl two black eyes." He turned toward Dhiraj. "Personally, I think field hockey could do with more fighting. Don't you agree?"

Dhiraj swung his fist at Redican's face. The former teacher juked at just the right moment to avoid the punch.

"We've come to blows already? There are so many more secrets to share." Redican resumed his deep concentration.

"We'll take you right back, Redican, I swear—"

Her father abruptly cut off and stared straight ahead.

She touched his shoulder. "Dad?"

The car drifted out of the lane ever so slightly. She whipped back around to see Redican staring at her father.

She screamed. "Your stupid game is so important you have to mess with the person driving our car?!"

Redican smiled through the strain before relaxing. Sheriff Norris jerked the car back into the lane, gritting his teeth. Jennifer looked back at Redican, who appeared even happier than before.

"What a thing to keep from your daughter." Redican licked his lips. "And I thought lawmakers were always honest."

Before her father could speak, Jennifer felt the words leap out of her throat. "I don't want to know. If there's anything my dad isn't telling me, there's probably a good reason."

Her father smiled over at her, though she could tell he was doing it through the same sharp pain that she was feeling. "Thanks, honey."

Redican laughed. "What an adorable father and daughter. It's a shame I won't get to see you two when you move to the west coast."

Dhiraj choked on his saliva. "He's kidding, right?"

Jennifer's head whipped over to her father. Her hand started to shake. "Move? Why would we move?"

Sheriff Norris glared at the rear-view mirror before attempting to console his daughter. "Nothing's in stone yet. I've just been applying for jobs in other cities that might pay more. It's all very prelim—"

Before Jennifer had a chance to respond, Redican's voice became robotic once again. "Take this exit on the right."

The sheriff's car was in the far left lane when he got the notice. With the skill only a lawman could possess, he merged through two lanes, snuck in between two cars in the third and sped ahead of one more before merging into the exit. As they got off the highway, the car pulled onto a high-end residential street with large houses and gardens that were more like art than shrubbery. Jennifer didn't recognize where they were in the slightest.

She looked over at her father. Jennifer never lost trust in her father's driving, but the possibility of them moving during her senior year made her question him about more pressing matters. She looked back at Redican, and the happy-go-lucky baddie who'd just taken a tour through their memories was gone, replaced by dead eyes and a stare.

"I was going to tell you if anything materialized." Sheriff Norris coughed. "I thought with a new job I could help you pay for college."

Jennifer put her hands over her eyes. "Dad, all my friends are here. Dhiraj is here. And I'm a senior!"

"But with college coming–"

In the midst of the conversation, Jennifer barely heard the click of Redican undoing his seatbelt. As the vehicle chugged along at 20 miles per hour, Redican opened the car door. "Erica's in trouble. I have to help her."

With that, the man rolled out of the moving vehicle.

CHAPTER
43

Ted's blood boiled as he watched Yoshi from across the room. The man had betrayed Erica and the entire light soul cause. If he'd been chosen as the living soul, maybe Ted wouldn't have had the burden of heroism, but the world would be in grave danger. It would've been like Adam, the living soul Erica needed to put down, all over again.

Ted circled to his left. "Did Senator Kable put you up to this?"

Yoshi slid his feet in the opposite direction. "I'm tired of following plans. The elders told me I was strong enough to be the living soul if I continued to follow the plan. No more plans."

Yoshi rushed Ted as soon as he finished speaking. Ted put up his hands and tried to push away Yoshi's first kick. The samurai's foot blew right by Ted's powers and into the side of his face.

Ted attempted to push off his feet and into the air. No such luck.

Yoshi grinned. "I suppose I've caught you on an off day. How fortunate."

The samurai ran for Ted again and swung his feet forward. This time, Ted slammed his wrist into Yoshi's ankle to block the kick. He scrambled backward.

The fight. The fight and the blood loss. I'm just too weak.

Ted looked around the dimly lit room. A beam of light shined down on a long metal pipe. He dove toward it and lifted the weapon into the air. It was heavy, but thankfully Erica's training had been focused on more than telekinesis alone.

Ted lifted the pipe like a sword, as Yoshi removed an actual sword from his sheath. The samurai whipped his weapon through the air and moved toward Ted. Yoshi swung the blade, and Ted brought up his pipe to meet it. The clanging sound reverberated throughout the room. Yoshi pushed back, but Ted held his ground.

"You know, Kikuchiyo wasn't my true friend." Yoshi leapt back and came in for another blow.

Ted felt the strain in his back as he repelled the strike.

Yoshi chuckled. "Kind of like how Erica doesn't really love you."

Ted's adrenaline doubled at the insult. "You don't know anything about us!"

He used his anger to go on the offensive. The pipe slammed into Yoshi's sword hand. The man let out a yelp of pain as he dropped his weapon, but he swiped the hilt out of the air with his opposite hand, almost like a reflex.

Ted swung his pipe again.

Yoshi parried with ease, despite the change of hand. He took a massive slice out of Ted's weapon with his sword, the blade lodging itself halfway through the pipe.

"When you die, she'll move onto her next mission so fast, it'll be like you never existed."

Ted screamed and put all his might into tossing the pipe across the room. Yoshi didn't expect the move, and his sword remained lodged in Ted's weapon as it flew into the adjacent wall. Ted took advantage of Yoshi's lapse in concentration, ducking under a half-hearted blow and jamming his fist in the samurai's abdomen. He let four more punches fly — two in the chest, one in the arm and one in the head. Yoshi went down to one knee.

"Maybe she only loves me because I'm the living soul. So what? It's more than you'll ever be."

Before Ted could react, Yoshi kicked with alarming speed at Ted's knee. He felt something tear inside, sending a shockwave of pain through his left leg. Ted pushed off his good leg and sent himself as far away from Yoshi as he could. The stabbing sensation in his knee repeated itself every second as he hobbled on one leg.

Yoshi stood up and walked slowly toward Ted. The hero hopped backward with each step the samurai took. Yoshi made a running motion, causing Ted to plant both feet. The pain forced Ted to fall down, his head nearly hitting the wall behind him. He scrunched up his face and did his best to ignore the agony.

Yoshi's smile was now firmly planted. He took a jog to the other side of the room to dislodge his sword from the pipe. His gait seemed to mock Ted's injury.

"The light souls will have no other choice but to give me the power. I'm the only one who can stop what's coming."

Ted used his hands to scoot backward. He rested his neck and spine on the wall behind him. Yoshi moved into position to deliver one final deathblow. Ted prayed that his powers would come back to him.

Please. Please let me have something left.

He felt something unfamiliar building inside him, but none of it seemed to manifest itself outwardly.

Ted pointed at Yoshi. "You're no true hero. You're a traitor who missed your chance. You'll never have the power. Killing me won't get you anything."

Yoshi gripped his sword tighter. "Maybe not. But at least it'll send a message."

The samurai wound up. Ted thought of Erica. He hoped that wherever she was, she'd be able to avenge his death. He closed his eyes and put up his hands. Ted heard the sword whooshing through the air, until it was drowned out by another noise.

Yoshi's scream caused Ted to open his eyes. Between the samurai and himself, a blue portal had opened on a diagonal plane. As Ted looked deep within the gateway, he could faintly make out Yoshi falling. The samurai still clutched his sword as he vanished out of view.

Unlike the portals he'd seen before, Ted could feel some kind of connection with this one.

I made this. I saved myself.

Ted stretched out his hand and the portal widened. He closed his fingers and the gateway closed completely. When he shifted his hand again, nothing happened. The portal had completely disappeared, taking his assailant along with it.

PART FIVE

CHAPTER
44

Jennifer's seatbelt pulled tight against her chest when Sheriff Norris slammed on the breaks. She turned to see a wide-open back door and Redican running onto the lawn of a massive property. Her adrenaline kicked in and she undid her belt to chase after the man.

"Honey, wait!"

Jennifer threw a thumbs-up over her shoulder to assure her father. She heard a pair of sneakers whacking against the sidewalk before Dhiraj reached her side.

He called over his shoulder with some difficulty. "Don't worry... Sheriff... we've got this!"

Jennifer cut around a bush carved in the shape of an elephant and picked up the pace. Redican was much more spry than she would've guessed. She barely caught a glimpse of him as he dashed between a lion bush and a set of trees at the end of one property.

She frowned at her cohort. "I'm sorry I didn't tell you about—"

Dhiraj put up a hand. "Later. I need to focus or I'll trip."

She nodded. "Fine, but don't slow me down."

His heavy breathing reminded her of a woman in labor. "It's moments like this... I'm glad... I got a treadmill desk."

Darkness was starting to descend and Jennifer was afraid they'd lose Redican as he dashed between more shrubbery. She looked over at Dhiraj.

One of his hands clutched at his right side, as if his lungs would fall out if he didn't.

"You okay?"

Dhiraj grunted. "Just a cramp. Couldn't he... give us directions... instead of... racing us there?"

Jennifer shrugged. "Maybe Erica's thing only works in straight lines."

They spied Redican in the distance. He didn't even wait for traffic to stop as he crossed a street at full speed. One luxury vehicle skidded to a halt and another honked, but Redican didn't slow down. Jennifer waved her apology as she and Dhiraj passed in front of the stopped cars. The vehicles, like the properties around them, were too rich for her blood. She wondered if Dhiraj had any pictures of this town on his vision board. Living here was certainly something to aspire to, though it wasn't her sort of thing.

Jennifer's feet hit grass, then road, then grass again. She started to make up ground. Or was Redican slowing?

After the seemingly endless chase, Redican came to a stop outside of an eight-foot-high brick wall. Jennifer halted just behind him, while Dhiraj collapsed onto the ground, his chest heaving up and down in rapid succession.

She put her hands on her knees and watched Redican make several unsuccessful attempts to jump and climb the walls.

Her eyes turned to Dhiraj. "You know, you're supposed to stay on your feet after a run."

Dhiraj coughed. "Sorry... can't listen... dying."

Jennifer offered him a hand up, but Dhiraj ignored it.

"She's in trouble." Redican started to pace. "She's in trouble and I need to help."

After catching her breath, Jennifer dialed up her dad and directed him over to the address. When he arrived, the three of them watched Redican wear a hole in the street with his pacing.

Jennifer let out a long, slow exhale. "You couldn't have come running after him, too?"

He smiled. "I thought I'd let you run for two."

A video screen on the wall interrupted their conversation. Jennifer hadn't noticed it before, as the monitor seamlessly melded into the brick.

"Excuse me. If you're here for Senator Kable, he's in Philadelphia preparing for the rally."

Kable's house. Of course.

Her father stepped ahead to the screen. "This is Sheriff Norris of the Treasure Sherriff's Department. We'd like to ask you a few questions."

Dhiraj put up his hand from the grass. "Tell her if they have any prisoners to let them go." He coughed again. "And ask if they have water."

The woman on the other end of the screen maintained a neutral demeanor. "I'm sorry, Sherriff Norris, but you'll have to come back in a couple of days when the senator returns."

Jennifer shook her head.

We don't have time for this.

"I'll take it from here, Sheriff." A man who had seemingly appeared out of nowhere put his hand on the sheriff's shoulder.

Jennifer's mouth hung upon. The pacing Redican was gone, replaced by an apparition who looked an awful lot like Senator Kable.

"Marjorie, could you let us all in, dear? I'm afraid I had to leave my car in the city."

Marjorie's eyes widened. "Oh yes, Mr. Senator. Of course."

The gates opened with a squeak. Jennifer and her father stared at Redican with amazement. He smiled. "What can I say? It's way easier to use the key than it is to break the lock."

Jennifer pulled Dhiraj to his feet. Redican disguised as Kable led the way to the front door. Marjorie greeted the group and ushered them inside.

"Senator." Marjorie's voice was laced with concern. "We're surprised to see you here. We thought that you and your wife wouldn't be back—"

Redican cleared his throat. "I'm sorry, Marjorie, but we're in a hurry. Can you take us to the girl?"

She looked at Jennifer and her father. Her eyes were wary. "All four of you?"

Redican scowled. "Please, Marjorie, don't waste my time."

She took her eyes from Redican's entourage and nodded profusely. "Yes, Mr. Senator. I'm sorry. Right this way."

Jennifer was amazed by the artwork and craftsmanship she saw on display throughout the house. It looked as though a different decorator had put together each room with a million-dollar budget. Despite the disparity between the rooms, they all still somehow fit together. As they were led down to a basement and a subbasement, Jennifer put her hands on the dark-stained wood that lined the walls. It was decidedly a house of money and secrets.

Marjorie opened a door at the end of a long corridor. Sure enough, Erica was there, lying in a bed with an IV attached to her arm. Jennifer ran past Marjorie and put her arms around Erica, who awoke with a start.

"Erica! Oh my God, I thought you were dead. Again."

Erica's eyes blinked slowly. "Jen." She looked up and met eyes with Redican disguised as the senator. "Why did he let you in?"

Jennifer turned back to see the man who resembled Kable change himself back into his true form. Marjorie gasped until Redican turned his attention on her.

"Be a dear and guard the door, won't you?"

Marjorie's eyes went dead. She nodded mechanically and exited the room.

Erica breathed hard. "So, he's not an evil senator, just an evil teacher. Great trade."

Sheriff Norris inspected the bag that was dripping into Erica's arm. "Evil or not, he led us right to you. What's in this?"

Erica tried to sit up in bed, but Jennifer had to help her get to that position. "Muscle relaxants. Sleeping meds. They've been pumping me with them since I got here."

The sheriff searched through the nearby medical equipment. He gingerly took out the IV and plugged up the hole with a piece of gauze and a nearby bandage. "Not anymore."

Erica smiled. "Thanks."

Dhiraj scanned the room. "Is Yoshi here, too?"

"He's on the senator's side. The gatekeeper is, too. And Sandra is his wife."

Jennifer's mind buzzed with the new information. "Evil waitress Sandra?"

Erica nodded.

"As if today couldn't get any stranger." Dhiraj sighed. "Are you okay to move?"

Erica took one step off the bed. As she wobbled, Jennifer couldn't help but remember half a dozen nights when she'd had to tend to her tipsy friend.

"I'll manage." Erica took a few deep breaths and shook her head to clear the cobwebs. "Let's get out of here."

Marjorie's scream from the hallway caused all of them to jump. The sound was followed by a thump as a man who vaguely resembled a masculine version of Sela Fortbright entered the room.

"Erica, I see you're up and about." He stepped over Majorie's body on the way inside. "Cal Fortbright, pleased to meet you."

He bowed low before smashing his hand into the wall. Splinters of wood zipped by Jennifer's face as she closed her eyes. When she opened them, she saw the distinct image of the dark soul tattoo on Fortbright's arm.

"Family." Erica took an unsteady step forward. "Of course. You turned your sister. We have you to blame for all of this."

Cal let his teeth show. "We could say the same, I suppose. I've been told to keep watch over you, and kill everyone else who arrives." He looked over at Jennifer and her crew. "I think I'll enjoy following my orders."

Jennifer gulped. Then she clenched her fists. "We're taking her with us!"

Cal Fortbright laughed. "I wasn't asking for volunteers to go first." He took two daggers out of his sheaths. "But you'll do nicely."

CHAPTER
45

Natalie and Christina tried their best to get a flight out of Ohio. With everything completely booked, they borrowed Harmless Sam's car and headed back to Treasure. When she took one last look at the lush, green campus, Natalie wondered if she'd ever see the school again.

"It's pretty sexy, isn't it?" Christina's smile lit up the vehicle.

Natalie nodded. "That's a good word to describe it." She let out a long breath. "I felt a little out of place, though."

Christina groaned as if she'd been hurt by the comment. "You're the sexiest of them all. You practically led the army of athletes against the bad guys. Everybody wants you back next year."

Natalie figured the school would say that about any top recruit, particularly one with some fighting skills. She wondered what it'd be like to leave Treasure for good. As the biggest fish in the smallest pond, she wasn't sure she was ready.

"I liked them, too."

Natalie was half telling the truth. Everybody at the makeshift party seemed nice, but she certainly didn't make any strong connections.

Christina pried. "But?"

Natalie wished perception didn't run in the Finley family. "But, maybe I can't have a normal life anymore."

Christina scoffed. "First of all, what life is normal? Second of all, what the hell do you mean?"

Natalie laughed. "Look, I know I could probably reach my full potential at a school like Southern Ohio, but maybe there's something happening here that's bigger than basketball."

Christina pursed her lips. "Nat. Just because you used to date Ted does not mean you have to be committed to him."

Natalie growled. "I know that. It isn't about Ted."

"Suuure." Christina made a kissy face. "I bet it has everything to do with saving the world and your high moral code or whatever."

Natalie grumbled and turned up the radio to cover up both their voices.

After a long trip with only one quick stop to use the bathroom, Christina pulled into Natalie's driveway and reached over to give her a hug.

"Nat, you've been training all your life for hoops. Nobody's forcing you to be a superhero's sidekick."

Natalie nodded. "I know. Thanks. And thanks for the ride. Get it back to Harmless Sam in one piece."

Christina pulled back and gave a fake confused look. "I have to give it back? I thought this was payment for us saving his life."

Natalie smirked. "Be nice."

"Always."

Before Christina was even out of view, another car pulled into the driveway. Travis hopped out and picked up her bag right away.

"Hey." Natalie yawned. "Don't expect a tip."

Travis kissed her on the cheek. "I was actually on a panty raid. I'll give you back all the other clothes, I promise."

She smacked him in the shoulder, and they went up to her bedroom. When she removed her light jacket, she inadvertently revealed the blood stains on her t-shirt.

"Jeez, Nat. Maybe you should go to a doctor."

Natalie rolled her eyes. "As if you haven't had worse during a game."

Travis inspected the injury. "We usually don't have to fight off giant lizards on the other team." Travis seemed content with the way the cuts had been bandaged. "It's almost like they followed you there."

Natalie nodded. "I'm just a magnet for crap these days."

Travis sat down on the bed and motioned for her to join him. When she did, his familiar scent filled her nostrils. Having him alone in her bedroom made her want to tear off his shirt. If she wasn't so beat up from the day's events, she might've considered it.

He put his hand on her leg. "I don't think you should do this anymore."

Natalie looked into his eyes. There was genuine concern there. The moment was a far cry from the anger-fueled lust of the college cafeteria kitchen.

"Do what?"

He sighed. "You shouldn't have to fight these things. That's Ted's job."

"The guy who used to run with the GHA actually wants Ted around?"

He squeezed her thigh. "I'm being serious."

"I know, but I don't have a choice. People could've died if I didn't—"

"But what if you'd died?! Where would I be then?"

Natalie couldn't believe it. She actually saw tears in Travis Conner's eyes. It gave her an uncomfortable feeling.

She inched away from him. "I'm sorry, but I'm not going to stop being who I am just because you'll miss out on getting some act—"

"I love you."

If Natalie's emotions were a building, Travis' last three words would've sent the entire thing crumbling to the ground. Her throat closed up. "What?"

"I love you, Natalie. I know you don't feel the same way, but I don't care. I don't want you to die."

She shook her head. "I don't have time for this right now." Natalie picked up her phone. "I've gotta go see where the others are."

She ignored Travis as she walked to the other corner of the room and dialed Ted. While the phone rang, she watched her boyfriend. His eyes were focused squarely on the ground. Ted's phone went to voicemail and she hung up. She tried Dhiraj.

Travis lifted his head. "That's all I get?"

When Dhiraj's phone clicked to voicemail as well, she hung up. "I don't know what you want me to say. I don't love you back? I don't appreciate you trying to stop me from helping my friends? What more do you want, Travis?"

The usual glimmer in his eye had faded. "I guess I hoped you would say it back."

Natalie's mind scrolled back toward the previous year's homecoming dance, when she'd said those three little words to Ted. She never expected to be on the other side of the conversation.

"Look, Travis." When she sat back down on the bed beside him, he sprung up.

"No. It's fine. Go get yourself killed by some monster." He walked to the door and put his hand on the doorway. "Do it for the world." He huffed. "Do it for him."

Natalie's first instinct was to toss the phone into Travis' face, but she resisted. Instead, she stewed as he stomped down the stairs and slammed the front door. Her stomach tightened as the phone buzzed in her hand. It was Ted.

"Hey." Natalie's voice caught in her throat.

Ted didn't seem to notice. "Hey, are you back?"

"Yeah."

She could hear Ted's smile through the phone. "Ever wanted to see a senator's house?"

CHAPTER
46

Erica tried her best to shake off the grogginess as Cal Fortbright approached Jennifer near the doorway. She watched as Dhiraj and Sheriff Norris formed a barrier between the dark soul and his intended prey. As much as she'd like to join the wall, she didn't have nearly enough energy to do so.

Erica spoke as defiantly as she could with the drugs coursing through her system. "Doesn't seem like something your sister would do."

Cal planted his feet and growled in Erica's direction. "And what exactly do you mean by that?"

Erica took a deep breath and another step forward. "After all the training she got, she'd probably be more confident. I understand why you'd go for the weakest person in the room."

Dhiraj cleared his throat.

Erica rolled her eyes. "Fine, second weakest."

Dhiraj nodded. "Thank you."

Cal changed direction and set his sights on Erica. "You think I can't handle a challenge?"

She crouched down. Even the slight bend of her knees made her feel off-balance. "I know you can't."

A dagger went whizzing toward Erica. She hadn't even seen him throw the blade. At the last second, she spun to the side and the projectile stuck deep into the wall. The dark soul came charging in Erica's direction. Instinct helped her to block a swipe with the other blade that was aimed at her head. She used all her strength to slam her hand into his wrist, and the dagger tumbled to the ground. Fortbright faked an ankle kick and punched Erica's chin so hard, she nearly made contact with the ceiling when she left her feet. Her back crashed into the wooden floor, causing a dull pain between her shoulder blades. As much as the drugs were killing her reaction time, at least they deadened the pain on impact. As Erica scrambled to her feet, she heard the sheriff pull the gun from his holster.

"Stay where you are." The sheriff tightened his grip on the weapon. "Back away or I'm gonna—"

Cal moved with unbelievable speed, ducking out of the sheriff's line of sight and crushing his hands with a powerful blow. The gun flew into the corner of the room as Cal sent a kick to the sheriff's gut. When he hit the ground, Jennifer stepped in.

"Get away from my dad."

The sheriff groaned on the ground as the dark soul approached.

"You've got quite the death wish, little girl."

Jennifer got into a low fighting stance. "I may be little, but I'm one heck of a distraction."

Cal Fortbright yelped in pain as his eyes shot downward. There was Dhiraj by their opponent's ankles, injecting a clear liquid through two syringes.

"I'm getting really good at these ground attacks." Dhiraj evaded Cal's efforts to kick him and rolled off to the side.

"You think that drugs can... stop... me?" Cal had a confused look on his face. He moved his hand in front of his eyes.

Erica assumed he was seeing things move just as slowly as she was.

She grinned. "Aw, gatekeeper's baby brother feeling a little sleepy?"

Cal closed his eyes. When they opened, Erica could see pure rage take hold. The dark soul grabbed Jennifer by the shirt and tossed her through the air. Dhiraj dove sideways to cushion her fall, only to take the worst of the impact. The sheriff remained on the floor. Erica looked from left to right.

Where's Redican?

Just as she cursed another wildcard element in the fight, Cal turned his attention toward Erica.

"Alright. Your turn."

As Cal dashed toward her, Erica spun to the side and gripped her IV stand like a staff. She twisted it at just the right moment to slip between the dark soul's legs. He tumbled, his face screeching against the hardwood. Erica wasn't fast enough to take advantage, but the drugs slowed Cal down enough that he couldn't counter, either. She imagined that from the outside, the two of them looked like prizefighters in the 12th round. They were on their last legs for sure.

Cal reached for Erica and pulled her in tight, preventing her from getting leverage. He wrenched the back of her hair toward the bed and smashed her head through the headboard. If her brain had felt cloudy before, it was a veritable thunderstorm of pain and confusion after the blow.

Cal stood above her with another needle in his hands. "Looks like I won the challenge."

"Not yet," a voice said from behind him.

Before Cal could turn around, both of the daggers pierced through the dark soul's chest. When he turned around to face his assailant, Erica could see the hilt of the blades buried deep in his back. She looked over Cal's shoulder, but she couldn't see anyone there. Then the air appeared to laugh as Mr. Redican materialized back into view.

"Sorry, Cal. But it's my job to protect the protector."

Cal Fortbright seemed to want to say something in response before his eyes rolled to the back of his head. The man collapsed, his body motionless.

Erica leaned against the side of the bed. Her ears rang from the assault as Redican walked over to her. Here was a man who'd nearly killed her. Now he'd just saved her life. Did that make them even? Before she could answer the question, the door to the room slammed open. Three police officers filed in.

"Freeze!" The burliest of the three pointed his gun in Erica's direction.

She and Redican put up their hands.

Dhiraj struggled to his feet. "Officers! Thank goodness you're here. You've missed some of the fun, but there's plenty of cleanup—"

"Get down on the ground!" The officer's voice continued to rise. "That means all of you!"

Sheriff Norris got up to his knees and flashed his badge. "Sherriff Norris, Treasure Sheriff's Department. Senator Kable was holding this girl hosta—"

One of the two silent officers kicked the sheriff back to the ground. Jennifer screamed and dove on top of her father to protect him from further assault.

"Don't make me repeat myself! Get down on the ground!" He clicked a bullet into the chamber. "Unless you need a little more convincing?"

CHAPTER
47

Sandra brushed her long hair for the hundredth time and moved onto the other side. She remembered back to Page's Diner, rambling off the names of the regular customers and their faces before getting to Ted Finley. She'd followed orders at Page's. She'd spent her personal life following men blindly. It felt like her second life as a living soul had gone much the same. Sandra went along with Nigel's plan to keep Ted occupied at the high school. She helped Kable destroy the police van carrying Stucky and Faraday. She even completely changed her appearance and shed everything she was to become a senator's wife.

When am I going to make a decision for myself?

The errant thought surprised her. Her stomach tingled and she looked back into the rest of the hotel room. Her husband was still on the phone discussing the rally. He could read thoughts and he'd called her on subordination before. She cringed when she imagined him tossing her across the room with his mind.

She neared her hundredth brushstroke on the other side when Senator Kable approached. He was handsome – the surgery and the expertly crafted mask made sure of that. His power knew no limits, which thoroughly aroused her dark soul side. She knew her devotion would be rewarded if she followed his plan to the letter, but she wished she could join him in the White House as well.

"You look wonderful, my dear." Kable kissed her neck.

Sandra felt goosebumps run all the way down her back. "It's just what you wanted. I wish everything you wanted me to do was so simple."

He wrapped his arms around her waist and bosom. For all the power he had, his embrace seemed to make her feel colder, not warmer.

"If the polls were more solid, we wouldn't have changed the plan." He grinned. "This is what's going to get us all the power we need to win the war."

Sandra placed the brush down on the marble countertop. She ran her hands through the hair that didn't seem like hers anymore. "It's going to get you the power. I'm going to be rotting in a prison somewhere."

He released his grip and let his hand caress her back. Sandra felt her pulse quicken.

"Even though you're the sweetest fruit on this world, you'll never rot." Kable smiled like he was pleased with himself. "You'll bide your time, and when Earth has fallen, you can resume your rightful place by my side."

Sandra looked into her husband's eyes through the mirror. "And if the plan fails?"

"If it doesn't work, it'll be because you didn't follow it to the letter."

Senator Kable walked into the other room, and Sandra followed. He'd made sure they stayed in a hotel with a presidential suite, as it made for good headlines. It was far too big for two people, but then again, the large and lonely mansion was even greater overkill.

"Honey."

He shuffled through the papers of the next day's speech. "Mmm-hmm."

"After we put the plan into action, can't I just escape instead?"

He looked back at her with a flash of malice.

"The story needs to be about my heroic act, not your escape and the country's manhunt." He turned away and looked out the window. The city lights flashed whites, greens and purples in the distance.

"I know you're making a sacrifice," he said, "but you'll be rewarded tenfold. It'll just take some patience."

She forced a smile. "Never my strong suit."

He chuckled. "I was like you. I wanted the world to burn and I wanted it to happen in a hurry." He opened up the curtains wide to bring in more neon light and the faint sounds of the city streets. "But you get a lot more satisfaction from destroying the world when you've taken the time to build it up first."

Sandra nodded and looked down at the carpet.

He lifted her chin. "I could've killed you in Treasure. Treat the rest of your time here like a gift. Even if you have to wear an orange jumpsuit for part of it."

Sandra focused on relaxing away the emotions. She kissed him on the cheek before he went on to other business. Sandra waited until he started practicing his rally speech out loud to let any more thoughts race through her mind.

I'll pull the trigger. I'm just not sure where I'll aim it.

CHAPTER
48

Natalie wrapped her arms tighter around Ted's waist as they zipped through the evening air. She remembered the last time he'd flown with her. They'd busted through the roof of a cave as she bled out from Nigel's stab wound. If it weren't for him, she would've been a goner for sure. The wind around them was so loud, she had to talk directly into his ear to be heard.

"How much longer?"

She could feel his muscles tensing against her body. Ted's training with Erica and his summer job had given him a lot more bulk. Gone were the pudgy love handles Natalie used to squeeze. They were replaced by the makings of a six-pack. She appreciated abs on a man.

"A few more minutes. Can't go full speed."

Natalie understood why. He was paler than normal, and some visible bruising on his neck and arms made him look like he'd been smacked around a bit. She also couldn't help but notice his visible limp before they took off as well. The no-nonsense glance he shot her at the time told her not to ask too many questions.

She nodded. "Okay."

"How was the school?"

Natalie figured the intricacies of her monster battle might be lost amidst the howling air.

"Busy. Worth considering."

He nodded. "What's Travis think?"

Natalie wanted to tell Ted everything. That's what she used to do, tell Ted and Dhiraj everything. Now that the latter was in the perfect relationship and the former was trying to save the world, she figured she'd leave out a few details.

"Fine with the school. Not with fighting baddies."

He laughed. Even with all the noise, she could tell it sounded much more hollow than normal. "I guess I have the opposite problem."

Natalie felt them begin to dip lower. It was half-exhilarating and half-terrifying to descend without a several-ton airplane surrounding them. As they approached the ground, several massive properties came into view — large, impressive houses with manicured lawns and iron gates at the end of the driveway. The image of plenty made her think of Travis and his family's financial troubles.

"It's weird who you end up with." Natalie closed her eyes as the ground grew nearer. "It's not always who you expect."

"Tell me about it."

They both stayed silent as Ted guided them to the ground on a patch of grass just outside Senator Kable's house. As much as the feeling of solid ground beneath her feet settled her, she felt her chest tighten when she took in the police cars surrounding them. They shared a glance and jogged to the front door.

The cops by the entrance recognized Ted and let him through. Natalie could hardly believe it, but the place looked bigger on the inside than it did from the outside. She wondered if they could fit two or three courts inside when she heard the commotion from downstairs.

"You're making a mistake! Ow, they're too tight!"

Ted and Natalie looked at each other and spoke in unison. "Dhiraj."

They hustled down the stairs and reached the busted down door. There the gang was, all in handcuffs. The only one who seemed to be resisting things was Dhiraj. An officer was trying to adjust his restraints.

"That's even tighter! Come on."

Ted walked to the center of the room as Natalie looked around the space. Her jaw dropped when she realized that Mr. Redican was sitting beside

Erica on the bed. She thought back to the prom catwalk and her inability to control her actions. Part of her wanted to find the nearest weapon and jam it through his skull.

Ted puts his hands on his hips. "Officers, what's going on here?"

The gang all began to pipe up at once, with Dhiraj and Jennifer leading the chatterfest. Natalie saw Erica smile silently.

The three policemen looked up. The strongest-looking of the three put a smile on his face. "Ted Finley. It's an honor."

When he extended his hand, Ted hesitated. "I'd be happy to share your hand, but you need to tell me why you're taking my friends into custody."

The officer's look changed back to one of duty. "Sorry, Ted. These guys were trespassing on private property. We're gonna have to bring 'em in."

Ted raised his eyebrows playfully. "Oh, Erica?"

Erica's smile grew wider. "Yes, Ted?"

"Can I break one of our long-standing rules?"

"You may."

Ted put up his hands. The officers reached for their ears, as if they'd just heard some kind of piercing radio feedback. Two of them groaned.

"What're you doing to them?" Natalie watched as the men struggled.

"Reprogramming."

The officers took their hands away from their heads and looked around as if they'd been teleported there for the first time.

Ted cleared his throat. "Gentlemen. If you please?"

Within the next two hours, the gang had been set free and rendezvoused around the kitchen table in Ted's house. Even though the whole Redican-being-free situation didn't sit well with Natalie, she didn't mind being in the same room with him. As long as they could stay as far apart as possible.

"Nat, you're up." Ted gestured to the head of the table and Natalie moved into place.

"I've figured out what Kable's up to. All of the attacks have been in states he needs to win for the election. He's trying to turn everyone against Blake."

Dhiraj scratched his head. "But didn't we determine that Blake sucks?"

Erica nodded. "We did, but Kable's got the gatekeeper and the dark souls on his side. Blake's the lesser of two evils."

"Barely." Ted grumbled. "Anyway, Nat?"

"I overheard the gatekeeper talking about the rally. That's happening in downtown Philly in less than 12 hours."

Sheriff Norris flared his nostrils. "There'll be thousands of people there. Roads closed down. If they attack then, it'll be a madhouse."

Natalie pictured dozens of beasts trampling Kable's onlookers as they tried to escape. It'd be like shooting fish in a barrel. Everyone in the room started voicing their opinion about the situation. Even Redican seemed to be piping in.

Dhiraj knocked his fist on the table and the gang quieted down. "Ladies and gentlemen." He placed an expensive-looking piece of equipment down on the table. "Welcome to the next generation of tactical software."

He touched a button and a holographic display filled the space between the tablecloth and the decorative ceiling lights. "While everyone was catching up, I brought up the satellite view and the building plans of the rally street. I plugged in our number of team members and assets. Unless you object, I think this could be our plan."

Natalie leaned into the display. There were little red dots sprinkled throughout the map of the block. She saw her name beside a dot on one side of the street. Underneath her dot was the word "evacuation."

Ted's face was incredulous. "How... how much did this cost, Dhiraj?"

Dhiraj waved away Ted's question. "Don't you worry your heroic little head, my friend. We paid it down by selling your movie rights. Which reminds me, you all need to sign these forms before you leave."

Later that night, Sheriff Norris had taken Jennifer and Dhiraj home. He also agreed to keep a close watch on Mr. Redican, whose role in the plan was apparently too important to send him back to the asylum.

Natalie sat on the couch with Ted and Erica. They were eating the last of the cookies Mrs. Finley had made for their "little meeting."

Ted recounted his battle on the bridge and his one-on-one with Yoshi.

"Before I knew it, the portal was gone, and so was Yoshi."

Erica shook her head. "Usually, the portal training comes last. It's amazing you were able to tap into that. Do you think you could do it again?"

He sighed. "I've tried. I can't figure out what I did to open it. Only how I closed it."

Natalie sat up straight. "That could come in handy if the gatekeeper goes portal-crazy at the rally."

Erica nodded. "Good point, Nat."

"Thanks. You two sure we shouldn't tell the police?"

Ted reached for the last cookie. "Kable obviously has some sway with them. Got them to come to the house to arrest everyone. I think it's better to do this on our own."

Natalie understood, but she'd certainly appreciate having a few dozen people with guns behind her. It helped in Ohio, that's for sure.

Natalie tried and failed to suppress a yawn. "Better rest up. Another long day tomorrow."

Erica got to her feet. "I'll see you out."

Ted waved as Erica followed Natalie outside. A fall breeze crept past them, bringing the smell of burning leaves along with it.

Erica put her hands on Natalie's shoulders. "You don't have to do this, you know. It's gonna be dangerous. You have a future to think of."

Even though Ted was the one with the mind powers, she wondered if Erica had taken a peek when Natalie wasn't looking.

"I know. All of this is part of my future, though. Hoops. The war. I have a responsibility to both."

Erica's smile was like a teacher who was proud of her student. "Good. We need you. I just wanted to make sure."

Natalie wasn't sure why, but she felt and followed the urge to pull Erica in close for a hug. It felt warm and mostly comfortable.

"Glad to be part of the team."

"Glad to have you."

When Natalie reached the final step, she turned back. She could Erica through the window, as the protector sat beside Ted and took his hand. Natalie smiled as her friends looked deep into each other's eyes. She ignored the temptation to call Travis and started walking home.

CHAPTER
49

Erica's body had almost completely fought off the rest of the drugs — Mrs. Finley's cookies seemed to help with that. She felt the enhanced strength return to her arms and legs. The warrior within her was primed for battle. And yet, sitting beside Ted took her mind far away from anything resembling conflict. She took his hand. It gave her much more than warmth.

"The last time we were alone feels like it was ages ago."

Ted's fingers interlocked with hers. "Right? I feel like Vott and Harding are going to bust through that door any second."

They both looked over at the entryway. Everything remained silent until Ted sighed. "I'm really sorry about the DHS. I shouldn't have trusted them and I should've fought harder for you to be there with me."

Some of the weight lifted from Erica's chest. "No, I'm the one who should be sorry. I trusted Yoshi. He got me captured and he almost got you killed."

He shook his head. "We're even. We both trusted untrustworthy people. That's over now."

"Now we just get to fight the evil people."

Ted appeared to have trouble smiling at that. He looked away and Erica brought her hand to his face.

"Hey, what's wrong?"

"I don't know how you do it. I killed that giant Lychos on the bridge, and I was inside its head. I died."

Erica squeezed his hand. "Dying is basically the worst. I'm sorry you had to go through that."

He pulled away from Erica and brought his knees up to his chest, wrapping his arms around himself. "It was so much pain. And darkness. How do you get over something like that?"

Erica drew herself close to him and rested her head on his shoulder. "I start over. If I thought of myself as a several-hundred-year-old person who'd dealt with all those deaths, I'd go insane." She turned her eyes up toward Ted. "I'm here. I'm 17." The nervousness spread through her stomach. "And I'm in love with you."

The next few moments lasted an eternity for Erica. First, Ted said and did nothing. She cursed herself for sharing her feelings. The panic dissipated when he tucked her hair behind her ear.

"I love you, too."

She stretched upward until her lips met his. After days of numbness, the kiss was almost overstimulating. To tell him that she loved him and mean it seemed to take everything to another level. For all the pain she'd felt in dozens of lifetimes, this one moment seemed to make everything worth it.

The next morning, Erica awoke with her face pressed to Ted's chest. She shifted her weight and realized they'd fallen asleep on the downstairs couch. The light from the sunrise streamed in between the blinds and into her line of sight. She let her fingertips glide down his t-shirt as she watched his eyes come to life.

He smiled. "Hey."

She returned the grin. "Hey, sorry I fell asleep."

"You have nothing to apologize for."

Erica let out a deep breath. "Okay."

A few beats went by without words as they shared a long look. Erica's heart felt fluttery.

Ted sighed. "Do we really have to go fight bad guys today?"

"I'm afraid so." Erica pulled him closer.

He kissed her on the temple. "We can't postpone?"

She laughed. "Sorry. Evil politicians like to stay on schedule."

A couple of hours later, the gang was stationed outside of a van that was made to look like an air conditioning repair vehicle. Sheriff Norris and Mr. Redican were the only ones absent, but they were in direct contact from one of the rooftops overlooking the rally. As part of the plan, Jennifer and Dhiraj would run surveillance from the van, using a network of tapped video cameras from stores on the street. Ted would take the air, while Natalie was prepared to shelter the rally attendees in a nearby building. Meanwhile, Erica would be the one-woman cleanup crew.

There were still two speakers until Senator Kable took the stage, so they figured they had at least a few minutes until the real show would begin.

Natalie checked her phone and tucked it back away with a sigh.

"Waiting for loverly to text?" Dhiraj asked.

Natalie and Jennifer whapped him on either shoulder and then nodded with a smile in unison.

"No prying." Natalie patted her hip, where one of Cal Fortbright's daggers lay in its holster. "Today's all business."

Dhiraj whined. "Aw, come on. Ted? Can't you just look through Natalie's brain for a second?"

Ted smirked. "Dhiraj, if you don't focus, I'm gonna tell everyone your darkest secret."

"I'm an open book."

Ted raised his eyebrows. "Pink. Unicorn."

Erica watched Dhiraj's face turn to one of terror. His voice grew meek. "Alright. I'll focus."

As the second-to-last speaker got on the microphone, the five of them huddled up.

Erica let out a deep breath. "We don't know what we're gonna be up against, but I know that with all of us working together, we can stop it."

The other four in the circle nodded.

"Everyone, take your positions."

Dhiraj put his hand in the center of the position. "Can we get a Team Ted on three?"

The other four slyly disbanded the circle and walked away.

"Aw, come on. You guys are no fun."

Erica stood next to Ted toward the back of the crowd. There were balloons, costumes and signs throughout the mass of attendees. Above them was a giant hanging banner that said "Kable for President" in garish letters. Erica might've been swept up in the fervor if she wasn't so concerned with figuring out how Kable planned to kill people. The others were in position and the senator was about to receive his introduction.

Ted put his hand on Erica's back. "Here goes nothing, huh?"

The anticipation coursed through her veins. "Yup." She caught his eye. "You know, I'm proud of you, Ted."

He grinned. "Thanks. I'm proud of you, too."

Erica took in everything that Ted was. A hero. A good friend. A man who loved her for who she was. It made her feel light to think like that. She hoped the sensation would last a lifetime.

"And now, the moment you've all been waiting for, your next President of the United States, Kit Kable!"

Thunderous applause filled the street. Erica wondered how long she'd have to wait before reaching for the concealed sword in her backpack.

After the applause died down, the politician straightened his tie and began his speech.

"There's been a lot of talk about heroes lately. From the men and women fighting wars overseas, to the firefighters and police officers making sure our streets are safe. From the doctors and nurses who are willing to battle a hurricane to keep our family members alive, to teachers fighting to pass on strong education to the next generation. We even have a real-life superhero with powers from another world who's helping us to fight the forces of evil."

Natalie grumbled over the comm. "Don't get cocky, Super Ted."

Ted touched his earpiece. "Yes, ma'am."

Kable continued. "But I'm not here to talk about heroes. I want to talk about the American people. We can't rely on heroes to fight our battle the way that President Blake has. If I become your next President of the United States—" Kable paused for another round of whooping, hollering and applause. "I will help you to fight your own battles. You won't be dependent on Ted Finley to protect you, because the White House will make sure you and your family are safe and sound."

As the next round of applause began, a small blue speck appeared high above the stage.

"You guys seeing this?" Sheriff Norris was sharp and prepared.

Ted nodded. "Looks like a portal's about to open."

When the gateway reached the size of a car, people from the ground began to spot it. Erica hoped it would stop growing, to no avail. It continued to get bigger and bigger and the crowd began to scream and run.

Erica spoke as loudly as she could without damaging eardrums. "Hold your positions."

Senator Kable played the part of scared Presidential candidate on stage. As two aids ushered him off, the enormous portal halted its growth.

Great. A whole army could get through that.

"Redican, Sheriff, do you two see anything coming out of there?"

"That's a negative," Sheriff Norris replied.

In the distance, Erica heard a roar through the portal.

"Guys, something's coming."

Ted flew closer to the edge of the gateway to see if he could get a better look. Static increased on the channel as he approached it.

"Oh, man."

Ted zipped back down to Erica's side.

"Did you see it?" Erica felt her pulse start to race. "Ted?"

"I did."

"And?" Dhiraj asked.

The sun shined against green scales as the beast poked its head out of the portal. Despite the size of the opening, the massive creature still had trouble squeezing all the way out. As it did, it snapped one side of the rope holding the "Kable for President" banner, which sent some of the crowd scattering to avoid it. Erica stared at the teeth and the wings, which were followed by a long, spiked tail. It let out a much louder roar, after crossing all the way over to Earth. The crowd beneath them picked up its pace and volume of screaming.

"As you can all see..." Ted's voice shook. "It's a dragon."

CHAPTER

50

Jennifer and Dhiraj had tapped into a combination of live video feeds and security cameras to get a comprehensive view of the entire rally. Despite a picture that left no angle uncovered, Jennifer could hardly believe the size of the creature that had just exited the portal. The beast was as long as a city block and wider than the field hockey field. Jennifer's mouth hung open and she couldn't tear her eyes away from the screen. While the creature's shiny, green scales drew some attention, Jennifer couldn't help but notice its extremely ugly face. The grotesque snout and teeth weren't going to win a dragon beauty contest any time soon.

Nobody spoke on the comms for a solid five seconds until Erica piped up.

"Actually, it's still a Draconfolk. Just a really big and nasty one."

Dhiraj glanced over at Jennifer. He looked twice as afraid as she was. "Weaknesses?"

"Can't fit in tight spaces." Erica sounded like she was all business. "Use your speed."

"Roger that." Ted didn't sound so sure over the comm.

Jennifer's eyes darted around the images on the screen. She tried to push the nervousness away. None of those emotions would help Ted now. She knew she had to think and act fast.

"Ted, there are some narrower streets to your three o'clock." She tried to steady her rapid breathing. "Play a little game of follow the leader."

Ted gulped. "All right. Let me get its attention."

The dragon had fully emerged from the portal now, which closed behind it. It whipped out its tail and stretched its body as long as it could go, as if it'd just escaped captivity. The creature swiped at a gargoyle statue perched near the top of one building. The screams of the crowd below doubled in volume as the statue plummeted. Before it got past the third floor, the gargoyle stopped in mid-air. The stone sculpture floated up toward Ted. There they were on screen: Ted Finley, a grey gargoyle statue, and a giant dragon all floating above the city streets.

"Hey, greeny." Ted's attempt to sound confident was somewhat lacking. "Catch!"

The gargoyle zipped through the air and nailed the dragon in the face. It roared loud enough to shake the pavement underneath the van. It was the kind of sound that'd make most people lose hope. The dragon flexed its hands and feet, revealing sharp claws that resembled metal.

As if he needed something else to be afraid of.

Ted sounded downright meek. "You guys think it worked?"

Dhiraj raised his eyebrows. "You sure as heck didn't make a new friend."

With that, the dragon gave chase. Jennifer watched the tiny image of Ted on screen as he flew between two buildings. She heard crunching sounds of structural damage as the dragon's body squeezed its way in after him. Windows smashed and glass rained down on the streets. Within a few moments, Ted was out of the view of all the cameras.

"I've lost visual on you, Ted." Dhiraj's voice cracked. "You better hope all these buildings have insurance."

"Hardy-har. I'll keep her busy. You guys just get everybody out of—"

The low pulse of the portals overwhelmed their comm links for a moment. The video feeds worked just fine, however, and it was easy to see over a dozen portals open up near the ground. In the space that had previously been filled with supporters, signs and chants for change, there were now figures from another realm. Among thousands of people running for their lives, normal-sized Lychos and Draconfolk began streaming out. Gurgles and howls from the creatures filled the streets as the beasts looked for prey they wouldn't have any trouble finding. In the midst of all the chaos, Jennifer spied a pale woman who she rightly identified as Sela Fortbright.

"Erica and Natalie?"

Natalie scowled. "It's crazy here, but people are starting to listen. Hey! This way, ma'am!"

"Three of the bad guys are nearby," Erica said. "Once I take 'em down, I'm going for the gatekeeper."

Dhiraj nodded. "Copy that. Everybody report back soon." He turned off their microphones. "Well, this is insane."

The second Jennifer looked over at Dhiraj, she couldn't stop herself from blurting it out. "I'm really sorry, Dhiraj. About the field hockey thing. I know I should've said—"

Dhiraj laughed. "You really want to talk about this now?"

Jennifer shrugged. "Can you think of a better time?"

Dhiraj nodded. "I could've helped." He fumbled with the video controls. "I don't know why you shut me out."

"It's just... you're so sure of everything. I didn't want to mess with your life."

Dhiraj looked into Jennifer's eyes. "I don't know anything. I work everything so hard. Trying to be the best and all. If I worked the relationship harder, I think we'd be okay."

She took his hand. "And I'll try to trust you more."

In the midst of the chaos, they kissed for a split second before Jennifer pulled away.

"What if I have to move?"

"Then we'll deal with it, cents." Dhiraj grinned. "Don't worry, I've got more than a few frequent flyer miles saved up."

Jennifer felt the tension melt from her neck and shoulders. "Good to know, dollar."

"And by the way, don't feel like you have to apply to the Boston schools. If you don't want to."

"I don't know." She winked. "I think I'll apply to one or two."

Dhiraj grinned and flipped their mics back on.

***

Even before the creatures emerged from the portals, Erica had a feeling they were coming. She drew the sword from its holster. The sharp pinging sound it made as it exited made her think of battles past. As much as she liked training, there was something about planting a weapon in the belly of a beast that made her feel so darn satisfied. Erica grinned and turned the sword in her hands.

"Let's go hunting."

She ran with full force toward the closest Draconfolk. It had its arms around a middle-aged woman letting loose a high-pitched scream. Erica stuck the sword right into its back. With a blue burst of light, the creature disappeared and sent the woman to the ground.

One down. About 50 to go.

The disappearance of their comrade caused two nearby creatures to look Erica's way. The Lychos dropped the teenager it was about to eat, while the Draconfolk pushed a mother and her daughter out of the way.

Erica licked her lips. "Didn't anyone ever tell you to say excuse me?"

The Lychos dashed toward her at full speed. Erica halved the distance and leapt into the air. Her blade came down on the creature's shoulder. The wolf clutched at the wound before the laceration turned a glowing blue and the creature burst. Erica grabbed her sword by its hilt and tossed it like a spear toward the chest of the approaching Draconfolk. It pierced the scales like a knife going through soft butter. The lizard exploded in light and the sword clattered to the ground.

Erica shouted a war cry. "Yes! That's three."

When Erica ran and rolled to pick up the sword, five more creatures descended upon her. Two Draconfolk moved to hold her arms behind her while three Lychos scratched at her legs.

"It's my party, and you'll die if I want you to."

With a guttural growl, Erica took out one by thrusting the sword straight behind her. She used the other Draconfolk as a springboard and flew into the air. With one windmill slice, she cut all three Lychos down before they vanished from existence. When the fifth creature reached for her, she sliced off its arm. The lizard gurgled in pain before its body and its fallen appendage both exploded in a blue firework.

"Eight. Piece of ca—"

A hard, metal object struck Erica in the back of the head, sending her face-first into the ground. She spied the heavy manhole cover to her left as she brushed off some of the grime on her shirt. A wound began to form right beside her contusion from the other day. She wondered if she'd have matching scars as she turned to see the dark black hair of Sela Fortbright. The powerful woman's eyes looked colder than ever.

"I think we've got a little family business to discuss, Protector."

Erica gripped the sword tightly with both hands. "I'd be happy to give you and your brother a reunion."

She ignored the throbbing in her head and ran toward the gatekeeper.

CHAPTER
51

Ted banked around the corner of the building so fast that he barely stopped himself from careening into a window. He righted his body and continued down the narrow street at full speed. The dragon pulled the same maneuver not a second later, tightly tucking its wings as it powered through the street. Ted could barely hear his comm link over the sounds of the buildings crunching behind him. The dragon howled in pain as its wings struck the metal, wood and brick of the buildings.

"Caution: wide load!"

When Ted banked around another corner, the creature flew straight up into the air to avoid the tight street. He looked above him to see the dragon flying back toward the open expanse of the rally.

"Oh, no you don't."

Ted tensed up his body and zipped through the air as quickly as he could. He felt the wind whipping against his cheeks as the dragon came closer into view. The beast was directly over the rally when Ted saw his opportunity to strike. The dragon had reared back in an effort to fly straight down. As it did, the beast revealed the lighter and softer scales on its stomach and chest. Ted willed his body to double its speed and aimed for the dragon's underbelly. He braced for impact and let his shoulder slam into the oily scales like a bullet. He felt the creature's organs shuffle during the impact.

The dragon let out a scream so loud, Ted's hearing short-circuited. But when the sound returned, so did the dragon's strength. It swiped at Ted, but he was able to duck the blow with ease. He clenched his fist and flew upward into the dragon's chin. The punch sent the dragon reeling backward.

"Dragon uppercut!"

As Ted prepared for one more blow, he felt all his muscles release at once. The powers that had kept him in the air to this point had shut down completely. His dead weight dropped like him like a stone out of the air, and all the confidence he'd gained from punching a dragon was replaced by fear and falling.

"Mayday!" Ted flattened his body to try to slow his descent. "A dark soul's blocking my powers. Helllp!"

Dhiraj squealed into the earpiece. "What do we do?"

"Catch me?"

Ted whipped past the tops of the buildings and knew there was little chance he'd survive the fall. If his powers didn't kick in, he'd be roadkill for sure.

"Ted!" Erica's voice came in through the comm. Ted wondered if he'd ever have a chance to hold her again.

He tried to access his powers with every fiber of his being. When nothing came, he screamed as the street approached and he covered his eyes with his arms.

Then something plucked him out of the air.

He felt a set of claws wrap around his body and hoist him onto a slick, oily surface. Ted uncovered his eyes and held onto the dragon's scales for dear life.

"What in the hell?"

A laugh pervaded through the comm links.

"Who knew?" Redican's smile was obvious. "Controlling a dragon's mind is even easier than a human's."

The dragon moved with lightning quickness beneath Ted's body. He was amazed that the beast who'd just tried to slice him to death was the only thing that kept him from splattering.

"Good work, Mr. Redican." Dhiraj sounded relieved. "Now what's say we take out some of those baddies?"

"With pleasure. Hang on, Ted."

Ted gripped the dragon's scales even tighter. The beast flew toward a pack of Lychos and Draconfolk that were terrorizing the Kable supporters. As it whipped its tail, Ted felt his body move in turn. He gripped his legs around the beast's body as it slammed the tail into about ten creatures as once. Ted looked back over his shoulder to see the beasts writhing in agony on the ground. He patted the dragon's scales.

"Who's a good dragon? You are. Yes, you are."

The creature roared with approval as it leaned back. Ted's body went almost completely vertical as the dragon kicked one of the Draconfolk back into its portal of origin.

"If we keep this up, maybe we can actually win this thing."

When the dragon went horizontal again, Ted saw a metal streetlamp flying toward them. The dragon shrieked when it saw the weapon and attempted to fly away, but the projectile was going too quickly and the metal pierced through the dragon's skin. The creature spasmed so hard that Ted lost his tight grip and fell to the ground. He landed thigh-first on the blacktop, sending a sharp pain through his leg and hip. Ted gritted his teeth and stood up.

Nothing broken. I guess I'm lucky.

The dragon's scream caught his attention. Ted looked back to see it collapse into a lifeless heap, cracking the pavement beneath it. Mr. Redican's screams simultanously shot through the comm channel. Ted winced and clutched at his ear. "Something's wrong with Redican." Sheriff Norris was nearly drowned out by the sounds of agony.

Ted frowned. "If he was in the dragon's head when it died, he's in a world of hurt. Take it slow with him."

"Roger that."

Ted limped to the creature's side. The streetlamp seemed to have gone right through the dragon's heart.

"Well, that's just not fair. How did that even happen, guys?"

"No clue, man," Dhiraj said. "Didn't even see where that came from."

Ted tried to use his powers to fly again, but whatever was blocking his powers before continued to have him on lockdown.

As he began to walk toward the stage, he heard a low gurgling rumble. The fear that coursed through him made him feel even more vulnerable than he already was. Ted turned around to see half a dozen Draconfolk approaching. His heart began beating at an incredible rate.

"For what it's worth, I was really good friends with your big sister."

The Draconfolk were unfazed. One of them let out a loud gurgle-scream and the others joined in unison.

"Sorry guys, I don't think lizard *a capella* is going to take off."

As one of the creatures lunged, Ted avoided its grasp and ran in the opposite direction.

***

Natalie called out to a group of stragglers.

"Get inside! Now!"

The group got the message and joined the other people Natalie was waving inside. The large office building had a massive lobby, which made it perfect for holding most of the overflowing crowd as they got off the street. It'd be safe, as long as the Lychos and Draconfolk didn't pursue. When she noticed a bottleneck, Natalie dashed inside and willed her throat to emit the loudest sound it possibly could.

"Move to the back! Make some room, people!"

To her surprise, the Kable supporters actually listened. Pride in her success grew within her. The shift to the back allowed several dozen additional entrants.

If only they didn't want a murderer to win the election.

Natalie pushed through the crowd and out the doors of the front entrance, where she came face-to-face with a Lychos. Her heart skipped a beat. The creature was looking straight through her, as if she was standing between it and a buffet.

Natalie drew her knife and pointed it at the creature. "Not today, White Fang."

The Lychos snarled and lunged for her. She rolled under the attack and crouched beneath a circular patio table covered with campaign pamphlets. When the beast came closer, Natalie pushed the table up with all her might. It slammed into the beast's furry chin, resulting in a yelp of pain. The wolf-like creature took a few steps back. Natalie hopped to her feet.

"That's right, wolfman!"

The Lychos rubbed at its chin before drawing its sharp claws. Natalie's eyes grew wide as she tightened her grip on the hilt of the dagger. The beast swung at Natalie, and she parried the first blow with the blade. The wolf continued to approach, and she blocked another swipe, though it continued to push her backward. One more attempt to cut her in two resulted in her spine pressing up against the stone of the building.

Natalie's pulse raced as she looked at the beast's hairy arm. "Gotta time this right or I'm kibble."

The Lychos growled and sliced at Natalie. She leapt up and out of the way of the claws, which lodged in the building's exterior. Natalie landed on the creature's arm and sprinted, doing her best to keep her balance on the hairy runway. Before the Lychos could shake her off, Natalie reached the beast's shoulder, deposited her blade directly into the flesh of its neck and jumped off. Natalie shoulder went crashing down on the concrete below. The blow knocked the wind out of her, but it wasn't forceful enough to jostle anything out of place. As she turned back toward the Lychos, she saw the creature clutch at its neck wound before falling to the ground. Natalie stood up and pumped her fist.

"I just blew your house down!"

As she went to retrieve her knife, she heard a growling sound from behind her. Her heart dropped. She turned to see two more Lychos approaching. They looked between their defeated comrade and Natalie several times and then bore their fangs in unison. Natalie pulled the blade free from the defeated creature's neck.

"There's more where that came from!"

A honking noise drew her attention behind the Lychos. Then came the screeching tires. When the two creatures turned around, they were met immediately with the hood of a fast-moving car. Natalie dove out of the way as the vehicle slammed into the front of the building, crushing the beasts against the stone.

Natalie stood up and surveyed the scene. The familiar car had been totaled with both airbags deployed. Travis stepped out of the car and rubbed at his neck.

"Man, getting around all those barricades was one hell of a trick."

Natalie wiped the knife on her pants, placed it back in her holster and ran toward her boyfriend. She kissed him hard, but he pulled back.

"Car accident victim here. Take it easy."

She smiled. "You can handle it." Natalie looked over at the two dead Lychos on the hood of his car. "You saved my life."

"I did, didn't I?" He put his arms around her waist. "I shouldn't have told you what to do. If you're gonna risk your frickin' life fighting bad guys, I'm gonna help you do that."

Natalie felt strange. There was no instinct to recoil at his public display of affection. For a moment, she didn't care that people might think they were in love. Maybe they were.

Natalie shook it off. "Alright, Prince Charming. Wanna help me get more people off the streets?"

He beamed. "With pleasure."

As they walked back toward the front entrance, Natalie took his hand and smiled back.

***

Erica swung again at Sela Fortbright, and once again the dark soul parried with her staff. After taking down eight creatures in less than a minute, Erica found the gatekeeper a much worthier opponent.

"You realize the plan's already in place." Sela swung at Erica's legs before she jumped the attack. "Nothing you do is going to stop that."

Erica flipped backward and planted her feet. She reset her grip and dashed toward the dark soul.

"Maybe not." Erica smirked before raining down a flurry of blows on Fortbright's sword. "But getting one more dark soul off Earth will make me feel pretty good about myself."

Sela went to one knee as Erica swung with more and more intensity. She felt impact after impact of weapon upon weapon until finally, her sword broke Fortbright's staff in two. She rolled away from Erica and stood up tall.

"We're going to win this war, Protector. Give up now and we'll give you more favorable—"

Erica dashed over as the gatekeeper monologued, and ran her through with the sword. She watched the steam rise up from the bloody wound. Before she could finish her thought, Sela Fortbright flashed with blue light and disappeared. All around Erica, the portals begin to close. There had been at least a dozen blue shimmering gateways, but one by one they shrunk into nothingness.

Erica tapped on her comm link. "How's everybody doing out there?"

"Redican's convulsing on the roof, but I think he's starting to calm down."

The big drawback to mind control.

"Keep him safe, Sheriff. Dhiraj and Jennifer?"

Dhiraj sounded calm amidst the chaos. "We're good."

"Ted?"

"I could use a hand! Near the stage."

Erica looked up and spied the platform in the distance. "On my way."

As she ran in that direction, Erica saw something strange. Despite the death of the gatekeeper and the destruction of the staff, one blue portal opened back up near the stage. It seemed to burn brighter than the others had. Something about it made Erica feel incredibly uneasy.

CHAPTER
52

Sandra grabbed a cameraman by the collar of his shirt and pulled him behind the stage. The man struggled, but he was no match for Sandra's enhanced strength.

"Mrs. Kable, what are you doing?"

She laughed when she thought about how she wouldn't be Mrs. Kable for much longer. The senator would see to that, labeling her as an evil dark soul who'd been manipulating his heart. He would play the hero behind the scenes of his rally-turned-massacre.

"Hold this position." She took the gun out of her purse. "Or I'll put your brain on the pavement."

The cameraman's hands started to shake.

"Start filming. And it better not be wobbly."

He nodded and began setting up his camera to film her. Sandra looked straight ahead as Kable's plot came into view. Terry the campaign manager had his arms around a little girl. Terry stared blankly. She imagined there was nothing resembling a thought in his head. The child had cute curls and even reminded Sandra of what she looked like in her youth. Tears flowed down the girl's face as she called out for her mother. Sandra felt the tears well behind her own eyes.

You're not human. Stop acting like you're human.

Sandra didn't mind the screaming and the carnage going on in front of the platform, but there was something about putting a little girl at risk that didn't sit well with her. She reminded herself that that if the plan went right, the girl wouldn't have a scratch on her. Kable would be the one with scars to heal.

"Are we in position?" Terry's mouth moved, but she knew it was her husband pulling the strings.

Sandra hid her reluctance and smiled. "Of course." She looked at the cameraman. "Time to point and shoot."

He nodded and the red light went on beside the lens. Sandra watched as her husband's head poked out from behind the side of the stage. He gave her the signal to begin.

"Ladies and gentlemen, I'm sorry to inform you that many of your friends and family members from the rally have perished. You've been caught up in the middle of a war and, unfortunately, you're on the wrong side. President Blake thinks that Ted Finley is enough to stop me and the other dark souls from killing every last one of you." Sandra pointed the gun at the little girl, whose cries grew in intensity. "He's here with us today, but he can't save everyone, particularly this future voter before us."

Sandra looked into the girl's eyes. The senator had told her that it had to be a child. When he ran in front to take a bullet for the girl, he'd be praised universally and she'd be the one serving the time. Regardless, the girl would no doubt be traumatized by the experience. Despite the bullet wounds, Kable would really be the only person to come out of this situation unscathed.

"She's going to die like all of you will, because President Blake can't protect anyone in this country."

Sandra clicked the bullet into place. "Goodbye, little girl."

As she prepared to fire, Sandra watched her husband run into place. For the viewers, the candidate would've come seemingly out of nowhere to protect the young child. He'd lie on the ground in a pool of his own blood, Terry would pass out, and Sandra would be left holding the bag. Kable's brainwashed guards were prepared to apprehend her immediately after the shots. Every second that passed seemed like an eternity. Sandra aimed the gun at the little girl's stomach. Her trigger finger hesitated, even though she knew her shots had to be timed exactly right. All in one moment, she saw the girl's tears, Terry's vacant smile, and the senator running forward to take the glorious bullets in his stomach. She'd gone from being a pawn in one game to a pawn in another game. With those bullets, she'd doom herself to a life of imprisonment.

As the cameraman filmed, Sandra moved her gun and pointed it at Kable instead. She fired six shots in rapid succession.

The first two projectiles struck the Senator in the midsection and the little girl bawled. Sandra felt the adrenaline ripple through her body. The other four bullets hovered in between Sandra and Kable. As her husband stood up, the bullets in his body dropped to the ground, though the wounds remained. The light seemed to dim around them as Kable pointed toward the projectiles.

One bullet zipped back toward Sandra, hitting her gun hand and causing her to drop the weapon. The wound stung as her blood dripped onto the ground. Kable moved his hand again, sending the second bullet into her opposite arm. Sandra winced and cried out. With two more flourishes, Kable sent one more bullet into each of her legs. She fell to the ground and fought against the pain. Sandra couldn't tell which of the wounds hurt the worst as she screamed in agony.

Kable stood above her. He carried one of the metal stanchions that had kept the crowd back.

Sandra let a laugh out in the midst of the pain. "I guess you can't control everything."

He smirked. "Maybe not. But I can adapt. If I can't be a hero, then at least I'll be a widower."

With that, Kable stabbed the top of the stanchion through Sandra's chest.

CHAPTER
53

The Draconfolk surrounding Ted were distracted by the sudden closure of the portals. Ted crouched down and leapt. His plan was to jump on the edge of the stage and attack. When his hop took him 10 feet into the air, he realized that whatever closed those portals had stopped blocking his powers as well.

Ted floated in the air above the lizards and grinned. "Put on your rally caps. It's time for a comeback."

He tightened up his muscles and sent a flying punch into one of the beasts. The blow lifted the creature off its feet and sent it into a building a half a block away. Ted used his powers to push away the next two before they could strike him. One skidded across the street until it slammed head-first into a metal pole. The other one crashed through a car window and remained motionless.

"Like riding a bike."

Ted focused his attention on the other three, but he need not have worried. A metal blade emerged from the stomach of the lizard in the middle. The beast exploded in a fiery burst of blue, revealing Erica behind it. Another two swipes and the other lizards were likewise vaporized.

Ted saw Erica's chest heaving up and down. The sweat dripped down her neck. For once, her hair didn't look like she'd just left the salon. From the confident grin on her face, he could tell that she was in her true element.

"Nice swordplay."

She nodded up at him. "Nice punch."

Ted jogged over to her and wrapped his arms around her back. She did the same. Despite the grime of battle, Erica remained as sweet-smelling as ever.

When Ted pulled away, he saw that the battle was mostly won. There were a few roaming Draconfolk and Lychos, but with his powers and his girlfriend back, they'd be no contest. There was still one blue portal that remained to the right of the stage. His breath calmed as the tension left him.

"So, we kill the last baddies, implicate Senator Kable and find a way to close that portal?"

Ted felt a sudden pain in his side. He reached toward it and found a sharp piece of metal sticking out of his shirt. Ted looked in the direction the weapon had come from. Senator Kable was bleeding profusely from the abdomen, but the wounds didn't seem to bother him nearly as much as the metal was stinging Ted. Kable opened his hand and thrust his fingers forward. Another sharp hunk of metal flew toward them, but Erica was ready. She kicked the projectile away at the last possible moment, and it clanged harmlessly on the ground.

Kable has powers?

Ted yanked the sharp metal out of his side, which sent even more pain through his body. He tossed the weapon in Kable's direction and used his powers to aim for a direct hit. The gleaming shard stopped in mid-air, just a few inches away from Kable's forehead. To Ted's surprise it didn't fall to the ground. It actually felt like something was pushing back against Ted's powers. As if it was an arm wrestling match for control of the object. Ted had never felt anything like it.

"What is he?"

Erica crouched low as Kable continued to approach. "I don't know."

That's when Kable invaded Ted's mind. Hundreds of voices called out at once in his head. His world became nothing but screams of terror and cries for help. He clutched at his head as if to pull the overwhelming noises out.

"Ted?!" Erica put her arm around his shoulder. "What is it?"

The sounds grew louder. He shut his eyes and concentrated on pushing away the cacophony of horror. When he opened one eye, Ted saw Erica running toward Kable. The senator blocked two punches and grabbed Erica by the throat, lifting her body above the ground.

Ted clenched his fists. "Go away!"

With that, the sounds faded from his mind. He concentrated on the muscles in Kable's arm. The senator yelped in pain as Ted broke the man's wrist. Erica fell to the ground, though she quickly did a kick-up and backed away. Much to Ted's chagrin, Kable began laughing. He looked particularly villainous with the eerie glow from the nearby portal lighting him from behind.

"But Ted, I was just having a chat with an old friend."

Kable took his good hand and pulled at his own face. As he peeled away the skin, Ted's stomach lurched. The senator tossed the mask to the ground and revealed that half of his face was red and shriveled. Ted was grossed out for sure, but the look on Erica's face worried him. Her eyes had seen it all, but apparently nothing like this. She nearly stumbled as she ran back to Ted's side.

"You need to run."

Ted flinched. "What?! We need to stop him."

Erica shook her head. "You're not ready for this. He... he's—"

Kable moved his broken wrist closer to his face. He focused intently on the injury before he flexed the hand. From what Ted could tell, he healed the injury just by looking at it.

"I'm like you, Ted." Kable grinned. "I'm a living soul, too."

Ted didn't understand. He looked to Erica. "What does he mean?"

She was near tears. "It's Adam. I thought I killed him. He's the one who's behind all of this!"

Ted recalled the story of Adam growing too powerful and Erica bringing a building down on top of him. It seems the killing didn't stick.

Kable chuckled. "My humble protector, I have you to thank for all of this. Faking my death was the best thing that ever happened to me."

Erica looked at Ted. A tear ran down her face. "Please, run."

Ted shook his head, but he wasn't sure what to say in response.

Adam moved closer. "You know, it's about time I returned the favor. Sandra had told me of your desire to die."

Suddenly Ted felt a pinch in his mind as Adam made a twisting motion. Ted saw Erica's neck turn all the way around with a loud snap as she collapsed to the ground.

His muscles shook, his mind filled with his own personal screams of agony. He bent down beside Erica and cradled her body.

"No. No, Erica. No!"

Ted searched within her mind and heart for any signs of life. There were none. The love he saw before him was broken in two. Ted gently laid Erica on the street and stood up.

Rage flashed through Ted's consciousness. Everything around him began to float up in the air. Metal stanchions, two-by-fours attached to trampled signs, and even a nearby security golf cart. Ted clapped his hands together and the items flew toward his adversary. The opponent flicked the items away with his own powers, and they went zipping by him and crashing into the ground.

Ted seethed. "I'm gonna kill you!"

He leapt off the ground and flew through the air. His head was aimed for Adam's midsection, but the senator caught him before he could make impact. Adam flew the two of them about 10 feet off the ground and threw Ted back toward the pavement. Ted halted himself a foot above the ground and barely rolled out of the way of Adam's foot as the senator propelled himself downward.

Ted reached with his powers for the senator's gunshot wounds. He tried to rip at the man who'd killed Erica and tear the flesh from his bones. He succeeded for a moment, until the senator put himself back together

Ted was about to lift the entire stage up to use it as a weapon when the senator made contact with his head. The first punch stunned him, but the next three put him on the edge of consciousness. He tried to swing back, but Adam blocked the blow with ease. Another punch to the back of Ted's head would have sent him toppling over if the senator hadn't taken a hold of his shirt. He dragged Ted toward the shimmering blue portal.

"Despite my grudge with her, she really was a good protector." Adam smiled. "You should have run."

Ted used all his facilities just to keep himself conscious. He stared into the abyss of the gateway. There was no telling what was on the other side.

I may just find out.

Adam pushed Ted high up into the air and threw him directly into the portal. Ted felt a wave of hot air as the blue surrounded him. Something stung his eyes before he completely lost consciousness.

CHAPTER
54

At the end of Erica's revised mission with Adam, she'd stayed near the fallen building for days. When there was no sign that the traitorous living soul was still alive, she remembered how she began to slip away. As a mission ended, so did the light soul's grip on its human body. The end was less painful than a forceful exit, but it remained similar. She'd feel something like an electric current go through her body before she was transported back to the Realm of Souls in her true form. At least, it was the closest approximation to her true form as she could get, given her miraculous existence there.

That's what Erica expected when she collapsed to the pavement. Only she wasn't dead. Erica reached for her neck, but it wasn't even sore. A bruise was beginning to form from where she'd made contact with the pavement, but otherwise she was alive and kicking.

But I heard my neck snap.

Erica pushed up to a sitting position and focused her eyes near the blue portal. She watched as Adam punched Ted multiple times in succession.

An illusion. He made me look dead so Ted would attack!

Erica tried to get to her feet in time, but it was too late. Adam lifted Ted into the air and tossed him into the portal. The living soul. Her mission. Her love. Ted disappeared before her eyes.

The senator saw Erica get to her feet and raised his eyebrows. "Now, I guess it's just you and me."

He cracked his knuckles and walked toward her. Erica suppressed her anger and steeled her mind against everything. The only way she was going to stand a chance would be to remain perfectly calm.

Out of the corner of Erica's eye, she saw something move across her field of vision. Unbeknownst to the villain, a second person had just gone through the portal.

* * *

Natalie stood at the ready. No more creatures had come their way since Travis took out the two Lychos. While he was an idiot for almost getting himself killed, she was glad to have him there. Natalie remembered her comm link and tapped at it.

"We can't really see what's going on out there. Can anyone report?"

There was radio silence for a long moment before Dhiraj piped up.

"It's not looking good, Nat."

Natalie furrowed her brow and looked at Travis. "I need specifics."

Jennifer sniffled. "Lost the comm on Ted and Erica when they got close to the portal, but the cameras... she hasn't moved."

Natalie growled. She motioned to Travis. "We've gotta help Ted."

"But what about the people?"

"Now you get a conscience? Come on!"

Natalie ran back toward the main street. It looked like the aftermath of a war. Fortunately, most of the blood and guts that'd been spilled had been that of the Lychos and Draconfolk. Natalie passed by the broken staff of Sela Fortbright as she came into view of the portal. A deformed-looking Senator Kable was punching Ted in the face. She cringed. The senator lifted Ted high into the air near the portal.

"He's gonna throw him in." Natalie's heart pounded. "We've gotta do something!"

She surveyed her surroundings. To the side of the portal, the banner promoting Kable's speech hung on the ground. While the rope that held the left side of the banner had been snapped, the right side appeared to be firmly secured to one of the buildings.

When Kable tossed Ted into the portal, Natalie didn't think. She ran. She heard Travis' footsteps close behind her.

"What are you doing?"

Natalie ignored him and reached the torn end of the rope. She wrapped it around herself and tied a perfect fisherman's knot. Natalie watched as Kable stepped away from the portal.

"Wait!"

Natalie prepared to give Travis a death stare, but there was too much love in his eyes. He ran up to Natalie and wrapped his arms around her. She felt a moment of hesitation.

He talked into her shoulder. "Be careful."

She pulled away. "Not my style."

With a wink, Natalie dashed off toward the gateway. She reached top speed in no time and dove into the blue portal like it was the deep end of the pool.

A strange sensation passed over her body. The air was dry and hot against her skin. Sand blew through the air, but she covered her eyes before anything could damage them. Behind her, she saw that the rope was holding firm through the portal. Natalie glanced down and saw a desert far below, but she didn't fall.

I'm floating.

As she braved looking ahead through the sandstorm, she saw him. Ted was motionless, though he floated as she did. Blood leaking from one of his wounds was likewise hovering in the air. She didn't stop to think about the physics as she tried to swim toward him. With each stroke, Natalie got a little bit closer. The sand shot into her mouth, but she refused to slow. With one strong kick, she reached him. Natalie took Ted under one arm like she was rescuing him from the ocean.

"All I need is a shiny, orange buoy."

All of a sudden, Natalie felt herself drop a few feet. She held on tighter to Ted as they stabilized. Natalie looked back toward the portal. It was shrinking.

"Not good."

Natalie used her free hand to grab around the rope. She pulled the two of them closer to the gateway, with a little assist from whatever was keeping them afloat. Natalie wrapped her legs around the rope and gave another tug toward the portal. They floated a little closer, but not close enough. The gateway continued to close in on itself, but they remained several feet away. Natalie felt the tug of gravity again, as whatever was keeping them afloat was gone. The fisherman's knot held with a jerk as they went completely vertical. Natalie clasped her hands under Ted's arms. They were stable, but stable wasn't going to keep them alive.

Natalie shifted Ted to one shoulder and tried to pull them up with her free hand. She couldn't budge. It was just too much weight to carry.

"We're not gonna make it."

Natalie looked down at the expanse of sand below. When she glanced back up, the portal was seconds away from closing for good.

* * *

Erica breathed a little more calmly when Natalie's rope seemed to hold up between the two worlds. Any one of a number of environments could await them. Erica could only hope that it was one that was habitable for humans. As Adam walked closer, she began to see the qualities of the living soul she'd once protected. He was confident and strong, but his awareness wasn't as keen as it needed to be. He hadn't even noticed Natalie's mad dash to the portal. Erica had tried to develop that particular quality in him; she was glad he'd never picked it up in the meantime.

Adam smiled and threw a punch. Erica dodged it and countered with her own, which Adam feinted with ease.

"You were stronger in the other body," he said.

"And you used to have a full face."

They continued swinging at one another for several exchanges. She knew he was toying with her. After a dozen blocked punches on either side, Erica finally connected after faking with one fist and jabbing with the other.

He nursed the forming bruise. "Enough!"

"You always were impatient."

"I think it's time to take your new brain for a spin."

Erica held her breath. She tried to calm her mind as she'd learned in Japan. She could feel the tendrils of his powers reaching through her thoughts, until they were gone completely.

He growled. "Let me in!"

Erica was confused. It didn't even feel like he was trying.

From a few yards to their left, Mr. Redican cleared his throat. "Mr. Senator, you've been impeached."

Erica couldn't tell what the object flying toward the senator was until it made impact. It was the massive wooden podium from the front of the stage. The senator couldn't react as the heavy stand slammed him right in the head and took him to the ground. Erica looked to the stage where Sheriff Norris and Travis stood panting.

Erica smiled. "Now that's what I call taking a stand."

Redican bent to one knee and held his head. Erica scampered to his side. "Are you—"

"He is very powerful." He waved her off. "The portal."

She looked up as the gateway between worlds started to close. Erica was already halfway between Redican and the portal when she heard a bullet click into a weapon's chamber.

"Stay right where you are, Ms. LaPlante!"

Erica did as she was told, but was surprised at the person who'd done the telling. Agent Vott of the DHS and several other agents had their weapons drawn. And all of them were pointing their guns at her.

"Ted Finley's on the other side of that portal, Agent Vott. Let me pull him back and then you can shoot me to pieces."

Erica took a step toward the shining blue circle, and Vott unloaded a bullet near her shoes. The sound of gunfire echoed through the street.

"I'm afraid I can't let you near that thing until we understand it."

Erica glanced back over her shoulder. "Redican?"

The former substitute teacher shook his head. "Kable was too strong. I've got nothing left."

She looked back to the stage before realizing that Sheriff Norris and Travis had stepped to her side. They took a stride forward and guarded Erica.

"Let her do it, Agent Vott." Sheriff Norris puffed out his chest. "You can take her in afterward."

Travis mimicked the sheriff's stance. "Leave her alone."

As Erica walked toward the portal, she heard the command that would change everything.

"Shoot all three of them."

One bullet hit Travis' side and went right through him, barely missing Erica behind him. As she ran for the portal, Sheriff Norris took at least two bullets judging from the sound they made upon impact. Erica reached the rope and began to tug. She could feel the weight of at least two people on the other side.

A bullet flew through the air and crashed into her leg. Erica squinted and continued to pull as the portal shrank.

Agent Vott put his hand up to wave off the other agents. Erica heard Travis and the sheriff moaning in pain on the ground, but she tried to focus all her attention on the rope.

Vott clicked another bullet into place and put the barrel up to Erica's head.

"I'm not going to ask again."

When she gave another tug on the rope, Vott pushed the gun even harder against her temple.

She growled. "Do you really want to be known as the guy who killed Ted Finley?"

Vott slammed the gun into the back of Erica's head and kicked her right in the leg wound. She lost her grip on the rope and fell to the ground. Above her the gateway closed at double speed. Smaller. Smaller. And then it was gone. The rope snapped with a blue glow and landed on the ground beside her. Everything she'd been doing to keep her mind calm exploded at once. Fear, rage and pain swirled like a tornado.

It's over.

"Erica?"

Erica wasn't sure where Dhiraj's voice came from until she remembered her comm link. Vott picked up the shining blue end of the rope and looked it over.

"Roll." Dhiraj's voice was sharp and fast.

"What?"

"Roll!"

Erica turned away from where the portal had been. When she looked, Erica saw the fastest moving van she'd ever laid eyes upon. She rolled to her left, as Vott dove out of the way on the other side of the vehicle. The van screeched to a halt and Jennifer popped out of the passenger side. She put Erica's arm over her shoulder.

"Let's get outta here."

Jennifer helped Erica limp back to the van, as Dhiraj and Redican assisted Travis and Sheriff Norris into the other side. Before the door closed, Erica looked back at the senator lying on the ground. The emotional ache made her physical agony even worse. When Erica tried putting weight on her leg, she felt like she might pass out from the pain. She slumped alongside the other two gunshot victims in the back and slammed the door of the van closed. Dhiraj put the van in reverse and hit the gas before Vott and his agents could fire a single retaliation shot. Erica looked through the side of the van as if she could still see the spot where the portal hung above the ground.

"I failed. Adam's alive and Ted's gone."

Jennifer put her arm around her friend. "We can get him back, right?"

Erica had tears in her eyes. "I'm not sure." Jennifer squeezed her friend tight as they sped away from the rally.

Sheriff Norris called in two favors and found an abandoned warehouse and an old buddy who was willing to help. Kelly, a former Army medic with a massive beard and kind eyes, stopped the bleeding and disinfected the wounds. Redican said that when his powers were recharged, he'd get them into a proper hospital with disguises. Erica made sure she was the last person to be treated. She wanted the bullet to stay inside her for as long as possible as a sort of punishment. She'd lost the living soul and one of her best friends, and she had no idea where they could be. The portal could have led anywhere. They might be dead already.

The gang moved locations multiple times over the next few days to avoid detection. They eventually made it out of the city to a safe haven: Kelly's family farm a couple of hours west of the city. It was peaceful and green out there. Jennifer had said it was the kind of fresh smell you never get in the suburbs. It reminded Erica of her village during her first lifetime. It was exactly the kind of place they needed to be to figure out what to do next.

Erica sat on an old wooden bench alone with her thoughts. Sheriff Norris was still in bed recovering. He, Kelly and Redican were talking about livestock or something else farm-related in the house. Dhiraj finally convinced Jennifer to leave her father's side and go on a walk to see some of the 30 acres that surrounded them. Travis came up beside Erica.

"Seat taken?"

She gestured to the empty spot and he took it. They both looked out into a field with corn as far as the eye could see.

Travis let out a deep breath. "You've been quiet."

She nodded. "Never got to thank you for taking a bullet for me."

"All in a day's work." He rubbed at his eyes. "Do you think Natalie's alive?"

Erica wished she knew the answer to that one. "I don't know."

Travis leaned forward. "If she is, do you have any idea how we can get her back?"

Erica let her back press up against the old wood and the bench creaked beneath her. "There's only one way I've thought up so far."

Travis turned toward her. "What's that?"

Erica pictured Ted. She thought of wrapping her arms around him and pressing her lips against his. The one way she might be able to save him involved her never having the chance to do those things ever again.

"I might be able to find them if I go back to the Realm of Souls." She paused. "And the only way for me to do that... is to die."

EPILOGUE

Razellia watched her youngest daughter play from the corner of their yard. It could hardly be called theirs, as everything was technically owned by their leaders, but it felt better for Razellia to claim some kind of ownership. Her daughter Vella had an unparalleled imagination. She was running around pretending to be a warrior who could slip between worlds with ease. Razellia thought about the rumors of the gatekeeper who'd been turned to their side. She didn't know what to believe. For all she knew, the war had been over for years and their leaders kept the truth a secret to continue oppressing them. It was amazing how many people were willing to live on scraps in order to serve a greater cause, even if they had no idea what the cause truly was.

Vella ran to one corner of a makeshift fence and stood upon it. When her daughter looked out into the barren fields, Razellia knew she saw grand mountains and massive oceans. She was able to imagine away the dust and the withered crops. Razellia wondered how her daughter contorted the ever-present smell of death into something more magical. Perhaps she conjured up the aroma of the sweet treats her father was able to obtain once every few moons.

How long has it been since she's seen you, Torrin? Would she even recognize you anymore?

Razellia's thoughts were interrupted by a sound resembling thunder high in the air. A flash of blue caught her eye. Vella shrieked with joy, as if her imagination had somehow manifested itself in reality.

"It's a gatekeeper! It's a gatekeeper!"

Sure enough, a blue marvel hung in the middle of the sky for all to see. It stuck out amid the gray dust clouds.

Vella ran up to her mother's leg and pulled at her dress. "Do you see it, Mom?"

Razellia nodded. "Yes, honey. Can you run inside and find your father's old scope?" She anticipated her daughter's protest. "We can get a closer look."

Vella let her mouth hang open in a smile before she dashed inside. Razellia wasn't quite as convinced the spectacle was worth smiling about. She strained her eyes to see more, but there was no chance without the scope. Several other members of her village had spotted the commotion as well. She even spied a child on the thin roof of his house trying to get a better look. Razellia's thoughts lay more with hopes the roof would hold than the blue phenomenon when her daughter handed her the scope.

"Can I look, Mommy?"

Razellia smiled and took the scope. "Let me look first, darling girl, and make sure it's safe for kids to look at."

Razellia let her eyes focus through the scope. As clear as day, the blue speck in the distance was a shining portal high in the air.

Why there? Why now?

Razellia absent-mindedly handed the scope to her daughter and propped the girl up on her shoulders.

"Wow!" Vella started laughing with glee. "It's so beautiful."

Until something comes out of there.

"Look, Mommy. A boy just came through."

Vella handed her mother the scope. Razellia looked back through the glass to see a boy with dark hair and a long, narrow face outside the portal. Surprisingly, he didn't plummet when he exited through the gateway. He sort of hovered there. Razellia noticed something on his side that dripped into the wind. Crimson blood was coming down his side.

Razellia gently lowered her daughter back to the ground.

Vella shook with excitement. "Mommy, can I look again?"

Razellia's eyes narrowed. "I'm sorry, dear, but there are some things only grown-ups can see. I promise I'll tell you all about it when you're done playing."

"But I'm done playing now!"

Vella's eyes were so cute and blue, it was tough to say no to anything she asked. But Razellia had plenty of practice saying no.

"You head inside and wash up, then."

Vella hung her head and walked into the house. Razellia knew she'd go right up to her room and look up from her window, but at least her daughter wouldn't have the detail of the scope. When she heard a gasp from one of her neighbors, Razellia looked back skyward. Through the scope, she saw that another figure had come out of the portal, this one with some kind of rope attached to her. Razellia knew right away that the girl was trying to rescue the boy.

Razellia saw the sand blow the girl back. The rescuer had a determined look on her face and willed herself through the air. With great effort, she finally put her arms around the boy and tried to pull them back toward the portal.

Razellia felt her heart speed up when the gateway started to close. She tore her eyes away from the scope and looked at her neighbors. They were all farmers and shopkeepers. What could they do to help?

But we have to try.

She watched as the two floating children went completely vertical. The girl struggled to hold onto the boy in the middle of the sky. She looked back at the house and saw her daughter's mouth hanging wide open.

"Vella, you close that window right this instant!"

Her daughter hesitated but eventually complied. When Razellia looked back toward the portal, it had completely closed, ripping the rope and sending the boy and the girl dropping out of the sky. Razellia's heart sank.

"No!"

A cloud of dust whipped around their bodies as the boy and the girl vanished out of sight and into the badlands. Razellia was afraid for their lives, but she felt something she hadn't experienced in a long time: purpose.

Razellia gathered her neighbors in the middle of the road. "We need to help those kids."

One of them laughed at the suggestion. "Since when did you get so generous?"

It was a good question. Most people in town were focused only on themselves. Razellia was no different, but there was something about those two. And the portal.

A kinder neighbor walked across the dirt path and placed her hand on Razellia's shoulder. "Not even the General could survive a fall like that."

Razellia slapped her neighbor's hand away. "Fine. Then I'll go out alone."

Once Razellia left Vella at the neighbor's house, she packed some food and water and began the trek to the badlands. It would take until suppertime for her to get there and back, but she had to know who these kids were and how they'd summoned the portal. Could one of them have been the dark soul gatekeeper everyone was talking about?

Razellia walked past a few shops, one of which had propaganda painted on the side. It was one of many such pieces of art throughout their village. This one showed the General of the dark soul army as an innocent boy prince. His black hair was coiffed with a crown, which was adorned with emeralds to bring out his hazel eyes. Razellia figured his long, narrow face was painted in dozens of different ways in countless villages.

When she walked past the edge of town, Razellia stared out upon the dusty wasteland before her.

"In the name of the General, if you two survived, I'll find you."

The dust kicked up around her heels as she began the long trek south.

About the Author

Bryan Cohen is the author of the *Ted Saves the World* series and a collection of creative writing prompts books. Bryan is a graduate of the University of North Carolina at Chapel Hill. In 2013, Bryan appeared on an episode of the nationally televised "Who Wants to Be a Millionaire." He did just fine.

Bryan lives with his wife, their cat Rocket, and their Netflix account in Chicago.

Learn more about Bryan at http://www.bryancohen.com.

37274567R00190

Made in the USA
Charleston, SC
31 December 2014